BLOOD PROMISE

ALSO BY T. G. AYER

Young Adult Paranormal

THE VALKYRIE SERIES

Dead Radiance

Dead Radiance Audio

Dead Embers

Dead Embers Audio

Dead Chaos

Dead Chaos Audio

Dead Wrath

Dead Silence

Joshua - Dead Radiance

Joshua II - Dead Embers

Joshua III - Dead Chaos

Joshua IV - Dead Wrath

Joshua V - Dead Silence

THE HAND OF KALI SERIES

Fire & Shadow

Blood & Gold

Time & Fate

Fury & Virtue

Spirit & Soul

THE DARKWORLD SKINWALKER SERIES

Skin Deep

Lost Soul

Last Chance

Blood Promise

Scorched Fury

Fate's Edge

Grave Debt

Oath Bound

THE DARKWORLD SOULTRACKER SERIES

Blood Magic

Demon Kin

Blood Curse

Demon Soul

Blood Moon

Demon Bones

Blood Born

THE DARKWORLD IRIN CHRONICLES SERIES

Retribution

Requiem

Resonance

Revelation

THE DARKWORLD ORIGINS

Pyros (Logan)

Ailuros (Kailin)

~

THE DARK SIGHT SERIES

Dark Sight

Cursed Sight

Vissarion

Shadow Sight

Dark Prophecy

Cursed Prophecy

Shadow Prophecy

~

THE APSARA CHRONICLES

Immortal Bound

Gods Ascendent

Dominion Falling

Vengeance Born

Last Legion

~

A SEASON OF ASH AND BONE

Heartfyre

~

Adult Sci-Fi

HANDS ASSASSIN

Death Dealer

Death Mark

Death Strike

Hand's Assassins Series

~

NEW ADULT CONTEMPORARY THRILLER W/A TONI VALLAN

Beautiful Collision

Beautiful Conviction

~

PSYCHOLOGICAL HORROR W/A TONI VALLAN

Dark Shadows

Splinter

Blood Promise

A SkinWalker Novel #4

Copyright © 2015 by T.G. Ayer

All rights reserved.

Cover art by Eduardo Priego

Editor: Gracie O'Neil

ISBN-13: 978-0995112551

BLOOD PROMISE

USA TODAY BESTSELLING AUTHOR

T.G. AYER

I FROZE AGAINST THE WALL, my fingers grazing stone slick with blood, my heart punching angrily against my ribs.

Why in Ailuros' name had I agreed to take this case, again?

I had a limited time offer from the Supreme High Council, the overseeing body of all paranormals, the oldest and most respected group in our known history, and I'd wasted five of those days thinking. And right now, I was leaning heavily in their direction. Beats the hell out of working for the peons, which was what Sentinel and Omega were.

A glance to my left confirmed Sentinel Agent Cassandra Monteith was still hunkered down beside me, the metal of her comms glinting in the weak light as she slammed her own bloodied fingers against the screen of her tablet. She'd been doing that for a little too long now.

"Where the hell is he?" I threw the question at her between clenched teeth, held that way because the cold, the intermittent rain, and the elusive vampire-demon were sufficient to chill any girl to her bones.

It was two in the morning and we were standing, backed up against the wall of a house at the edge of a village, huddled there beneath the low eaves of the thatched roof. The meager protection against the drizzle was a relief against the rain. Not that it made me any less wet as drops slithered down the back of my neck, making their way down my neck and into the neck of my turtleneck, dampening what little warmth I had left in my body.

I edged closer to the corner of the wall to peer out across the Scottish moors, and snorted through a nose already partially Panther. "And here I thought your outfit knew what they were doing." A sniff of the wet air produced nothing. As frustratingly nothing as the last time I'd taken a whiff of good Highland air.

"We do. It's just this damned blood."

Behind me, rough fingertips scraped against the fabric of her jeans as Cassandra tried to wipe off the still-slick blood. The mess belonged to the vamp-demon we'd spent the better part of the last day tracking.

Unsuccessfully.

Cassie had gotten off a shot with her fancy demon-revolver, but had only managed to spill some of his blood. And all that got us was confirmation of his species, not to mention fingers stained with his disgusting blood. Vamp demons were a strange sub-species, their hemophiliac condition only amped up by their vampiric cells—cells which consumed them from the inside unless they fed regularly.

I grunted, more than a little pissed off. "Freaking demon's got a sixth sense or something." I glared at Cassie as if it was her fault. "He seems to know where we are, and when we're about to grab him. Disappears like a freaking ghost at the last minute, every single time."

Cassie narrowed her eyes at me. "I thought you'd amped up your demon-tracking skills thanks to your sister's visit to the Graylands?"

She had a point. Saving Greer from the demon lordlings who controlled the dead world had enhanced my awareness of my own skills. Probably the reason Sentinel wanted me on the job in the first place.

And here I was thinking it was my winning personality.

Too bad for this demon that I wasn't just a wraith-hunter anymore. He could run, but he couldn't hide.

Not from me.

"It looks like it's time to break out the big guns." My voice, though grim, fell flat on the moist Highland night. I straightened and leaned my head back against the cold stone.

Cassie rose from her crouch and faced me, her usually straight blonde hair frizzed by the wet air.

"What exactly do you mean?" Her steel-gray eyes flashed a wary, what-the-hell-are-you-thinking look.

I unzipped my sodden parka and dropped it on the driest patch of ground I could find, then knelt to unlace my hiking boots. "We're just wasting precious time. My panther can catch him faster. With all this rain, my nose alone isn't up to the job."

Cassie squinted at me. I ignored her as I unzipped my jeans and slid them off my hips, hissing as the air slapped a coat of icy wetness over my pasty thighs.

She made an odd strangled sound in her throat and looked away. "I'm particularly glad I'm not the one bare-arsed naked in this bloody weather."

She slid past me, swapping places as I wrangled my black jeans off my bare feet and began to slide out of the dark turtle-neck sweater which was my last failed barrier against the climate.

She peered around the corner and gave a frustrated groan. "Still no sign of him. Where the hell is he hiding? I swear he's using some kind of magic. It's likely the only thing able to help keep him hidden from us."

"Either that, or somehow he knows we're coming," I said

dryly. Dropping my final pieces of clothing onto my backpack, I straightened, feeling a few unmentionable bits begin to slowly freeze over. I gave a quick shudder. "Right. Here goes. I'm going to shift. Once I've transformed, keep your distance. You'll be familiar to me, but animal instinct can sometimes override my human awareness, so no sudden moves. I can't be held responsible if I eat you."

When I tilted my head to Cassie, and caught a glimpse of her face, it was enough to tempt me to break what little cover we had and burst out laughing.

I didn't give in. "I'm kidding."

Cassandra breathed. "Heavens. You're so terribly funny."

"I try."

An inelegant snort burst from her regal nose. "Next time, please don't."

I smiled and began the shift.

Muscles tightened, icy hot. Skin grew taut, and stretched slowly. Pain ripped through every inch of my body, from the tips of my ears as they lengthened and grew fur, to the hollows of my eye sockets as human gave way to full feline, night vision changing the countryside to varying shades of sharply contrasted grays.

A few strangled, painful minutes later, I stood on all fours, a mere two feet off the ground, giving my massive black panther body a relieved shake.

I gave Cassie a cursory glance, noting the tightness in her neck, and her scent that stank of nerves. That it didn't stink of fear was a true credit to the woman. I liked her even more now than I had when she'd helped save my ass from Illyria the wraith-bitch not too long ago. Cassie's ability to shape-shift had been a true asset to us in the past, and we'd become friends.

The scent of vamp-blood tainted my paws and I strove hard to ignore it, to compartmentalize that area of my brain that wanted only to give in to the call of the wild.

Regardless of species, demon blood had a particular scent. My advantage was that this demon was a vampire, a blood-sucking creature that didn't hesitate to break the law and slide through the veil to partake of the warm offerings that many an innocent female, or male, would willingly provide.

Too many people were so gaga over vampires they fell easily for the charms of the demon-vamps instead of looking harder for the real thing.

As I slinked past Cassie, I brushed against her. Too late, I hoped it would be a reassuring contact rather than making her wet herself with shock. Then I turned the corner and set off on a loping run.

My paws hit the ground, sliding on the smooth stones as I sprinted along the narrow path that cut through the moor. A low stone wall appeared on the rise and I launched myself over it, the move smooth and elegant, as if I'd done it a million times before.

Only recently had I begun to allow my panther more face time. Since Greer's death, I'd slowly learned to appreciate my feline side, my sister's troubles having made me understand the true value of what I had inside me, more now that I'd lost my sibling forever.

Icy rain began to pelt my long back, hitting my fur with vicious slaps, as if frustrated it couldn't penetrate to my skin. Now that I was no longer cold, I felt a little righteous, my shift a middle finger to the universe.

Strangely enough, the downpour didn't hinder my sight, I blinked and ran, my gaze fixed out on the rolling dark hills that surrounded the shallow valley. A small forest of trees grew to my left and I headed up across the grassy hillside.

I drew in a deep breath as I reached the top of the rise and caught the faint trace of demon-blood mixed with cold ash. I frowned. It was probably only the residual odor of the blood that had been on my fingers. I would've preferred not to have touched the substance but doing so had helped me know how warm it was and whether our prey had survived his injuries.

Pity he had.

The heavens decided, at that moment, that they'd had enough of throwing buckets of water upon our heads and dried up so suddenly I found myself squinting up at the dark night. It was probably totally natural here, but to me everything seemed strange and foreboding, and wrong.

Where I was concerned, suspicion tended to be a good thing.

It usually saved lives.

I concentrated on the smell, breathing a little deeper, staring that much harder into the darkness. Something blurred to the right of the valley below and I moved slow and careful down the hill. My paws made little noise on the wet grass, and my body seemed to slide between the low growth without making a sound.

At the bottom of the hill stood a drab, dilapidated old hut, its gray surface broken, its mortar so crumbled that many stones had fallen out and left gaping holes in the wall. The roof too showed a number of missing sections, like tired mouths yawning to the open heavens.

The tap-tap of water dripping onto stone told me the hovel would be just as cold and wet inside as out here. Guess our demon wasn't on the smart side at all.

Somewhere along the hillside an animal cried, and my panther ears pricked to attention. It was a cat's cry and though I couldn't be sure what feline species it belonged to, it sounded more like an invitation than a warning. But I held myself stiff, cutting through my panther's temptation to investigate.

I padded around the broken wall to where a half-open door hung precariously from a rusted hinge. A mere breath from me would be enough to send it to the ground. The narrow space was just wide enough for me to slide inside the darkened interior without having to test my breathing theory.

Inside, the hovel was silent. A glance upward showed me the once well-thatched roof was now bare straw, moldy and broken, over rafters swollen and split in so many places that I'd bet it would collapse under a sparrow's weight.

Up near the rafters something shifted, and pale light gleamed on a ragged spider's web. The shifting image morphed into the web's now seven-legged owner. Even higher up, scurrying flashes of darkness confirmed the presence of rats.

Great.

Even in panther form, I hated the vermin.

Demons I could handle.

Rats? Nope.

I clicked across the floor, my sharp claws hitting the wet stone and echoing loudly around the room. Another doorway, this time free of anything remotely door-like, led to an inner room, this one no drier.

I froze, suddenly sure I'd heard something move. I felt, deep in my gut, the presence of someone or something. I tasted his scent on the air, and it led me to the far corner of the room, drawing my attention up toward the shadows within the high thatched roof. I squinted, the world a multitude of shades; gray and shadow and night, as my panther located the demon, and conveyed it to my human brain.

I'd discovered long ago that panther sight and hearing could overwhelm me, so I'd learned to blend it well. Now the sensations were not a total shock to my system.

Helps when you finally accept the panther side of you, doesn't it?

My eyes narrowed. My prey crouched on an old cracked rafter so swollen from the rain that it looked ready to burst into shards of toothpicks especially with the demon weighing it down.

He watched me too, his head tilted to the left, his demon eyes glowing amber. It was clear that he wasn't sure what to make of me.

I smelled no fear on him either. And that was certainly a mistake. He should be afraid of me.

His white protruding canines—yes, vamp-demons had them too—glinted as he grinned down at me.

It was easy to see why humans mistook this creature for the legendary vampire. His glamor didn't help either. Soft blond hair that hung to his shoulders, deep green eyes, a muscled tanned physique that would make him instantly sexy. He'd have plenty of fodder on the streets of Glasgow, let alone in cities as big as London or New York.

It certainly made sense that Sentinel would want to be rid of him. I found it refreshing that they hadn't requested we bring him back to headquarters. Omega had that particular requirement on all the missives they'd sent my way. Not a palatable job when I was forced to hand over a potentially innocent person—demon or otherwise—to Omega. They possessed a stained track record for experimenting on their own, one I wasn't comfortable with.

But, as pleasing as the instruction was, it didn't contain fine print regarding innocents. Something I planned to discuss with the higher-ups the first chance I got.

The barest hint of sound drifted to my ear. It wasn't much, probably the shifting of a stone against the path, or the brushing of clothing against the stone wall that surrounded the abandoned hut.

Cassie.

When the demon stopped grinning and simply disappeared, my panther's gut churned with the same fear my human self experienced.

I spun around and loped to the nearest window. I launched myself through the bare casement, its glass and framing long gone, and landed smoothly on the bare sand outside the hut. I stiffened as both my sense of smell and sight worked in tandem.

Across the yard, the shape of the demon shifted.

He'd stopped running and disappeared into a shifting smudge of darkness, only to reappear halfway up the hill to the left of the house, as if he'd taken a mere step away.

We'd been right about his uncanny ability to elude us.

He'd Jumped.

CHAPTER 2

*N*OW IT MADE SENSE HOW the slippery vamp-demon had managed to evade us for so many days. He'd disappeared off Cassie's radar one too many times for it to be a coincidence, and it had bugged me to a point that I'd begun to suspect that Sentinel, or someone else, was setting us up.

Paranoid much?

On the plus side, we'd managed to get close enough earlier that evening—by walking past him in a run-down old pub over in the next town—to place a tracking device on him. Vamp-demons didn't seem to mind when chewing-gum got stuck under their shoes. Or, in his case, army boots.

He still hadn't found the bug, but since Sentinel's equipment appeared to be on the fritz, it hadn't helped us locate him.

Gritting my teeth, I scrambled across the yard, knowing my midnight dark fur would make me melt into the evening. I flew across the low stone wall, landed softly on padded paws, then slunk toward a stand of trees on the hillside up ahead.

Vamp-demon scent drifted down toward me, proof that he wasn't smart enough, or experienced enough, to at least remain downwind. Either that or he thought he was too smart. I'd put my money on the latter.

But right now, Cassie was my first concern. Although her main role with Sentinel was as an Appereo, a rare type of mage with the ability to shapechange and turn herself invisible at will, she was still essentially human as most mages were. I could smell her human scent pretty strong on the soft breeze that filtered down the hill. The demon would close in on her faster than I was able to run.

Pity I couldn't jump too.

I loped to the top of the hill and flew over another low wall, landing a few feet from where Cassie hunkered down out of sight of the hut, both our backpacks at her feet.

I took a step toward her but I was too late.

The demon shimmered, twisting shadows slowly forming into the creepy vamp. He stood, profile to me, studying Cassie who was halfway onto her knees, her invisibility beginning to shimmer, distorting the air around her.

The demon's teeth glinted and I sprang at him. Cass's eyes flickered in my direction but the demon must not have much of an instinct going on. Granted, all he saw was a black panther. But how many black panthers lurked around the farmlands of Scotland?

Cass flickered into nothing but the demon wasn't to be bested so easily. His fingers snapped out, sharp black nails sprouting in a blink as he wrapped them around Cassie's invisible neck.

Cassie shimmered again, visible now, eyes wide. Something was wrong. He could teleport and now he had the power to see Cassie while she was invisible.

This was not happening.

The demon laughed, tightening his grip. Cassie was unable to get away from him. The bastard must have some sort of spell on him that held her in this plane. That we hadn't expected.

Cassie let out a furious grunt, using the force of her solid state to tug away from his razor-sharp grip but all she managed was to topple over the fence. Which wasn't the best idea. It saved her ass, but it also meant the vamp's claws sliced into her skin and tore a good portion of her flesh open. Thankfully, the injuries weren't mortal; it would take a good deal more than that to threaten the life of a high-level paranormal like Cassie.

And, the demon seemed to be the I-like-to-play-with-my-food variety. A good thing in this case or—judging by Cassie's shocked face and her grimace of pain—maybe not.

She paused, raising her the fingers of her right hand closer to her comms, but the vamp wasn't as stupid as she'd hoped. He grabbed the earwig and flung it into the grass.

It landed a foot in front of me.

I stood frozen in the darkness considering my next move. If he really meant to kill her he was taking his time. Any sudden move on my part could finish the job if I wasn't careful.

I studied the location of his nails in her throat, the lines of the blood trails on her skin, the ragged flesh where he'd torn her open. Cassie gasped as he tightened his grip, her bulging eyes searching wildly for me as he held her neck stiff preventing even the slightest movement.

When he leaned forward I thought nothing of it until I saw the glint of a sharp lengthening canine. Okay, so he wasn't going to muck around after all.

I sprang at him, aiming parallel to the stone wall to allow Cass to fall on this side of the fence if he suddenly let go of her.

He didn't let go.

I hit him broadside. His head snapped around, eyes shocked and furious at the interruption. When he realized his attacker was the black cat he'd so recently dismissed he didn't release his prey. He fell sideways, hitting the ground hard, his fingers still clamped around Cassie's neck as he dragged her with him.

She shrieked and I sank my claws into his arm. But he was a

stubborn bastard. My presence didn't seem to discourage him and he only gripped harder.

And as she lay very still beside him, Cass made a strange, hair-raising sound. The sound of dying; last gasps, final desperate breaths before the end.

Not on my watch.

I shifted my paws and threw my weight forward onto his neck, keen to provide him the same treatment he was meting out to Cassie.

Your turn, asshole.

The vamp-demon grunted, lifting his shoulder as if that small action would dislodge my claws. When I didn't move he rolled onto his back, lifted his knees and kicked his feet into my abdomen.

As prepared as I was for his reaction, the force of the blow still winded me. For all his scrawny appearance, he packed a wallop. I grunted, and it must have sounded too human for any kind of feline because he gave me an odd, worried glance.

Sounded human, huh?

Too bad. His new position gave me more claw to skin surface area than my previous angle had, and I took advantage of it. I pulled my razors free and then plunged them into the base of his throat. My paws thumped hard on his chest side by side, and I pressed with all my weight. I'd break his sternum. Stop his ugly heart. Rip into his throat deep enough to drown him in his own blood—

A bit on the vicious side, aren't you, Kai?

With his full attention on the basic need to live, the demon's survival instinct finally kicked in. He dropped his hold on Cassie.

Part of my brain registered that she was no longer dying but wheezing and gagging for breath, the ragged breathing and hollow coughing of my poor, near-suffocated partner.

But I didn't have time to celebrate. As I sucked in my own breath a shudder rippled through me. My gut twisted, as a red haze began to fill my vision, fear gripped my throat. I might have saved Cassie but the bloodlust of the walker had finally come to claim me.

I'd danced around bloodlust since I'd shifted. It had been easy enough to avoid—until blood started to flow. Now that sweet, coppery scent began to entice my inner feline. Soon it would be a raging frenzy.

Usually the blood call forces the human-to-feline change. But because I was already in cat form, my visceral need was more powerful, a deep-throated bellow to my panther's wilder nature.

A call for the kill.

I strained against the call, the pull of pain in my teeth, the ache in my bones. I'd heard of this type of bloodlust. It went deeper than just being a walker. It was a more primal, unadulterated animal instinct that demanded dominance. I'd heard tales of walkers going over to the darker side, giving in to the primal need and never being able to come back to normality.

The walker could return to human form, but the bloodlust came home with her, and she'd have to spend the rest of her life fighting it. I didn't want that for my future. I had too many things to consider.

Too many people I cared about.

I stiffened my resolve. Tightened my jaw—

Cassie's fear filled my nostrils and her strangled cry brought me back to awareness.

I blinked.

My jaws were clamped tight around the vamp-demon's neck. Horrified, I spat him out, scrambling backward on my hind legs.

No. No.

One moment, I was a hulking black panther stricken by bloodlust. The next I was a very naked female, pale skin streaked with blood.

CHAPTER 3

I CHOKED, SHOCKED AT WHAT I'd almost done.

Huddling on the wet ground, I watched as Cassie crawled to the demon and studied him, pressing a hand to her wounds. They trickled a thin stream of blood but I was sure she'd been through worse.

Paranormals were a tougher brand of human.

She looked up at me and shook her head, her pale-gray eyes wide and bright. "He's too far gone. He'll be dead in a minute or so."

I opened my mouth, then closed it, unsure what to say. And she understood.

She got to her feet, dabbing her neck with fingers before giving them an annoyed glance. Then she wiped her bloody hand on her equally bloody jeans, grabbed a fistful of clothes from my backpack, and threw them at me. I snatched them out of the air. "Put something on before he dies of shock instead."

I glanced down at him.

Death for a vamp-demon was always a slower process than for a human. This one's neck was a mess, and thick black blood seeped into the ground beside him, but he still seemed to be in control of some of his faculties. His eyes especially. Despite being moments from death he studied me. Leered at my naked body.

Cassie snorted, searching the grass for something; probably her comms. "Or before he dies of something else." She grinned as she found the device and dusted it off before inserting it into her ear.

I shook my head, trying not to think about the anatomy of a vamp-demon, and proceeded to dress as fast as possible, more concerned with the cold than the dying creature.

When I'd finished, I stepped closer to study him. I wasn't usually the morbid type but he was still conscious.

"You're her," he rasped, his voice rumbling.

"Her who?" I asked. I already knew what he'd meant. When he didn't respond, I said, "If you'd stopped when I told you to then you'd still be alive."

He shook his head, coughed, and splattered blackish blood all over my boots. "I know your type. Kill before asking questions."

"Not the way I operate. You didn't need to attack her." I pointed a thumb at Cassie who stood beside me, glaring at the reddened tips of her fingers as they continued to come away from her wounds bright and wet. She was taking longer than normal to heal and she didn't seem to be the patient type.

"She would have killed me."

"Damn straight I would have," Cassie snapped, colder than the night air.

He cocked a weak eyebrow. "See?"

"Cassie."

"Okay, well, if she had insisted I would have left you alive." Cassie shrugged, her expression a confused mash-up of guilt and regret.

"See?" I repeated his word back at him and got a look of regret for my trouble.

Not that it helped. He was still going to die.

"Well, I'm on my way out, but you can still save him," the demon whispered, his voice still gritty but now a tad weaker.

"Save who?" I asked, leaning over him.

Cassie's grunt warned me not to get too close but it didn't matter. His eyes, blank and fixed, stared unseeing into the black sky.

"He's gone," said Cassie.

"No shit."

Cassie grabbed her rucksack and threw it over her shoulder. "What's with you?"

She pressed a white bandage to her neck and from the pink speckles it looked like her wound had finally stopped bleeding. Although Cassie was primarily a shape-changer, I knew, from spending a few days in her company, that the power to change form helped her to heal too.

"Nothing's with me," I snapped, reaching for my backpack. "He's dead."

"Yeah. He's dead. So maybe keep your distance before he goes poof in your face."

I grunted and turned on my heel. Vamp-demons didn't go poof, as she well knew. They merely disintegrated to ash and had to be dealt with using a good old broom.

I was about to tell her to take me home, when a low sound caught my ear. Tilting my head, I glanced at Cassie, in silent question.

She narrowed her eyes and frowned as my ear shifted slowly from human to feline, its pointed end pricked to pick up even the merest hint of sound.

There, again.

I shifted around toward the sound, finding myself moving back in the direction of the hut.

It came again, low. Pained. Agonized.

The hairs on the back of my neck stood on end as I launched

into a run. Cassie hurried down the hill at my side and we took the low wall like the trained agents we were.

Or rather, Cassie was a trained agent, I was merely housebroken.

We neared the hut and separated, Cassie pointing around to the side of the building. She'd enter through one of the empty window holes, while I crossed familiar territory, paying even closer attention this time around.

Outside, there had been a hollow note to the cry. When it quivered through the building this time my panther ear and my instinct told me to search below the floor.

I moved slowly along the floor, sweeping my foot left and right, shifting soil off the stone. Where would I find the entrance to a cellar in a place like this?

Moving into the second room I saw Cassie slipping over the empty sill. She closed in and we stood still waiting to hear the cry again. When it came—plaintive, mournful, and very loud—I shivered. So did Cassie.

The walls around us were bare, the rafters in full view, so again we were left with the floor. I began to stomp the surface of the dirty stone until something clanged beneath my weight. I toed the dirt away.

There under the soil-covered surface lay a thin square metal panel. Made to look like the stone of the floor, it blended into the surrounding rugged tiles aided by darkness and shadows.

In the daylight it would be harder to hide, but I assumed our demon hadn't cared. Considering the abandoned state of the property he wouldn't get many visitors.

I crouched in front of the panel and slipped a finger underneath it, before hiking a brow at Cassie.

She nodded.

I heaved the panel up and took few steps back in case we were peppered with gunfire. In case this was a trap.

But no bullets flew out of the black hole, only that pitiful sound again. Cassie dug around in her rucksack and retrieved a heavy-duty flashlight. She flicked the switch and white light flooded the coffin-sized space below.

A young man lay there, all protruding ribs, pointy elbows, and knobby knees. He was curled in a fetal position, his matted hair almost dreadlocked, dark arms hiding his face, his gasps somewhere between relieved and terrified.

I touched Cass's hand and she aimed the light away, leaving just enough illumination to cast a soft glow into the burrow. I knelt at the edge, afraid to touch him in case he panicked.

"Are you okay?" I asked. Despite lowering my voice, I heard the sound echo within the room and inside the hollow dug-out.

Stupid question, Kai.

But it seemed to pull the boy from his panic and he shifted his hand from his face, revealing one very black eye.

And one very ravaged neck.

It didn't take a genius to figure out the kid had been turned.

Cassie sucked in a breath.

"Whatever you're thinking right now," I told her, "stop." I kept my attention securely on the boy, but my voice was hard and low, and meant business.

"Kai, it's protocol."

Protocol meant humans that were turned were considered a liability to be terminated at will. An archaic rule that I certainly didn't agree with.

"You know what you can do with your protocol."

Cassie snorted. "It's okay for you. You're not exactly 'on the books'."

"Just tell them I didn't give you a choice."

"And reveal to all and sundry that you have me by the brass ones?"

"They're brass?" I asked, a grin in my voice.

She clicked her tongue. "Just get him out of there before I change my mind."

I didn't respond, just sank to the floor and put one foot in the grave beside the shivering boy. His shoulders shuddered as I leaned forward and rested a hand on his bony arm.

I'd barely touched him before he sprang away, slamming his head into the back end of the box so hard that I could have sworn I heard something crack. Closer inspection of the tangled mop covering his head told me he'd live.

"I thought you said you were going to save him?" Cass peered into the hole. "Sounds like you're going to kill him anyway."

I gave her a blistering stare and returned my attention to the terrified boy. Up close, he had more than just dusky skin and deep black eyes going for him. Give him a few meals and a hot shower and he'd be positively cute. If a little dead.

I wasn't sure how to deal with the damage to his neck, but that wasn't a priority. Waiting only until he stopped shivering I moved in a little closer. Little by little, I managed to ease my way into the hole.

No danger here, kid. Just your neighborhood kitty-cat come to curl up and purr.

I'd made it all the way into the space thinking the feel of human warmth might help him when he looked up at me, his obsidian eyes gleaming as he studied my face.

This close, I recognized the signs of starvation, the blue-black veins, the dark rings beneath his eyes . . . and the grayed, almost lifeless skin.

I stiffened, but I wasn't going to back away now. I refused to think he was so far gone that I couldn't help him. It wasn't his fault that he'd been turned.

Or was it?

I shook that thought out of my head. "Look, I'm not here to hurt you. And he's dead, okay."

The dark eyes went wide.

So he understood English.

Progress.

"We need to get you somewhere safe. Can you sit up?"

He paused for a few seconds, his hands trembling while he considered my offer. Knowing his master was now truly dead seemed to have a positive effect on his terror.

He gave a tiny nod, so small a movement I almost missed it. Sliding an arm behind him I ignored my instinctive flinch and my panther's discomfort. I just waited, supporting him as he tried to lift himself upright.

Time seemed to move in slow motion as he progressed to his knees and then to sit on the side of the floor. With him out, I glanced up at Cassie and gave her a short nod.

She rolled her eyes, her version of 'finally'.

Then she pressed the button to the comm in her ear and summoned Larsson, our on-call teleporter who materialized within seconds, his red hair a stark contrast to the drab day.

He took my arm and we jumped from the grotty hut.

CHAPTER 4

*L*ARSSON TRANSPORTED US DIRECTLY TO the Sentinel offices. Then he disappeared with a smile at Cassandra and a short nod to me.

Not a small-talk kinda guy.

The light from Cassie's flashlight bounced around the room and she shut it off and stowed into her backpack. Though we'd jumped time-zones, inside the room time didn't seem to matter.

The room was intimidating, small, square, filled with a gigantic mirror and steel walls. Screamed interrogation.

And I worried that the boy would panic, but he kept his eyes on my face as if the sight of me was enough to calm him. Odd that I would have a reassuring effect on anyone.

The boy wavered on his feet, his knees threatening to collapse under him. His face seemed paler, if that was possible. Cassie and I grabbed his arms before he toppled over and plunked him down on the nearest chair.

We didn't have long to wait before the door slammed open with a crash.

The kid sprang to his feet, clutching my arm so hard his

ragged nails bit into my skin and drew blood. But I didn't brush him off.

My attention fixed on the man who strode inside. He was tall. Maybe a full head taller than me. Muscles bulged under the cotton of his long-sleeved white shirt and he'd dressed like he'd grown up wanting to be a spy. The only thing missing was the dark glasses which I suspected he'd left behind on his desk, wherever that might be.

Good thing he ended up being a spy because he looked far too grumpy to be the kind of person to live a life that didn't make him happy. He'd be a danger to his fellow man.

"What the hell is going on here?" His voice rang around the room, the metal helping to bounce the sound ominously around us.

Cassie's cheeks paled slightly but she stood her ground. "We had a survivor."

"A survivor who has set off every alarm in the building." His voice grated on my ears.

"What did he do to set off the alarms?" Cassie might have sounded sweet but there was a cold edge to her tone.

"Where do I start?"

"Paul—"

"Don't Paulson me." Dislike and resentment simmered in both words and tone. "Just because the people upstairs want her doesn't mean she has the right to break all the rules."

His voice was iron.

I didn't know him and I already didn't like him. "He's my problem. Not yours. I'm not asking for Sentinel's help. There's a guy I know who will be more than happy to take him."

Paulson's black eyes widened. "You think that because you have a solution to the problem, it's okay to break our rules?"

Really didn't like him.

I stepped into his personal space. Stabbed an index finger into his chest. "Look. Paulson." I spit it at him. "Those are your rules. My rule is 'Don't kill innocents'. Which is why he's here." I jerked my chin to the poor kid who'd remained utterly silent during our exchange.

Paulson glared down at where my finger drilled into his sternum.

I didn't move, and when he lifted his gaze back to mine his eyes were hot, hard, and bitter. Enemy. If he hadn't been one before he was now.

He twisted away to face Cassie, breaking my contact. "Just get him the hell out of here," he grated. "Before I decide to throw the three of you into Decontamination." And he stalked off.

I listened to his retreating footsteps. Paulson, for all his bluster, couldn't do anything about my choice except to make a lot of noise.

Like Cassandra, he and Sentinel had little control over what I did that wasn't entirely case-related. The case was the vamp-demon, not its victims. They didn't care about the victims beyond the fact that they might be a danger to society. Our young vamp didn't look like much of a threat. Even Paulson with his panties in a bunch knew as much.

Right now, Paulson, in his ignorance was making a huge case for me opting to work for the High Council.

I turned back to Cassie. "Friend of yours?"

She pursed her lips and glared at the empty doorway. "Walter? He's not all that bad, really." Then she sighed. "To be quite honest, he's a right arsehole. There is really no way to say it nicely."

The boy let out a soft sigh, and collapsed, my lunge toward him too late. I couldn't grab hold of him in time and he hit the floor with a thud, his grayed skin a stark contrast against the black tiles.

Cassie sighed and held out a hand. "Here I was thinking I should follow protocol and bring you two to Sentinel first." She snorted in disgust. "Come. Let's get the boy to safety before Paulson changes his mind."

I grabbed onto her hand and leaned forward to hold onto the kid. "Can you get Larsson to take us straight to Storm's place?"

She nodded and within seconds Larsson appeared and whisked us from the room.

CHAPTER 5

WE REAPPEARED IN THE SPARSELY-decorated waiting area of City Deep, Storm's shelter. Storm, who had no last name as far as I knew. The same Storm who was a friend of Grandma Ivy's, and who—early in my career when I'd needed direction—had pointed me at Tara for weapons.

Storm was formidable, an Immortal who devoted his time and considerable clout to City Deep, the city-based clan that comprised all species, welcomed all strays, and helped them get back on their feet by teaching them the necessary skills for a fresh start.

Storm seemed too good to be true, but he wasn't. He was the best of the best and we were all so glad for it.

As our feet met solid ground, I tightened my grip around the boy's bony frame. Cassie helped me lift him and seat him on the sofa behind us.

"Watch him," I told her. "I'll fetch Storm."

Cassie arched her brows. "What? You trust me alone with him?"

I rolled my eyes and hurried out of the small front office and across the corridor to Storm's office. The place was quiet, as evenings always were with Storm placing priority on homework before fun.

Storm had taken over a small hotel on the Southside and converted it into his own shelter for kids. Dozens of homeless children lived here under his guardianship. They attended the local school and got themselves back on track all while he ensured they behaved themselves. So far, he seemed to be making a success of it.

Lily and Anjelo were both excellent examples of his success.

Storm had saved Lily Marks, my Lynx walker sidekick and friend, from a life on the streets. But for his intervention she'd have probably died of a drug overdose. Many Walkers who struggled as she had with an inability to shift fully, often turned to drugs.

Anjelo Alvarez, on the other hand, had left Tukats—our panther clan home in the mountains—to follow in my stupid footsteps. Thanks to Storm, he'd been able to steer clear of a lot of trouble until he reconnected with me.

He'd remodeled the entire ground floor of an old hotel, sectioning off areas for his personal apartment, maintenance, and office-space for himself and Chloe Murdoch, his Healer Mage assistant. The lobby he'd converted into the waiting room in which Cassie now sat with the boy, and the old restaurant into a general dining and common room for the students who drifted in and out of the place.

The old hotel rooms had been converted into dorms for the dozens of people he took under his wing.

His door sat ajar as I reached it, a sure sign he was available. I knocked lightly against the frosted glass that made up the top half of the door and waited only seconds until a deep, sexy voice bade me enter.

I pushed the door open and walked in to find Storm was not alone.

A girl looked up from the side of Storm's desk, her hands

filled with a stack of files. Her heart-shaped face, and deep brown eyes were familiar.

She gave me a shy smile and waited. Without the pasty makeup it would've been easy for me not to recognize her. But a few weeks back she'd been standing on the side of the road, barely sixteen, wasting her life away in the world's oldest profession.

Her pimp had turned out to be a wraith whose life I'd happily erased, probably leaving his prostitutes with nobody to force them to keep working. I'd given this girl Storm's card for the Shelter and told her to come to him if she needed anything. I thanked *Ailuros* she'd actually listened to me.

"Kailin," said Storm as he got to his feet. With his looks the man could be a supermodel—the cheerful smile on his way-too-beautiful face, the wide strong jaw that inspired trust in the kids and people around him, those deep eyes that let everyone know how much he cared. All that beauty and he spent his time here, helping people. Gorgeous and admirable.

"Hey," I said, coming to a halt in front of his paper-strewn desk. "You need a secretary."

"I have one," he waved a hand at the girl. "And we have *you* to thank for sending Niki to us."

I gave her a warm smile. "I'm so glad you came."

"You remember me?" she asked, her cheeks reddening.

I grinned. "Of course, I do." I jabbed a thumb at Storm. "Has he been good to you?"

"Better than I deserve," she said, her eyes darkening.

"We all deserve better than we think we should get," said Storm, his tone gently chiding as he watched her. She gave a small smile and he continued, "Now Kailin, what can I do to help?"

"I have a new addition for you," I said. "But only if you want him. I'm not entirely sure you will, so I haven't left him on your doorstep in a cardboard box and taken off. He's in the waiting area with Cassie."

Storm nodded and rounded his desk. "Very well. Let's have a look at him."

He hurried off toward the waiting area with Niki and I close behind him. I wasn't sure she should witness Storm's assessment, but he knew me well enough to know chances were high I'd be bringing him a paranormal. His decision.

Just inside the door, Storm stopped and glanced back over his shoulder. "Niki, if you can get that filing finished, then you'll have plenty of time for your Chemistry homework." It wasn't a suggestion, but he phrased the command so nicely no one would argue with him.

Niki nodded and began to turn away. Then she stopped and looked straight at my face. "I want to thank you for what you did that day. You didn't need to save me, considering how I spoke to you. But you did, and for that I will always be grateful."

I smiled. She'd been a foulmouthed little creep that night and even Lily hadn't been impressed. But Niki had made the right choice and listened. Gotten out of the game. "I did what I always do. And you can thank me by making a good life for yourself. You've got a nice start here."

"I will. I promise." She did one of those little finger-waves and headed down the corridor.

I watched her leave, her thin body now slightly more rounded after a few weeks of decent food and no drugs. I gave a small nod as one success story walked off, then turned back to the waiting area hoping Storm would agree that another potential success story sat on his sofa.

The boy lay on his back on the sofa with Storm bent low studying his neck. Cassie stood a few feet away hovering a little like a protective parent.

I joined Storm. "How bad is it?" I asked, afraid of the answer.

"It's not reversible." His words killed the air.

Hope drained from me as if I'd been mortally injured. "So we can't save him?" Poor kid.

Storm shook his head. "Not from the vampirism. But once he's healed, we can rehabilitate him to live a relatively normal life in society."

My gaze snapped to Storm's face. "But he's been turned." Even *I* didn't think it was possible for a vampire to survive in the normal world.

"He's been turned, yes. But, with help, he can get back to a more healthy stable state. We can give him the support he needs. He hasn't spoken yet, but I'm pretty sure he's too old for school so we can find him some kind of proper work to do."

The boy's gaze shifted to Storm's face. "Hack . . ." he whispered.

Storm frowned and looked questioningly at me.

I shrugged. "Hacker?" I asked and received a weary nod from the boy.

Storm smiled as the boy watched him through half-closed lids. "Good. I have some IT work that needs updating."

That teased a smile from the kid. Encouraging.

"What's your name?" asked Storm.

"Baz," he rasped. "Sebastian Ross."

"Nice to meet you, Baz," I said giving him a nod over Storm's shoulder.

Storm straightened. "Right. We'll get him settled and I'll have Chloe come and give him a once-over." He turned to Cassie. "Infirmary?" he asked.

She was about to take Baz's arm when a gentle voice spoke from the doorway. "Niki said you needed me."

We all turned around. Chloe Murdoch stood in the doorway radiating calm as if it was something she sprayed on every morning like a fragrance. Her soft auburn curls were piled up on her head, delicate tendrils drifting to her shoulders. In her fifties she could easily pass for thirty.

I gave her a happy grin and gestured to the sofa. "Yes. The boy. Baz. He needs you."

Chloe went straight to him, and placed her pale hand on his dark arm. "Right, young man. All you need to do is relax. I can feel the tension and fear in you. You don't have to be afraid of anyone here. We are all here to help you."

When Baz glanced at Cassie, I stifled a snort.

"Yes," I said, keeping my features neutral. "Even Cassie."

His gaze flicked from Cassie's weak but encouraging smile, to my face, and then up to Chloe's. I'd bet the older woman's kinder features were much more attractive than either of ours. Poor kid had been through far too much.

His shoulders sank into the cheap satin pillows beneath him, as if an invisible layer of tension had weighed him down for all this time and had only now been lifted.

Chloe crouched down, her hand stroking his shoulder inches from his ravaged neck. "How do you feel?"

He nodded and his teeth glinted white against his dark skin. A soft smile if it were possible to ignore the sharp point of his canines.

"Tell us about yourself." Chloe continued to stroke. "That way we can get you the best kind of help."

"I'm from London." He said it a little defensively, his well-educated accent becoming more pronounced. "Born and bred."

And I understood. People of color didn't fit that well into the general *idea* of a highly educated Londoner. You'd think more along the lines of white. But for me, born-and-bred was enough.

When nobody challenged his claim, not even the only other Brit in the room, he said, "I went to Eton, studied programming. But I f— . . . I mean I was stupid. This guy got in touch with me on a programming forum. Wanted some sort of complicated code. We met. And yeah, now, I'm here."

"Was it the demon we killed?" I asked softly.

"You killed him?" He seemed to want confirmation even though I'd already told him the demon was dead.

"Yes. You don't have to worry about them anymore." I focused my attention on him. "How long were you in the house?" I didn't want to ask him how long he'd been beneath the floor.

His mouth twisted. "About two months. They took me there when I refused to write their program. I heard them say that once they turned me, I'd have no choice."

"Did you write it?"

He shook his head. "You killed him and the others will find the place empty when they get back."

Cassie was already hurrying out of the room, phone in hand, to let Sentinel know that more vamp-demons were expected at the house.

"What was it they wanted you to do?" I asked softly, hoping he had the energy to keep talking. Judging by the gray undertone of his dark caramel skin, I didn't think he'd last much longer. And neither did Chloe. She gave me a stern glance.

Baz cleared his throat. "Hack into MI6."

The silence in the room pierced my ears.

"Why?" asked Chloe, now too intrigued to stop him.

"A terrorist," Baz said "One of their own. He was in trouble with MI6 and on their kill-list. He wanted off."

I'd bet he did. "Did you give them anything?"

He grinned. "Just a program that keeps going into an endless loop. They'll figure it out eventually but for now they will think it's working."

"Clever," said Chloe as she got to her feet. "Now, I think it's time you got some sleep. When you're rested, you can shower and change. In the meantime, we'll find a healer for that wound and see if we can also find someone to remove some of the virus."

"Remove it?" I asked, as Baz rested his head back on the sofa. Our questioning was taking a toll on him.

Chloe lifted a shoulder. "Only some of it. One of our skilled healers would be able to suck it out of his system, but he'd still have the virus in his bloodstream. He'd have to have regular visits as it builds up, but it will enable him to live a fairly normal life."

I blew out a sigh of relief just as Cassie entered the room.

"It's been fun ladies and gentlemen," she said. "But duty calls." Storm and Chloe nodded at her. Baz lifted his head from the pillow. "And you," she told him sternly, "behave yourself. Don't make me come back here to sort you out."

"Yes ma'am," he said with a weak smile.

It didn't take anyone long to see through Cassie. All bluster, but just a big marshmallow inside.

She looked at me, giving her comms a tap. "Do you have a minute, Kai?"

As Larsson appeared, I said, "Sure." I gave the small group a wave. "Take me home. I need a shower."

Cassie nodded, took my outstretched hand, and we melted away into the ether.

CHAPTER 6

THE SHOWER IN GRANDMA IVY'S en-suite was running when Larsson dropped Cassie and me in my living room.

I felt a rush of anticipation as I dropped my backpack beside the kitchen counter and headed to the sink. Seeing Grams when she came home, however brief her stay, was something I looked forward to and our teatimes were a pleasure I couldn't miss.

Even if we had company.

Things had been crazy for the last few weeks, so nuts that I'd barely noticed the absence of Cat, our pet feline. The last time I'd seen her was before I'd been thrown into the wraith world and found out my Mom was still alive. After that shock to my system I'd barely had time to think about mundane stuff like cats who have the habit of running off for weeks on end.

It's true when they say that dogs have owners but cats have staff.

I spent a few moments diligently scrubbing remnants of the demon's blood from my fingers before grabbing the kettle and filling it for tea.

"Ivy," Cassie said, giving the closed bedroom door a glance.

She knew Grandma Ivy Odel pretty well. "Tell her I'm sorry I can't stay and chat. Sentinel wants me back at the vamp's hovel, overseeing this op."

She kept her backpack firmly on her shoulders and gave me a twist of a smile. "Have you thought any more about Sentinel's offer?"

I glanced up as I switched the kettle on. "I've given it a thought or two."

How was I supposed to turn her down? The Supreme High Council's offer to join the Elite Corps was much more enticing than anything Sentinel or Omega could offer. But it would remain confidential until I confirmed my decision.

Cassie sighed.

"Why?" Although Cassie was a new friend she'd already gotten pretty close to me, and I suspected it was purely because I missed Tara's comforting presence so much. With my Fae bestie gone off to *Ailuros*-knew-where, I felt a bit on the lonely side.

Cassie pursed her lips and then slid onto a stool and faced me. "Look, I am probably not supposed to tell you this, but the offer won't be on the table forever."

I didn't say a word, just pulled cups and saucers from the cupboard above the counter and laid them out. My pointed finger at the cups got a 'no' from Cassie.

"You're special," she continued. "We all know that, but even for the Ni'amh, offers don't stay offered when you keep refusing."

I stiffened. "So you know?"

She shrugged. "Most agents who need to know, know. I was tasked with looking after an agent who we'd once thought was the Ni'amh."

"My mother."

Without missing a beat, she continued. "And when we discovered the interpretation of the prophecy was wrong and indicated you, we went with it."

"And now?" I asked, narrowing my eyes.

"And now that we know that *you* are not the only savior, we've planned accordingly."

I smiled faintly. "Good to know."

Somehow I'd felt dethroned when Grams had confirmed the prophecy's interpretation had been slightly skewed. Although, if I were honest, I much preferred to be part of a team than to carry such responsibility alone. If the shit hit the fan it would be nice to have company in my shame.

"There are a few people on the upper rungs who—" she hesitated, "—*disagree* with this offer."

Disagree. Pulling out of my thoughts, I grabbed a knife from the top drawer and selected bread, butter, and cheese from the fridge. "Like Paulson?" I grinned as I buttered a slice of bread.

Cassie made a rude sound. "Paulson is ruled by his male parts. When he calms down he'll realize he would have probably made the same decision you did."

I hiked my eyebrows. "I thought you guys played by Sentinel's rules?" I just couldn't picture Spy-Man-Paulson doing something nice. Or even something for someone other than himself.

She shook her head, her blonde hair glinting as it danced around her shoulders. "We do. For the most part. But Sentinel doesn't insist we do things that are wrong, illegal, or against our moral code. If you were on the payroll you would have still been able to make that final choice to save Baz."

"Really?"

"Really."

This was sounding a heckuva lot better than Omega, especially since I was still reeling from the discovery of their underground facility. How could I possibly come to terms with the knowledge that Omega had been holding and experimenting on my mom?

"Do you have any information on their facility?" I asked her.

"Irreparably linked to Omega," she said. "They're dicking us around right now, but the Supreme High Council wants to get to the bottom of it. Omega is guilty. Once the charges are formalized the whole organization is in trouble."

I thought of Logan, of Saleem, and my stomach tightened, the buttered bread forgotten. "Not all their agents are guilty of wrongdoing."

Cassie nodded. "The High Council knows that. They aren't just going to arbitrarily label people as guilty. They would first require proof. And as for the teams on the ground, they're just the worker bees. The council wants the queens."

The kettle whistled. I switched it off barely registering the noise. My mind remained fixed on my two friends who'd get vaporized when the whole Omega thing blew.

I sighed. "Who knows what else they've been doing that they're currently scrambling to sweep under the floorboards."

"You have no idea what Omega is suspected of," Cassie said sadly. "The list of offenses is longer than my arm."

"Then find the evidence and make it stick," I said. "To the guilty. Just be careful how you do it, Cassie. Too many innocent people are likely to get hurt."

She got to her feet and reached for her bag. "I can vouch for Sentinel. Their heart's in the right place. And you should trust them. I do."

"So . . . you think I should say yes?"

"Of course." She winked. "Join the family business."

I nodded wondering if Mom would consider rejoining her old team. It would make sense if they were offering her her old job back—especially after what she'd been through. If I were in her place I'd be chomping at the bit to slide a knife across Omega's collective jugular right now.

"Right," she said. "That's me. Now I've really got to get my arse moving." She sketched a salute as Larsson appeared. This time he smiled before they faded into nothing.

I stared at the empty air, hoping at least some part of my heart would tell me what to do.

I wasn't stupid. I knew I'd refused Sentinel because it wasn't Omega. Omega meant Logan, and any other choice would have conflicted with our relationship no matter how either of us tried to avoid it.

But Sentinel and my family had a long history, so joining their ranks would mean I'd be following in my family's footsteps.

I shook my head and reached for the can of English Breakfast tea leaves. No. Omega was under investigation. Sentinel was doing the investigating. Now wasn't the time to take a position with Sentinel. The last thing I needed was to be tasked with tossing Logan and his friend out on their butts.

The Elite Corps was looking better every day.

I grinned as I spooned tea into the teapot and covered it with boiling water.

Butts or arses, everyone's behinds were on the line.

CHAPTER 7

I'D JUST PLACED THE TEACUPS on the dining table when Grams exited the bedroom, her pale skin pink from the heat of the shower and her white-blonde hair curling at her temples. The fact she was wearing her gray sweatpants and hoodie was a comfort. It meant she was home for the evening.

"Kailin, dear." She reached out and pulled me close and into a tight squeeze. Grams was a hugger and I didn't mind at all. "You look tired," she said against my cheek.

I nodded as I disengaged from her arms and reached for the bread and cheese. Setting the plate on the table, I made a face. "Sorry. I didn't have anything else in the fridge for dinner. Been in Scotland."

Grams laughed, her face brightening as she shook her head at me. "You forget, I have my spies."

I snorted and pushed the sugar bowl toward her. "Of course, you do."

"Was that Cassandra?" she asked as I handed her a spoon.

"Perceptive of you."

"She has a particular way of forming her vowels and consonants."

Yeah, that and the fact that Grams' panther nose worked just as well as mine.

I rolled my eyes. "Gee, Grams. Speak straight. I'm not old enough for old-people-speak."

"Watch it, young lady," She gave me a mock glare and then lifted her cup to blow lightly on the steaming surface. She took a sip. "This is good. Hits the spot."

It certainly did. I drank deeply, enjoying the sweet warmth as it slid down my throat. All that time in England and not a drop of tea to drink.

Then again, was Scotland part of England?

I frowned, then sat back noticing that my fingers were still gritty with vamp residue. "I need to be clean. Demon blood gets into all the wrong cracks and crevices."

I felt a little guilty gulping down the food, but the longer I sat there the more time I spent wondering if I was giving off any kind of demon stink.

When Grams sniffed the air and twitched her nose, I grunted, swallowed the last of my tea in one long gulp and stalked off to my room.

Her snickering followed me all the way into my bathroom.

FIFTEEN MINUTES later I padded out of the bathroom in bare feet. I was clean. My hair was clean. I was wearing my 'at home relaxing' sweatpants and hoodie. Could the night get any better?

I looked up and stopped in my tracks. No. But apparently the night could get worse.

Gram was busy running a pale pink lipstick over her lips as she peered into the mirror we'd hung on the wall behind our front door. No longer in her comfortable clothes, she was dressed in a dark green skirt suit. A pair of black heels sat neatly beside the door.

"What . . ." I trailed off as Corin Odel, dressed in a dark gray suit, rose from the sofa with an equally dark look on his face.

"It wasn't me, Dad."

The words fell out of my mouth, but when a smile broke through the shadows in my father's eyes I was glad of my inability to hold my tongue.

I went to him, received his hug, gave him mine. "What's wrong?"

"Get dressed."

Not a night at home then. "Don't tell me . . . Walker High Council meeting."

"I raised a smart girl," he murmured as his phone beeped. "So proud."

That earned him one of my dark glares but as he was busy swiping his screen and answering his phone it was totally wasted.

I spun on my heel and headed back to my room to change. A few minutes later I returned wearing a deep burgundy skirt suit, carrying black pumps in one hand and running the fingers of my free hand through the mess that was my hair.

As black as Mom's, it was as unruly as hers if I didn't blow dry it into some semblance of decency first. Having left it to dry while I'd dressed, it now stuck out like a mane around my face as though I were more lion than panther.

When I reached the table, I held onto the edge for balance as I slipped my shoes on. Then I bent and grabbed my satchel.

"You are not taking that old thing to a meeting of the High Council," Grams said in a voice of ice and iron.

I rolled my eyes. "Of *course* not Grandmother. I'm just about to get my *purse*."

Total lie.

"Good save," Dad murmured from the sofa.

"You're not helping," I snapped and returned to my room for a more acceptable carrier-of-useless-stuff.

There was no time to fix my hair. The Walker High Council wouldn't care anyway. I grabbed my purse and headed for the door.

CHAPTER 8

I DON'T KNOW WHICH UNSETTLED me more—attending a Walker High Council meeting, or actually setting foot in Justin Lake's home again. Memories of the last time I'd been in the place gave me the shivers. The word 'tense' didn't come close to describing it.

Tonight, however, Justin, the blond Cougar Alpha, who also happened to be both Iain's brother-in-law, and my teenage crush, was too busy herding people around, and met my gaze for only a few seconds as Grams and I entered the room. He didn't need more time though. His golden eyes bore into mine and conveyed a thesaurus of emotions. None of them meant 'happy'.

I sucked in a breath and sent him a short smile, trying not to remember his kiss, or his marriage proposal. He acknowledged my greeting with a nod of his blond head, then hurried over to my father who was standing stony-faced beside my brother Iain. They were an impressive pair, all wide shoulders, and white blond hair. Justin murmured something in Dad's ear. A moment later both Dad and Justin had disappeared into the crowd while Iain took a seat at the back.

Tonight was certainly different from the last meeting. Instead of a small number of Alphas, today the room overflowed with spouses and the immediate families of Alphas from all over the North American continent.

As chivalry hadn't yet died for the walker male only the females occupied the available seating. Members of the High Council were the exception. They'd sit at the head table at the front of the room. Those called on council business would take seats at a smaller table at the side.

At the moment both tables were empty, but places against the walls were filling up as the non-councilmen arranged themselves for the best view of the proceedings.

Well, the non-councilmen and me.

Ignoring Grams' hesitation, I put a hand on her shoulder and gently pressed her down into the last available chair. She patted my fingers before I let go.

The air moved next to me and I looked up to find Mom standing there, her white pants-suit glowing pearlescent.

"What are *you* doing here?" I whispered, shocked to see Mom attending a council meeting. To my knowledge she'd never been invited to one. She was human, of course.

Mom shrugged. "I was summoned," she said, making light of the formal invitation.

I wasn't fooled. For the High Council to summon a human was not a commonplace thing, so it didn't take long for me to scan the crowd and gauge the number of eyes flickering in our direction, a few expressions of surprise at Mom's presence.

It was a harsh reality to be faced with the fact that my mom's species had been widely known and accepted, by everyone except for me. And more the fact that so many of them seemed accepting of her, and concerned with what her presence meant.

A few chairs to Grams' right a heavyset blonde woman leaned forward. Mary Hevers, the wife of the lynx alpha of Montana. She waved her fat fingers at Mom and curved her lips in what she probably hoped would be construed as a supportive smile.

Her lips lied.

Or maybe I was better at recognizing fake than most. Always being the one on the sidelines had taught me to watch for those little tells that gave away what people really thought—even when they were silent. Especially when they were silent. Words mean little. Actions speak the truth.

If you know what to look for.

Tonight Mary held her jaw tight, her spine tighter. She knew something, the thin smile on her face filled with glee and triumph. I glanced at Mom and the tightness at the sides of her eyes told me that she too was very good at picking up emotional tells.

I took a tiny step closer to Mom and relaxed a little when I felt her arm curl around my waist. I didn't want to be seen comforting her because that would have made her look weak in front of all the other Alpha wives. And my mother was not weak.

Instead, I leaned into *her* comfort, glad I was there to be a support during what I felt was going to be very bad news.

Across the room, Dad now sat at the small council table placed along the wall at a right angle to the main conference table. The light from the ancient chandelier above him lent a hooded, shadowed cowl to his face. Beside him sat Alfred Gordon, cougar alpha of Texas, whose wife was Fae. On his other side sat Jem Gumble, Lynx alpha from Maine. His wife, Elaine, was human.

Human and fae. Not walker. I was beginning to see a pattern.

All three men sat very still, blank-faced, not looking at each other or anyone else. They too knew something was wrong but perhaps not precisely what. The meeting hadn't started yet.

"What's going on?" I muttered.

"Exactly what you *think* is going on, sweetie."

I turned to the owner of that voice of dripping ice—Denise Farnsworth, wife of one of the High Council members—but she'd dropped her little poison bomb and moved away, spine stiff, skin pale as if blood was in scarce supply.

I glared after her. "Who does she think she is?"

"High Council wife," was all Mom said.

The crack of gavel hitting block in the now stuffy room pulled everyone's attention to the head table and the—now seated—High Council.

I gave the room a quick, sweeping study. From the expressions on the faces of various general members it was clear some of them knew what was on the meeting's agenda and not all of them agreed with it. A few looked downright upset. But here they stood, in spite of their unhappiness.

It was massively clear who was in control here, and it was the council members whose forefathers had been elected into their illustrious positions decades ago.

Grams often said that it was high time new members were elected but few walkers, Alphas or otherwise, were powerful enough to go against such an ancient tradition.

And yet I too had to stand by and watch as the Walker High Council bound the strongest people in the history of Walkers.

This cannot be happening.

Council Leader Joseph Marsden got to his feet and swept his pale gaze over the gathered Alphas. He stood there for a moment, spine stiff, his hands behind his back like some great leader instead of a power-hungry, turkey-necked wannabe. He loved holding court, this overbearing old creep. As he spoke his throat wobbled, loose skin shivering, making my stomach turn.

I knew what he was going to say before he spoke, and I listened in cold horror.

"Alphas of the United States, wives and family members. We, the High Council, welcome you to today's meeting and would like to extend our heartfelt appreciation for your immediate acceptance of our invitation."

I called bull. I didn't think they'd sent *invitations*.

A rumble across the crowd confirmed they agreed with me.

"Just get on with it," someone complained from the back row. Marsden's face tightened and he cleared his throat. "We have received every communication from the alphas regarding our last discussion and we have finalized and passed the Addendum to the Codex of Rules laws. Now we have an unpleasant task to perform."

As he spoke he moved away from the head table and went to hover over the trio of stony-faced alphas at the smaller table, like an overgrown vulture. Dad watched him, his expression unwaveringly cool.

"According to the tenets of the new law," Marsden continued, "all alphas in a relationship with, or married to, a non-walker will have their alpha statuses revoked forthwith."

Forthwith? Who even said forthwith anymore?

But Marsden wasn't done. "Alphas Odel, Gordon, and Gumble," he toned solemnly. "It is my sad duty to relieve you—"

The noise of movement behind him drew Marsden's attention and he swung away from the seated alphas to glare at the crowd. Fae Marcia Gordon and human Elaine Gumble were on their feet and moving along their rows toward Mom and me.

What was going on?

"Point of order," Mom said clearly and took a step forward. "I believe what you're about to do is a violation of the law."

He stared at her down his nose. "Really, *human*? What do you know of our laws?"

"I know that under the new addendum it's illegal to relieve an alpha of his position if his wife is no longer with him. We"—she gestured to Marcia and Elaine—"are no longer with our husbands."

"What?" A pallid man to begin with, Marsden managed to blanch a few shades whiter and his eyebrows hiked up as far as they could go. "What are you talking about?"

Behind him, Dad, Gordon, and Gumble snapped their dropped jaws closed and tried to look as if this was old news.

"I am saying," said Mom, speaking very slowly, "that I am not with my husband. We've been separated for a good long while now. Everyone is well aware of that." Mom shrugged. "Not sure you can punish a man for his past before a law came into being? I don't believe so."

Marsden's color had turned from white to dangerously red. His gaze shifted to Gumble's wife. "Is this true, human?"

A curvaceous woman with bright yellow hair and a face as round as an apple, Elaine could have played the role of Viking lady on any stage. She gave Marsden a coy smile, her eyes glowing dangerously despite her seductive expression.

"If you kept up to date with the welfare of your people," she said sweetly, "you'd be well aware that Jem and I have had a rocky relationship this last year. As a matter of fact, I moved out two weeks ago. Or did your underlings not tell you?"

Wow, she was daring.

Apparently Marsden hadn't been aware of the Gumble's rocky relationship. It was just as well Marsden had his back to the table because, judging by old Jem's expression, he hadn't been aware of it either.

Marsden, struggling to control his swiftly rising fury, moved his attention to Gordon's wife. "And you, fae?"

Marcia stood very still beside Mom, her rapid pulse beating at the base of her neck. Then she laughed, a humorless, croaking sound.

"If you think marriage to that old goat is fun then think again. I'm with these girls. I'm better off with him as my alpha than as my husband. Thanks to your law I've finally been given the perfect opportunity to toss his wrinkled old ass out of my bed."

Someone snorted.

A couple of people in the back row were unable to control their laughter, and around us a good few were struggling to hide their smiles. Even old Gumble himself couldn't stop the corner of his lip from curving before he sobered into alpha blankness.

But I couldn't laugh. It wasn't simply my reaction to the sudden breakup of three alpha marriages that sobered me. It was knowing that Marcia, who exuded youth and beauty courtesy of her Fae genes, had been married to 'the old goat' for decades. Now, because of Marsden and his ilk, she and Gordon would be denied their last years together. It was cruel.

"Enough!" Marsden snarled, and the laughter in the room died. He swung back to face the three almost-ex-alphas. "Is this true?"

Together, as if choreographed by a master, each man gave him an arrogant, very alpha, inclination of the head.

Our marriages. Our business. You're incompetent. Oh yeah, that nod said it all.

Marsden stood still for another moment, but I could see his face. It was a strange shade of purple and he looked like he'd swallowed a bowlful of jalapeños.

I hoped my parents, the Gumbles, and the Gordons knew what they were doing. Lying to the High Council was a dangerous game.

CHAPTER 9

THE ONLY THING THAT BROKE the icy silence in my apartment was the low bubbling of the kettle.

Why does it seem like I am always making tea?

Dad sat on our sofa, hunched over staring at the floor, his fingers threaded, elbows on his knees. Mom rubbed his back, her expression sad but determined.

He cleared his throat. "You shouldn't have done that."

"Of course, I should have," she said

"I've only just gotten you back." His voice sounded strained.

She sighed, a soft breath of sound. "There are more important things than us."

He shifted his gaze to her face and the look he gave her drew hot tears to my eyes.

But Mom seemed unfazed by the raw pain in her husband's eyes. She patted his cheek. "We have all the time in the world for *us*. Right now, the clans are troubled and they need *you*. Besides." She grinned. "A sordid affair with one's ex is far more interesting than boring old marriage."

Dad gave a harsh laugh and shook his head. He, like Grams and me, was still recovering from shock after Mom's little performance with her two comrades. Iain, unfortunately, had to attend to business in Tukats.

I snorted. "I'm still not sure I believe what you did."

Mom shifted in her seat and glanced over her shoulder at me. Never before had I seen her slim build, her clean profile, her dark hair, as being so much like mine. And so human.

"Would you have done any differently?" she asked softly, her hand never leaving Dad's shoulder.

Grams moved past me and began to prepare the tea, leaving me with no option but to answer Mom.

"Fine," I said. "I would have done the same thing. But you three seemed to have had it planned."

Mom smiled and got to her feet. The pearlescent silk of her suit pants clung to her hips as she strode to the kitchen to make her coffee. She'd never been a tea girl. "The alphas have been expecting something like this since the last High Council meeting."

"You spoke to Marcia and Elaine?"

Mom nodded. "We were well prepared."

"But you didn't bother to tell us," Dad said, his voice rough.

Mom lifted her gaze from the coffee machine to him, her fingers hovering over the switches. "Giving you three advanced warning would have guaranteed the High Council's win. You know as well as I do that you would have shot us down."

Her words fell like hot rocks onto snow. Devastating.

"High Council really wanted you out," I told Dad hoping he'd explain why.

His face paled a little, but when he didn't answer, I decided to ask my questions up front, "Have you heard anything? Rumor mill? Grapevine? Underground?"

He glanced up at me, and the truth was written in his guilty face. "You've known all along."

"Of course he did, dear," said Grams from my side. She

elbowed me gently out of the way and, with nothing left to do with my hands I went to sit beside Dad.

"What are you going to do?" I asked him.

"He's going to keep on going, as if nothing happened," Grams said before he could reply. "While he does that, *we* are going to deepen our investigation."

"You and Mom?"

Grams nodded. "I have feelers out. Marsden and his cronies still have an agenda."

"We've got a hacker working on their servers," Mom said. "We're just waiting to find something damning, but"—she shrugged—"So far nothing."

Grams sighed. "Only hints and implications. Nothing concrete. They seem to be covering their tracks too well. Even the big guns are coming up empty."

"Sentinel is on this?" They had to be, surely.

"Like a bear all over a honey pot."

As our laughter subsided, Mom said, "I'm going to stay here for a while. Dad and I can't be seen living in the same house."

I raised my eyebrows. It went against nature when parents grew up and moved back in with their kids. Would this mean I'd be kicked out of my room?

Mom's mouth curved into a secretive smile. "Do you still have your key, darling?"

It was my house. Of course I did.

"Of course, I do," my father said.

Huh?

"And in all this time you never once used it?" Mom's voice held a hint of accusation.

What?

"You left," Dad said tiredly. "You made it clear we were done. Whether it was to protect our children or not, you said we were done. Why would I use it?"

What. The. Hell?

"Because it's time you both grew up." Grams marched over and placed the platter of teacakes and pastries on the dining room table. "I'm tired of watching you two kids going around and around in circles. You did what you did at the time to protect your children. That's it. They don't need protection any longer. So be done with the past, and start thinking about the future." She skewered Dad with a don't-mess-with-me glare. "Use your key."

My parents turned to stare at Grams, their expressions a blend of shock, annoyance and gratitude.

I stared at Grams too. But not in gratitude. Would I ever get the image of my parents having sneaky sex like a couple of hormonal teenagers out of my brain?

No. No, I wouldn't.

"Food," I said, feeling nauseous. I waved both hands at the trays like a demented magician. *Don't think about it.* "Food."

Dad got to his feet, giving me an odd look, and walked over to Mom. After a moment of silent communication, he placed a hand around her waist and guided her to a seat at the table.

She patted the chair next to her and he took it. Grams and I joined them.

For a while we limited the conversation to asking for the sugar, the teacakes, the pastries. Finally, though, we had to move to the real issues. Dad started the ball rolling.

"So," he said, sounding resigned. "What the hell am I supposed to do while you ladies do the groundwork?"

"Gather the Alphas and start preparing," Mom said. "Do your own investigations to find the traitors. Someone from the clans is feeding information to the High Council and that info is being used against us. We need to know who the mole is."

I cleared my throat. "And target those High Council members who looked like they were sitting on hot coals. Not all of them were thrilled with the new Addendum or with what Marsden had planned. Surely they would be the first to turn on him as long as they were promised discretion and safety?"

Dad shifted his attention to me, his expression impressed. "I hadn't noticed their discomfort, but I think that's going to be my first order of the day."

"No," Mom said. "It's not." She had a strange smile on her face, and when he raised his eyebrows she fluttered her eyelashes at him. "Don't forget, we have an affair to carry out."

Don't think about it.

"Do we now?" He leaned back with a cheeky smile.

They looked like two kids in love. So cheesy, yet so cute.

If they were someone else's parents.

"You get your key," Mom said, "and I'll meet you downstairs."

They both got to their feet, Dad heading for the coat-rack and Mom to my room where she'd thrown her coat and purse.

"Downstairs?" I echoed.

"Yes," she called from my room. "My apartment is downstairs."

What?

"Your apartment is *downstairs*?" I squeaked. Couldn't help it. I didn't even know that the downstairs apartments were occupied. Grams and I had had the building to ourselves since I moved in a couple years ago.

"Yes, honey." Mom emerged from the room, coat in hand, her bag slung over her shoulder.

"*Your* apartment?"

"Is downstairs." She smiled at me, at Grams, and slid her arm into the crook of Dad's elbow. Then they both glided out of the apartment as if they hadn't just dropped a bomb on me.

Don't think about it.

I gave a delicate shudder, and the door clicked shut behind them.

CHAPTER 10

O'HAGAN'S WAS NOISY BUT I needed to be out of the apartment. It wasn't because my parents were having their illicit affair one floor down.

Or was it?

I just needed a change of scenery that didn't include demons, or families falling apart.

I wrapped my fingers around the glass of golden liquid and stared at the aged whiskey. Why the hell did I even order the stuff? It wasn't as if alcohol had any effect on me. Walkers were immune to the effects of any alcohol or regular drug.

But I was in a bar after midnight. Drinking seemed the thing to do.

The air changed, and drifted warm against my skin as someone slid in beside me.

I glanced up and smiled.

Logan pressed warm lips to my cheek, then nuzzled my neck.

"What's a girl like you doing in a place like this?" he mumbled against my skin, his spiky stubble tickling me.

"Of all the corny lines in the existence of corny lines, that's the one you use?" I laughed softly. I had to admit it had been cute. Or maybe Logan was just that cute.

He raised his head, his dark messy hair standing up in all directions, and grinned. Then, as he studied my face, his smile disappeared. "What's wrong?"

"Crap."

"Crap?" He frowned. "What kind?"

"All kinds. Bull. Fans. Deep in it. Take your pick."

"That bad?"

I nodded as I twisted the heavy-bottomed glass.

He sniffed at my whiskey. "Strong stuff."

"Not for me."

"I know," he said with a sigh. "Care to share? Or do you want to keep staring at it?"

I smiled and slid the glass toward him. As he sipped I studied his face, noting the darkness smudging the skin beneath his reddened eyes.

"You still dreaming?" I asked, gently.

"Yep."

"Anything new?"

"Nope."

"Saleem?"

"Meeting me here."

I nodded and sat back wondering what the Djinn had to share that was important enough for them to track me down. Logan's presence was no accident, then. Saleem's involvement made it more important than a chance chat.

So I didn't push. I'd seen Logan struggling with his dreams, confused by memories that weren't memories, and I prayed he'd find some form of release. He needed low-key interaction and I was happy to comply.

Gold and bronze sparks of light flickered in the shadows of our booth and the djinn appeared in the seat opposite us as if summoned.

Saleem grinned, his dark features matching the sexy smile as he solidified. "Hey gorgeous."

"Hey, yourself." I smiled back. He was pretty sizzling for a humanized demon. "Where have you been?"

"Around." He glanced at Logan, his black eyes glittering. "Busy."

Busy must have been fairly bad because for the briefest moment Saleem lost his glamor making the swirling tattoos on his skin starkly visible.

"Is everything okay?" asked Logan, his eyes not leaving his friend's face.

"Not really."

"Did she take you?"

Saleem nodded, then glanced at me. "Mel took me to find my mother."

"And?" I urged. Mel Morgan was not only the djinn's main squeeze—a pairing that I definitely approved of—but she was also probably the most powerful SoulTracker of them all. Mel moved through the veil like Larsson did, but with more skill and power. She could also astral project.

"She's being held at a compound outside of Virginia."

I didn't press him but my *and?* hovered in the air between us.

"And," Saleem said "I saw something I hadn't expected."

Clearly he needed a prod. "Which was?"

He sighed and ran his fingers through his shoulder-length black hair. "Familiar faces."

"Familiar faces?" Logan leaned closer, his appropriated drink now forgotten.

"Familiar *Omega* faces."

We sat in silence for a while, but none of us were shocked.

"Not surprising," I said. "Not now that we know they had everything to do with my mom's abduction."

"It's possible they've been holding *my* mother since before they roped me into working for them."

Saleem looked so defeated I felt a pull of sadness in my gut. Betrayal by an organization you trusted isn't an easy thing to bear.

"Did you see her?"

"Mel did. She's fine, but she doesn't look very happy." Saleem's face remained expressionless. He kept his hurt inside, a lot like Logan did.

I turned to Logan. "So Omega is suspect. Do you think they could have something to do with those memories of yours?"

"Memories?" asked Saleem.

Logan's grimace made it clear he thought I shouldn't have said anything in front of the djinn, but I shook my head. "Tell him. You need all the help you can get."

Logan jaw tightened but he relented and gave Saleem a quick précis. Vivid dreams that felt so real they were more like memories. His strong feeling that the girl was real. That she had something to do with his past.

"Have you considered," I said slowly, thinking aloud, "that she might be your sister?"

As I spoke, Saleem glanced at me, his expression odd.

Logan's face seemed more haggard than before.

"Of course you have," I murmured, my mind spinning. "Okay, maybe your memory has been tampered with. We all know Sentinel and Omega both resort to that kind of thing to protect innocents. They must have mages capable of doing the job."

"I'm not an innocent," Logan said.

Naturally he'd missed the point. "You *were* when you were twelve."

I spoke softly as he pushed away from the table and leaned against the back of the seat. He rested his hands on his thighs, running his palms back and forth along his jeans.

"Maybe," I continued, watching those restless hands, "they wanted to protect you from the truth."

He stilled. "What truth?"

I swallowed hard, reached for his left hand and threaded my fingers through his.

"That she's dead." I held his fingers tightly, keeping them as close to me as possible. "Have you considered that maybe she died in that fire? Maybe the memories were wiped so that your mind could heal."

It certainly made sense. To me at least.

Now he looked more than haggard. He looked sick. His head jerked left to right, a ragged negative.

Saleem snorted and we both snapped our attention to him. "What?" I asked, my voice curt and cool.

He raised his eyebrows, then shook his head. "Considering the fact they are holding *my* mother"—he jerked a thumb at his chest—"and that they abducted and experimented on *your* mother" —he stabbed a forefinger my way— "I wouldn't put it past them to be responsible for killing someone *you* love."

When he said the last 'you' he pointed at Logan. "She could be your sister," he said gently, his eyes never leaving Logan's face. "Or even a friend. But she must have meant something to you. Omega seems to be in the habit of taking people who mean a lot to us. If I were you, I wouldn't trust them right now."

"I wouldn't trust them at all." I didn't even try to keep the ice from my voice. "At *all. Ever.*"

The silence stretched across the table, a blanket of daggers. Sharp, tangible, painful.

Logan picked up my glass and downed the last of the drink. He set the glass back on the table a little harder than was necessary. Cleared his throat. "I don't plan to trust them."

"Have you thought about joining the High Council Elite?" I was supposed to have been gathering my team. But things had gotten away with me these past couple of days. They'd given me a week to decide, but if they really wanted me, I didn't think a few days more would matter.

Saleem looked at me, outraged. Even Logan stiffened—the

instinctive reaction of faithful men to the suggestion they should betray their oaths. But slowly, their expressions changed.

Oaths worked both ways. Omega had sworn loyalty and faithfulness too. Tonight the results of those broken promises cried alone in a compound in Virginia, whispered through Logan's dreams.

Logan cleared his throat. "We haven't considered it." He shared a glance with Saleem. "Not until now."

"What if we investigated on our own?" Saleem said.

"That's dangerous, don't you think? An organization like the Supreme High Council provides backup in case you need it." I was beginning to sound like Cassie.

Logan shook his head. "Saleem is right. Let's approach this from a different angle. *If* we change sides and *if* there is a mole in the Corps then our families may be in danger. If the girl is my sister and she's dead, then all they have on me are memories. But *if* she's alive somewhere—like Saleem's mother—then we'll be endangering both of them. We can't risk it."

"So we stay and keep on as normal." Saleem seemed to have already made up his mind. "We don't raise eyebrows. Then, on our own time, we investigate the shit out of this whole thing."

"I'm in," I said.

Two pairs of eyes snapped to my face, expressions incredulous.

So flattering.

I tensed at the look in Logan's eyes, the one that said clearly that he didn't want to endanger me. But, as I glared back at him, my shoulders tense, ready to jump down his throat, he sighed.

"Fine," he said.

I raised an eyebrow at the single word of assent.

"And Mel is in too." There was a smile in Saleem's voice as he spoke the SoulTracker's name.

I hid a grin. "Good," I said. "At least with the two of us on the case *something* will get done right."

That set the two of them laughing, and I just sat there, uncomfortable at the sound. Not because they were laughing but because this laughter wasn't joyful. It reeked of desperation.

And fear.

CHAPTER 11

AFTER O'HAGAN'S, LOGAN, SALEEM, AND I ended up at my apartment.

They had spent an hour hatching their plans for Omega and an investigation into its involvement in their personal lives.

I'd spent that hour staying out of their plans for Omega, biting my tongue when Logan talked about finding Jess and demanding she tell him what she knew. As Jacinta Carnarvon—an enigmatic Titan—would know a lot more than she was willing to share, I doubted he'd be as successful as he wanted.

She was one of the Immortals, a being that had lived for thousands of years, and one who just happens to be guardian to Logan.

Also, she happened to be employed by Omega.

Even now, Logan had no idea that his partner was a Titan whose role was to protect him. Though Jess had confessed as much to me, she still hadn't told me why he was so important that he needed a Titan to watch over him.

They were still mulling things over when Saleem whisked Logan home leaving me to clean up the kitchen on my own. Which I resolved by heading to bed.

I was still drowsy, squinting at the gleeful morning sunshine streaming through the windows as I made a mental note to ring Mel and talk things through with her as soon as I'd dried the dishes, but I was wiping and putting away the last plate when a knock sounded on my door.

Hurrying to the door, I sniffed the air, finding nothing untoward on my threshold. But when I swung the door open the identity of my visitor took me aback.

Nerina.

It figured. DeathTalkers had no living scent.

My stomach gave a twinge as I forced a smile on my face. "Hello, Nerina," I said and waved her inside. "Come in."

The last time I'd seen the DeathTalker I'd just made a deal with her High Priestess in return for a portal key to take me to the Graylands, an in-between plane where the dead remained if they didn't move on to the next life.

DeathTalkers engendered a feeling of dread in most people, including me, but I knew Nerina better than any of her sisters. DeathTalkers were inherently immune to human emotion—or so went the general opinion. Which is why her behavior was worrying. It told me general opinion was very wrong.

Nerina wore the requisite gray robes, the hood covering her gray-white hair and shadowing the features of her pale face. But today the serene calm she always carried with her was markedly absent.

Her fingers shook and she folded them tightly in front of her waist.

"Are you okay?" I asked, guiding her to the dining table rather than to the sofa. Nerina didn't seem the lounging type.

She sat across from me, so still that I wondered if I should urge her to talk. Instead, the words, "Would you like some tea?" fell out of my mouth.

What the hell was it with me and tea these days?

She shook her head and twisted her fingers together.

At last she shifted in her seat and raised her eyes to me. Eyes that had been clear and pale with milky irises the last time we'd spoken were now reddened, the way human eyes got when you cried for hours on end.

"What happened?" I asked softly, really worried now.

She lifted her chin the tiniest bit. "I have a message for you, Kailin Odel."

Why so formal?

I gave a "go ahead" nod, and she took a thready breath, as if she'd been waiting for my permission to speak.

"By order of the High Priestess of the DeathTalkers of the North American Continent you are hereby summoned to fulfill your Blood Promise."

The words rang out across the apartment and I could have sworn I heard Lady Kira's imperious voice overlaying Nerina's voice.

Not too long ago when I'd needed a way to get to the Graylands to save my sister Greer, I'd been forced to appeal to the DeathTalker High Priestess. She'd given me a key that allowed me to traverse the veil between worlds, and in return she'd extracted a Blood Promise.

And Lady Kira was calling in her marker. Of course I had little choice but to respond. I'd known when I'd struck the bargain that one day I'd have to fulfill my end of it. I just hadn't expected it to be so soon. Or sound so ominous.

Because the girl's tone was worrying.

"Of course I'll come," I told her. "But what's wrong? You can tell me."

I waited while Nerina bit her trembling lip. When I leaned closer she jerked her head away, and I figured she had no authority to tell me what I wanted to know.

That left me with one choice. To go to the DeathTalker estate and find out for myself.

 S SOON AS NERINA LEFT, I hurried to my room to change. Soft slacks and an oversized tee were not the clothes I wanted to wear when going head-to-head with the ice-priestess.

I drew on a pair of formal black pants, a silky long-sleeved blouse, and my leather jacket—a concession to normal working attire.

I was pulling on a pair of black high-heeled ankle boots—and wondering why I even bothered to dress up for a woman who neither liked nor respected me—when someone knocked.

This place was Grand Central Station all of a sudden.

I stifled a grumble and headed to the door, only mildly appeased to detect Logan's signature scent on the air.

I'd gotten into the habit of sniffing before I opened the door, and before I entered the apartment. I'd let my guard down once and paid for it. My wood floor still bore the marks of my abduction by a band of crazed Walkers.

Lesson learned.

I opened the door and though I was in a hurry, one look at his face sent me straight into his arms.

He'd held back last night while Saleem had been with us, and now the truth of his emotions showed in his eyes.

He crushed me tight for a moment and then I leaned back so I could read his expression. "I wish I could help you remember."

He grabbed my butt, gave it a squeeze then looked over my shoulder his expression a little chagrined.

I laughed. "Don't worry. Grams won't catch you in the act. She's off somewhere investigating something."

I pulled him inside and closed the door. "I can't stay, sorry. I'm on my way out."

"That's fine. Just came by to thank you, and to tell you not to worry about me." There was an odd note in his voice.

I thought I knew why. "You heard about the High Council meeting."

He nodded. "I have a high clearance level."

"Figures," I said, as I zipped up my boots. "I was going to tell you, then Saleem came and . . ."

"You don't have to explain." His crooked smile flashed. "You always put everyone else first. I'm used to it." He curled his arm around my waist. "So how was it?"

"Awful. You should have seen Dad's face." Then I laughed softly. "And wonderful, too. Three non-walker women threw the pack law back in their faces. It was brilliant."

He chuckled. "I heard. A lot of people are impressed with them. So what happens now?"

"Now the couples stay away from each other until things settle and they have a better handle on where the clans stand in relation to the High Council."

I leaned back to study his face, my stomach a little queasy as I wondered if I could trust him with the whole truth.

His eyebrows rose. "Sounds like they got it bad for your dad. What'd he do to them?"

"What makes you think he did anything?" I asked, unable to keep the defensive note from my voice.

"Well, they aren't likely to have picked his name from a hat. Whether he did something on purpose or it's just because he is the man he is, they have a reason. Find that reason, then you find the way to break them."

Good point.

Logan ducked down to scan my face, took my chin with gentle fingers. "Nothing you say to me will ever be repeated beyond this room."

"Really?" I patted him down, shoulders, hips. Butt. "What if you're wired?"

He frowned, seriously considering it. "If I am, I actually have no way of knowing. So good point. Let me verify our security before you say anything you regret."

I frowned too. "I didn't mean—"

He shook his head. "Kai, it's got nothing to do with anything you said. If I'm bugged, something I hadn't even considered until now, then I'm a danger to us all. What we discussed at O'Hagan's could have incriminated us."

I shook my head. "I'm just not sure that either you or the djinn are buggable."

"What do you mean?"

"You guys are both hot."

He smiled. "What can I say?"

"Shut up." I smacked his shoulder, then skipped around him and headed into my room where I grabbed my messenger bag and returned as fast as I could.

"I meant your body temperature. I'm not sure any electronics can survive that kind of contained heat. Not unless it's the NASA kind. And that's bloody expensive."

"Both Sentinel and Omega have access to a lot of money."

I sighed. "Just great." There was a very real possibility that all my secrets were out there for anyone to see.

"So where are you off to?" he asked too brightly.

"The DeathTalker Estate. To see Kira."

Silence stretched between us as a flicker of flame flared in Logan's eyes. It wasn't often that his fire showed.

Not good.

"She collecting?"

"Yup. And something big is going down. Nerina was so jittery, she looked like she was about to explode into shadows."

"I'm coming with you."

I lifted my chin. "Not on your life. You saw how angry she was the last time you tagged along. How many hours did you wait outside for me?"

His cheek twitched, as if he didn't care that the high priestess had made him wait more than two hours outside her library.

"You're not coming."

Logan's eyes narrowed. "Fine. If you don't take me, then at least ask Lily to go with."

"Just to make you feel better?"

He almost blinked.

I grunted. "Fine," I said ignoring the surprised arch of his eyebrows as I dug into my bag for my phone and texted Lily to come over.

Knowing her, she'd bring Anjelo and I'd have to kick him out before dragging her with me.

Fabulous.

Just fabulous.

CHAPTER 13

THANK GOODNESS I'D GIVEN LILY a key to my apartment. One more knock on the door and there was no telling how safe she would have been.

She flung the door open, kicked it shut and staggered in hunched under the weight of her rucksack.

"Did you rob a bank?" I asked, tapping my finger on my wrist as I leaned against the kitchen counter, arms crossed. I'd gotten tired of pacing.

Lily rolled her eyes. "Almost." She set the rucksack on the table. "I brought whatever I thought would be needed." She opened the flap and untied the mouth. "What do you think?"

I walked over and peered inside. Laughed. Shook my head. "We're going to see a high priestess, not to fight the whole wraith army."

Lily sighed, looking from the bag to my face then back again. "Can we fight the wraith army *after* we see the queen B-word?"

"Empty it and let's go. We don't want to keep the B-word waiting." It surprised me Lily had actually used a clean version of the term. She'd never been one to couch her thoughts in niceties.

"No Anjelo?" I asked.

Lily jerked her head. "Nope. He's otherwise occupied."

I stopped in my tracks and turned around.

I'd known Lily long enough to recognize when something was bothering her. Her inability to shift had always been a chip on her shoulder but she'd learned soon enough that I wasn't the judgmental type. Having her at my side in a fight had taken getting used to but now I used her skills to my advantage.

And she'd become more than just a sidekick.

I waited until she caught up with me at the front door. Then I blocked her exit. "Talk."

Lily gave the way out a longing glance over my shoulder. Then her shoulders sagged. "Oh, all right. Anjelo's been in a mood since we got back from Wrythiin."

"Mood?" I prompted, hoping I wasn't going to have to pull every detail out of her like some deranged dentist.

"Yeah. I think he's taking it bad. You know, the whole how-could-I-have-trusted-Illyria song. You'd think he had feelings for the bitch."

That's more like it.

I shook my head. "I don't think it's that, and nor do you."

She shrugged. "Maybe. Yeah, okay. But she played him and he risked your mom's life with his carelessness. That's more or less what he believes."

With a sigh, I set my hands on my hips. "I should have gone to talk to him but I've been crazy busy with all the hell that's breaking loose. It didn't cross my mind he'd be taking it this hard."

"Not your fault."

"It's not *his* either and it's time he faced it."

"I've tried to make him face it," Lily said. "Believe me, I've tried. But it's like he can't hear me."

I snorted. "Yeah, that's usually the case with the people we care about the most. We don't listen when they talk because we take them and their opinions for granted."

Lily's mouth turned down. "You think he still cares?"

So *that's* what was really going on.

"Lily," I admonished as I walked toward her. I held onto her shoulders, tipping my head to meet her gaze. "You know he cares. His feelings haven't changed. He's just taking longer than most to adjust. Guilt is a difficult burden to bear."

She nodded, sniffed, shifted her gaze. Anjelo wasn't the only one taking it hard.

"Look. If it makes you feel better, I'll go talk to him after I see Kira." I spoke softly, hoping she wouldn't take it the wrong way.

She turned to face me, her eyes shining. "Yes. That's probably the best thing. He'll have no choice but to listen to our Alpha, right?"

Their Alpha.

I'd forgotten that Anjelo had declared me his alpha before he'd ended up being pulled into the wraith plane. Now it looks like Lily had taken up the same standard. It probably wasn't legal to acknowledge an alternate alpha and I wasn't sure how I felt about it since it meant he was divesting himself of my father as his pack leader. Too late now.

"Right," I said. "No choice. Let's go."

I slung my messenger bag over my shoulder and headed out of the apartment and toward the stairs, a pensive Lily in tow.

No choice.

Heading for the stairs, I wondered when I'd grown up and chosen to stop using the rickety fire-escape at the back of the building?

Sure, it had always been untrustworthy and its rusty bolts had had me clinging on to both walls and guts a few times as I teetered above the street.

Could that need for excitement, for the rush of death-defying stupidity, have had something to do with my panther's needs? Since I'd chosen to give her more freedom, time to run as a cat, perhaps I no longer required the rush of adrenaline that came with choosing to risk becoming a chalk outline on the pavement below.

Who knew?

But even that rusty-lattice web of doom was better than the Birdcage. I could deal with troubled teens and a certain Death-Talker B-word, but nothing—not even imminent death—would get me to choose that clunking monstrosity over the stairs.

CHAPTER 14

I DIDN'T HAVE A CAR, so we'd run to the meeting.

What was the point of a walker owning a vehicle anyway, when they run like the wind?

Oh yeah, for times when you want to appear cool, calm and collected instead of looking like you'd been hit by a windstorm.

I should have thought this through, but it was a little late now.

The street outside my apartment was deserted enough but we made for the back alley. None of the surrounding buildings had windows facing the alley.

There, Lily tightened the strap of her rucksack. She'd only removed the heaviest weapons from it. Good thing even Pariahs —walkers who couldn't shift into their animal form—could run or I would have had to leave her behind. *Then* she'd have been mighty peeved.

I gave the nod and we both set off, Lily following close behind me so she could see where I was going.

It was difficult to enjoy the scenery as we went. Our speed meant most things passed by in a blur while wind dragged our hair away from our faces and flattened the fabric of our clothes against our bodies.

Still, what would have taken forty-five minutes in a car took us a mere fifteen.

I slowed as we approached the final turnoff, hung a left, and jogged along the dusty road. A few moments later, however, we were deep into a forest of elms and ash, following a shadowed trail. The trail ended at an imposing pair of black iron gates set into a twenty-foot high wall of rugged gray stone.

As I'd expected, the gates opened as we approached, their grating sound of metal-on-metal setting my teeth on edge. High on the wall a security camera swiveled to follow our progress as we entered the property.

Behind us, the gates grated shut.

We followed the graveled drive hedged in by expansive green lawns to its end—an impressively large stone castle complete with three towers, one on each front corner and the third on its back wing. With its dark, diamond-shaped paneled windows the castle looked foreign, with edges of fantasy and danger. Not at all like something that belonged on United States soil.

We walked up the steps to a large, ornate door. As I reached out to knock it, like the gates, it opened before us. A small woman, wrapped and hooded in stone gray, her eyes trained on the honey wood floor held the door open with one hand and gestured down the wood-paneled hall with the other.

I knew the way but I followed her gesture, taking a left to the waiting room outside Lady Kira's library. Then I dropped my messenger bag on the rich mahogany coffee table and sank into the dark leather of the sofa, prepared to wait.

Lily, on the other hand, took her time joining me, studying each painting and artifact along the route.

"Do you know what *that* is?" she said, pointing a finger over her shoulder at what looked like an old pottery relic. Her voice, low and breathy, trembled with awe.

"What?" I asked, not really interested.

"It's the remains of one of the oldest DeathTalkers," she whispered.

I rolled my eyes. "Lily, they wouldn't have their predecessor's remains hanging around in here. It's not as if it's a mausoleum."

Lily narrowed her eyes and set her rucksack on the floor beside me. "It said so on the card."

"What card?" I asked staring at the door to the library. Was Kira going to make me wait as long as she had on my last visit here?

Lily pushed my shoulder to get my attention. "The card in front of the urn. It said the name of a DeathTalker ancient." She shivered dramatically.

I sighed and aimed a pointed glare at the library door. "Can we talk about burial urns later?"

"Sure," she said, flicking the urn a watchful look over her shoulder. "But you have to admit it is *muy* creepy."

"*Muy* creepy?"

Her mischievous grin flashed out. "Anjelo is back."

I smiled, then ignored her.

Thankfully, a mere ten minutes later the library door opened and Nerina came out. Her expression said she wasn't very far from hugging me breathless.

Okay, then.

"Only you may enter, Kailin." She spoke softly, her expression apologetic.

As I rose to my feet I felt Lily tense. I didn't recall telling her she'd actually meet Kira with me. I'd only asked her to come along, and even that had been simply to placate Logan.

I glanced at her, a question in my eyes. Lily shrugged, nonchalant now she saw I wasn't bothered by Kira's demand.

I took my messenger bag and followed Nerina inside the large high-ceilinged library, and got my first surprise.

Kira was not alone.

The dark-haired high-priestess stood near floor-to-ceiling windows, and was flanked by two more DeathTalkers.

Kira's pitch-black eyes stared down at me, cold and arrogant, but since the last time we'd met I'd grown thicker skin against the woman's barbs and feline insults.

"Welcome, Hunter," she said.

What? No cat insults?

I inclined my head.

She ignored my lack of verbal greeting and gestured at the woman on her left. "This is Gaia, High Priestess of the European Council."

Gaia smiled, her pale eyes glinting with a hint of blue. She was tall and thin and seemed a thousand times nicer than Kira.

"Well met, sister Hunter." Gaia dipped her head in a shallow bow and I did the same.

"And this is Sini." Kira allowed no time for more social conventions. "She controls the African Continent."

Sini, a dusky woman, was wrapped in gray cloth too, but she wore what appeared to be a turban. The cloth wrapped around her head and hung loosely about her face to hide her features.

She cast her honey-dark eyed gaze over me and her smile was tight. Only when I returned it did she relax. Maybe Kira hadn't given her much of a welcome either.

"So," I said, to help move things along. "I take it something bad happened."

Kira arched a pencil-thin eyebrow. "Hence your summons."

That put me in my place. "Summons? Don't you mean your request? I need no compulsion to honor a promise freely given." I wasn't about to let her walk all over me.

Gaia smiled and so did Sini, so it was probably a good thing Kira didn't glance sideways. I wasn't clear on DeathTalker hierarchy so any one of these three women could be the highest ranking.

"Nerina, if you please?" Gaia's soft tones managed to fill the large room. When Kira kept her lips in a thin line, saying nothing about Gaia taking over, I wondered if Gaia ranked higher or if the women were working to a common plan.

When Nerina came to a stop at my side, Gaia said, "Kailin, in order for you to fulfill your blood promise, we wish for you to see an incident through the eyes of the deceased."

I blinked.

Nerina slipped her hand into mine and drew me to a long leather sofa. Sat me down. Held out a tiny cup.

"May I ask that you drink this? It is Elven Mead. It will assist in the mind-meld, allowing you to relax to a level which most humans are unable to access."

I glanced at Gaia, but her encouraging nod bolstered my courage. I took the cup and sniffed the contents; a silvery-gray drink that looked like mercury and smelled of copper and ozone.

Weird.

I dipped the tip of my tongue into it. It tasted cool and minty, like icy spring water steeped with peppermint.

More weird.

Finally, I drank it all in one gulp and handed the cup back to Nerina realizing too late that I hadn't asked how much to have. Her calm expression told me I'd done the expected thing.

She placed the cup on the floor at her feet then sat beside me and took hold of my hands. Her skin felt smooth and cool. She smelled of mint—or was the mint taste in my mouth affecting my sense of smell?

"Now keep calm, relax." Nerina's voice slipped through my thoughts. "Just lean on my energy and I'll take care of you. Afterward you may feel a little ill so we will leave you to rest." Her fingers tightened on mine. "Ready?"

I gave a tiny nod and then felt a strange pull on my energy as whatever Nerina was doing sucked all the strength from my body, all the breath from my lungs.

My heart stuttered in my chest as I closed my eyes. It took

real effort to force myself to calm down, to heed Nerina's warning.

Calm.

Shapes danced in my vision, shadows that coalesced to form furniture and people, like a strange dream.

A street.

My ears caught sounds, laughter, a car roaring past. A tin can skittering on the blacktop.

A large room came into view, what looked like a bar stripped of its furniture and booths. A bunch of kids. A pool table. A game with colored balls set up on the playing surface. Not a single pool cue in sight.

A girl stood by the side rail, her short aquamarine hair tipped with bright green, her slim form covered in silver-studded leather that matched the dog-collar around her neck.

She leaned over the table, swayed her butt from side to side drawing a few whistles and more raucous laughter. I got the sense it was all good-natured because she smiled, rested her elbow on the side rail, aimed, and sent a burst of energy at the eight ball. The eight-ball hit the black with a *crack* and then both of them spun over the playing surface and into the far corner pocket.

As shouts roared through the room, cheers and jeers alike, a taller, spiky-haired man drew closer to her. Smiled a sensual smile.

"Are they all here?" His silvery eyes were oddly colored and didn't mesh with his olive skin.

The strangest of this was I could see each individual feature and yet when I tried to get a picture of his face, it just blurred, as if the viewer had gone cross-eyed.

The blue-haired girl tilted her head and looked over the man's shoulder as another couple of people entered from a shadowed back door. "Now they are."

She pulled her attention back to him and tipped her head to

study his face, a frown creasing her smooth brow. "So what was it you wanted us all here for? Something you wanted to tell us?"

He nodded and looked around at the gathered people.

There were about a dozen young adults, a mix of races, but I sensed all paranormal or fae. The girl used energy. At the back a short Asian boy bounced lightning in his palm while his friends nudged him to stop. A second girl, reed thin and pale, glowed a soft blue.

It was only then I registered that my view of the room had adjusted. I'd become one of a crowd shifting toward the rest of the group as instructed. From where I now stood, I could look the silver-eyed man in the face.

He gestured for the girl to join her friends and though she frowned she obeyed. She hadn't even turned around before he straightened to his full height, locked his knees, he drew his hands forward, palms out and then flung a bolt of energy directly into the crowd.

Screams shattered the air around me, ripped the insides of my ears. Pain ripped my flesh and eyes. I smelled ozone and fire, and white-hot power.

And then it all went black.

$\mathcal{I}$ ROCKETED TO MY FEET, gasping for breath, my brain throbbing with the drumbeat of my pulse and my mouth tasting of metal and vomit. I wanted to run but I was surrounded by mist and shadows. Surrounded by enemies. Blind. *Helpless.*

"You are safe," said a calm voice from the mist. "Breathe."

Nerina.

"Breathe," she said again. "Slowly, Kailin. In. Out. In . . ."

I breathed, wrapping an arm around my midsection, as if the mere gesture would encourage my churning gut to settle.

A few moments passed before my vision cleared enough for me to recognize the hazy blotch in front of me as Nerina's face. She must have jumped off the sofa when I did.

She seemed unaffected by the vision. I, on the other hand, was a twisted, confused wreck.

"What the *hell* was that?" An inane question. I had a pretty good idea what I'd witnessed.

Nerina took my shaking hand and guided me back down to the sofa cushions. "I apologize," she said when we were both seated. "I know what it feels like to see such a thing for the first time."

I wasn't troubled by the vision itself, just the content. "Why couldn't I see his face? I know what he looks like, even his eye color, but his face . . . It was indistinguishable."

Nerina nodded. "We also found that strange. We think it may be a type of psychological block. Perhaps Kira blocked it out. The trauma . . ."

"Did they all die?"

Nerina nodded. "We were able to see what happened in the room well after what you were shown. DeathTalkers have a greater awareness of the world, even after death, giving us greater flexibility with what we can see. After he killed them he simply left. It seems he was certain enough that they were all dead."

"How many?" My voice still shivered. Much more to Death-Talkers than I'd ever hoped to learn. Right now my head hurt too much to think about the specifics of mind-melding.

"Twelve."

"Hunter."

The word vibrated with tightly-controlled fury.

"Yes, Kira?" I blinked and the rest of the mist cleared away.

What the hell?

She stood before me now with dark circles under her eyes, and slight tremor rippling through her stiffly-held frame. She looked as though the last few minutes had sucked out her arrogance and strength and left behind a fragile shell.

"You have had enough time to recover," she said, and no matter what her body looked like there was nothing frail in that granite voice. "Now I will have your word. You will find that monster and kill him."

I stared at her, my ears ringing. She wanted me to assassinate someone? Given what I'd seen the killer do, I was inclined to hunt him down anyway. But having Kira—anyone—use a Blood Promise to force me to kill was a different thing entirely.

Before I could tell her so, Gaia came to her side and slid an arm around her shoulders. "Come. I think it's time you rested a little. You need your strength."

Kira glared at her but didn't shrug her off. Instead she submitted without complaint and let Gaia guide her out of the room.

Through the open door I caught a glimpse of Lily. She frowned at the two DeathTalkers and shot me a questioning look. Before I could respond, the door closed.

"You do not have to do this," said Sini.

I angled my body so I could look up at her. "Of course, I do. I made a Blood Promise. I have no choice."

Although it sounded like I was reluctant to fulfill the promise, she must know it wasn't because I thought the dead shouldn't be given justice.

Sini shook her head, a sad smile curving her full lips. "Kira is not herself. Grief blinds her."

I glanced at the closed door, pieces slowly falling into place. "She knew one of the people he killed?"

Sini sighed. "Your vision came from a DeathTalker teenager. Kira's daughter, Mika. Her youngest, most rebellious child."

Kira's daughter? Blood drained from my cheeks and when I turned back to Nerina her twisted expression said she understood exactly what I was feeling. "I'm so sorry."

"Mika was rebellious long before she came into her powers." Sini sounded regretful as she continued. "She and her mother had numerous arguments. Finally, the child left the estate to live on her own. She still attended her school but refused to live at home."

"Where was she . . . when it happened?" I asked softly.

"In Cicero," Sini said. "On the outskirts of the abandoned quarter. A set of loft apartments above a bar and restaurant; all abandoned, of course. The young people fend for themselves and though Mika had money from her mother she refused to use it."

"Did she and Kira reconcile?" I asked, this time feeling sick to my stomach for a totally different reason.

Nerina shook her head. "It was only after her death that they made their peace." She spoke softly as if she was afraid Kira would hear.

I hoped Kira didn't have the ability to hear through walls. I didn't handle grief well myself. The idea that an enraged, grieving mother might come running back into the room and demand I kill for her was difficult enough. Facing that emotion from someone who disliked me—and who I didn't care for either—somehow made it worse.

I got to my feet slowly, feeling my stomach tilt but not as badly as it had. Beside me, Nerina rose too.

"Tell Kira I will find her daughter's murderer and fulfill the promise," I said. "The killing felt like . . . part of a plan to me. He needs to be found before he strikes again." And before more paranormals died.

Sini nodded, her honey eyes troubled. "Unfortunately, the problem is not limited to this one incident."

That stopped me cold. "He's killed before?"

She nodded again. "Gaia and I are here because we both have reports from our territories of similar incidents. When Kira told us about her child's murder, we decided we needed to call a High Council meeting to discuss our next steps."

Her mention of the DeathTalker High Council reminded me of our trials with the Walker one, and I only wished our council members were as amenable as Sini was.

"A worldwide attack on paranormals?" I asked, not bothering to hide my shock.

"It does look that way." Sini's face grew darker and it was clear that the death of Kira's child had hit them all hard.

I nodded. "I'll uphold my end of the bargain and fulfill Kira's request but I can't promise to kill them all." I had to make *that* clear. "However, I'll do whatever I can to help. That includes using all my resources to find out who's behind the attacks and to stop them."

Sini did another shallow bow. "I believe you are just the person for this job, Kailin Odel." I noticed she didn't call me 'Hunter'. "We are grateful for your help, even if it is under duress."

Grim determination flooded my veins. "As harsh as it sounds, this is no longer only a DeathTalker problem. He killed other paranormals as well as Kira's daughter. Have you spoken with the other high councils? Warned them?"

Sini shook her head. "Not yet. Kira wanted to guarantee you would eliminate the killer first, before we brought in every other clan and group."

"I saw mages and fae in that room," I said softly. "They were all killed by the same man. It's only fair to give all the high councils warning." And especially the Supreme High Council. They'd want the Elite in place as soon as they knew about this.

"I hear what you are saying," Sini said. "But Kira is the one who holds your debt and it is she who saw and experienced the terror and pain of her own child's death. Nobody else in that room was capable of revealing what happened. No other parent will see it, feel it, live with the agony of it as she will."

I understood. "Which is why I will do my best without involving any of the other groups initially. But I will try to warn them against future attacks."

So the Elite would have to wait.

She nodded. "I understand. And may I say again how grateful we are. Kira may not show it but she, too, is very thankful. Nerina?"

Sini must have given her some silent instruction because Nerina bowed. "Let me show you out," she said. "And you must tell me if you need anything from us."

I frowned, "Like what?"

I turned back to Sini to say goodbye. The high priestess was no longer in the room.

"Weapons," Nerina said, drawing my attention back to her. She handed me my messenger bag and walked with me. "Assistance."

"DeathTalkers have weapons?"

She shrugged as she opened the door and let me pass through to join Lily. "Not modern ones. But we can provide funds for the purchase of new weapons and ammunition."

Lily's eyebrows flew up at the prospect of buying new weapons.

"Don't worry about it yet," I said. "I think we have enough guns and ammo to get the job done." Nerina smiled, once more her serene and unaffected self. "And you mentioned assistance?"

The smile faltered. "We will send reinforcements should you need them."

"Good to know." She hadn't looked too enthusiastic and I wondered what she would have done had I said I needed them now.

Nerina turned to Lily. "Thank you for waiting so patiently. I hope you were well taken care of?"

Lily patted her stomach and grinned. "Yes thanks. Someone gave me hot chocolate and some tiny burger things she called chicken sliders."

I just shook my head and started down the hall.

Nerina returned to the library.

We knew the way out.

"What the hell was that all about?" Lily muttered as we walked.

I shook my head. "Nothing good."

"She's calling in her marker right?"

"It's a Blood Promise." I said dryly. "But even then, this case is not something we can walk away from."

"It's a case?"

"More than a case."

"And we have no choice?"

I shook my head as we jogged down the castle steps to the drive. "Nope."

Just like those murdered kids, we had no choice.

And this time I didn't have a problem with what needed to be done.

CHAPTER 16

OUR RETURN TRIP WAS FAST and silent, and both Lily and I extracted what little peace we could get from the exercise.

Because I wasn't looking forward to being alone in my apartment—too much on my mind—we went to O'Hagan's instead. Even with everything that had happened, I managed to have lunch on my mind.

We took our usual booth, the one with the most shadows, the one furthest from the door. As we sat, a short, brunette waitress sashayed over, bright eyes matching the bright smile on her lips, both equally cool and expressionless.

As she took our order of steak pie for me and nachos for Lily, she scanned us both head-to-toe and up again.

Her inspection left Lily stifling a giggle.

When the girl headed to the kitchen Lily leaned over. "She looks interested in you," she whispered.

I shrugged my messenger bag onto the seat beside me. "About as interested in me as she was in you."

Lily frowned, watching the waitress as she bussed tables her gaze returning to our table every few minutes. "Yeah. That's not *interest* interest. That's more like she recognized us from somewhere."

Recognition. "Exactly."

Lily had hit the nail on the head. I shifted so I could keep an eye on the waitress as well as the rest of the room. So far everything else seemed normal.

The waitress, Del according to her name-tag, returned with our soft drinks, Lily and I exchanged glances. Definitely odd.

We'd been coming to O'Hagan's for ages and had had no negative experiences with the staff. Fynn, the owner, knew us all by sight. So did his regular wait staff.

But Del was new.

"Keep an eye on her," I said as I sipped the frothy chocolate shake. "There's just something off about her."

"Same," was all Lily said as she pulled her tablet from her bag and began swiping.

I was on my phone, scanning my emails when Del returned with the food, her black eyes studying us with the intensity of a scientist studying bugs.

"Enjoy," she said as she placed the plates and baskets of fries on the wooden table.

"You're new here, right?" I said.

She nodded, the lines at the corners of her mouth deepening in a tight smile.

"Where are you from?" My cheery smile did nothing to increase the warmth in hers.

"DC."

She was certainly a talker.

Across the table Lily rolled her eyes while manhandling her nachos.

"Well, I hope you enjoy your stay with us." The woman was hard work. Even Kira was more forthcoming.

Del nodded, analyzed my face again, then left, giving me at least half a dozen glances over her shoulder.

"Well, at least we know she isn't a walker," I said as I fell on my steak pie, snagging the buttery flakes that attempted to escape my plate. The run to the estate had kicked my hunger up a notch.

"At least we know your nose still works." Lily grinned.

I ignored her, finished my meal, and leaned back in the booth to relax. Something that just wasn't happening.

"So what are we going to do?"

Apparently Lily wasn't able to relax either.

"Do about what?" Anjelo said as he slid into the booth beside her and curled his arm around her waist.

She stiffened the tiniest bit but Anjelo seemed not to notice as he fixed his hazel eyes on me.

"Sorry I've been scarce," he said. "Just catching up on stuff." When I raised my eyebrows, he continued. "When I disappeared into Wrythiin, Storm took me out of school and applied for a homeschool permit on the off-chance I survived. Good thing, too. So I've been studying hard these past weeks trying to make up."

I was impressed with his fortitude. Or was it Storm's unbending will he'd submitted to? "So, you making headway?"

"Yep, although I have been neglecting the people in my life." His voice echoed an apology.

Lily looked relieved. "We understand."

Anjelo watched her face for a second, his doubt all too visible. Then his stiff spine softened and his mouth quirked up at the corners. "So, Kai. What's going on? What are we doing about what?"

No reason not to tell him. "What *we* are doing is fulfilling my blood promise to Kira."

Anjelo's eyes popped. "You *can't* be serious. The woman is a freaking viper."

"I am well aware," I said airily. "Unfortunately, as it's a Blood Promise, I've agreed."

He paused, his eyes shifting from my face to Lily's and then back again. "Agreed to what exactly?"

"A DeathTalker girl was killed recently along with several other paranormal kids. Kira wants me to eliminate the killer." I lifted a shoulder. Not a big deal.

A scowl darkened his brow. "Why would Kira ask you to kill this person?" Then he made the connection. "Is the girl one of hers?"

"You could say that," said Lily drily. We both knew he thought we were talking about one of Kira's DeathTalker acolytes.

"I feel for her." His sarcastic tone indicated he didn't.

"What do you have against Kira, anyway?" I asked, watching him closely.

Anjelo shrugged. "I was friends with one of her daughters. She went to Crawdon High. Same homeroom."

"Was she?" said Lily, folding her arms and looking concerned.

I sighed, now worried about Anjelo's reaction. "The kid who was killed is Kira's daughter. The woman is devastated."

He paled, but said nothing.

I pressed. "Which daughter did you know?"

His Adam's apple rose and fell as he swallowed hard. Lily looped her hand through his elbow. "Mika."

Tears pricked behind my eyes and I struggled to blink them away. "I'm so sorry, Anjelo. It was Mika."

Anjelo's shoulders bowed and his skin went a little gray. He sat there, so still it was painful to watch, while he processed the news. Lily sat beside him, her hand tight on his arm.

"Did you know her well?"

A ragged laugh escaped his lips as he nodded. "She was a bit of a rebel. Nobody could tame her."

"Was she still at the school when you left?" I asked, giving Lily a glance. "Did you know her too?"

"No." Anjelo answered even as she shook her head. "Lily

didn't know her. Mika left before Lily started. She couldn't take the pressure of trying to conform, and she'd started to turn."

I nodded. "I hear it's tough on them when they come of age. Grams once told me they call it the first death. I gathered from the description that it wouldn't be an easy thing to experience." Much like a walker's first shift.

He shrugged, but his eyes had gone dark and I wondered if he'd cared for the girl. "Her mother was giving her a very hard time. She disapproved of Mika mixing with us. Even though we were all paranormal we weren't DeathTalkers. DeathTalkers, according to Kira, are superior to the rest of us."

I could almost hear Kira saying precisely that. "It's such a responsibility."

He snorted. "Yeah. I ran into her after school one day, and she told me to stay away from her daughter or else. Not long after that, Mika left. We never heard from her again."

His voice was back to ragged and his eyes glinted wetly. Then he shifted his gaze and met my gaze without flinching. "What happened?"

I hesitated, deciding at the last moment that a detailed description here and now was a very bad idea.

"The killer seems to have joined their group. He'd been hanging out with them for a while. Asked for a gathering of all the members under some kind of pretense. The kids were gullible enough and they came."

"And all died?"

I nodded. "He had some sort of power but he didn't appear to be paranormal. He obliterated the entire group within seconds, then disappeared."

Silence hovered over our table like a cloud while Anjelo absorbed yet more bad news. I'd given him enough to understand the deaths had been brutal. I didn't plan to elaborate further.

Suddenly he lifted his chin, his shoulders tensing as his grief transitioned into anger at me. "Why the hell did you make this blood promise in the first place?"

I controlled my expression, maintaining outward serenity. "Because it was the only way to save Greer."

"Greer." Anjelo snorted. "Why am I not surprised?" His eyes narrowed. I knew what he was thinking, could see he was holding back.

"I know you didn't like her," I said. "But, if it makes you feel any better, she said she was sorry. She asked me to forgive her." I smiled and reached out to hold his hand. "I forgave her."

"She had a lot of problems," said Lily softly. Lily understood Greer more than we all did. "She was struggling with some pretty big emotional weight."

Anjelo waved it away. "That's no excuse."

"I know. It isn't. I don't take my frustrations out on people. But not everyone who can't shift can control their emotions."

Anjelo's eyebrows rose. "Greer was Pariah?"

My turn to be surprised. "Did you not know?"

His eyes shifted to me. "How would I know if nobody told me?"

I looked from him to Lily. "You didn't fill him in?"

Lily shrugged. "It wasn't my story to tell. I knew you would tell him sooner or later. And besides, he's had his own burdens to bear."

"*He's* sitting right here," snapped Anjelo, his golden eyes glowing a little as his panther stirred. "And what burdens are those?"

"Illyria."

He stiffened. "She's not my burden."

"Then stop making her one."

"*She* isn't my burden. *My* actions are."

"What actions?" I snapped. "Trusting the person who saved your life? She deceived you, yes. She deceived me too. I trusted her until she stuck her blade into my gut. Do you see me living with everlasting guilt?"

Anjelo shook his head. "You wouldn't have trusted her if I hadn't vouched for her."

"Don't be stupid. What about Cassie? She could have confirmed that Illyria was a two-faced bitch. But even *Cassie* was fooled. We were all smart enough. Illyria just happened to be a high-level psycho. She had everyone fooled. Even Wren'do didn't know and he was in love with her. He remained as her second in command thinking she cared."

Anjelo stared at me for a long moment, seeming to consider my words as if the truths had never occurred to him.

Maybe they hadn't. "Have you really been blaming yourself all along?"

He blinked. "She stabbed you. She gave your mother to Omega to be tortured."

"Ah. I see." I nodded, understanding now. "You feel responsible for what happened to my mom?"

His head shifted so slightly that I almost didn't recognize it as a nod.

"Anjelo, can you please stop with all the self-blame. This is all on Illyria. Even Mom knows that." I sighed and smiled. "Have you spoken to her?"

"Who? Illyria?"

"No. She's dead."

"Oh, your mom."

"Yes, Anjelo. My Mom."

Even Lily was smiling and shaking her head.

"What makes you think she'd want to see *me*?" he asked. "It's not like I did anything to save her."

Did he really believe that, too?

"Mom remained alive and safe because of your determination to find her. Illyria had her agenda, but she needed you too, so she kept Mom alive. Whatever you did while you were there worked to keep Mom alive and well." My eyes narrowed. "Are you sure this isn't an ego thing?"

"Ego thing?"

"Yeah. She made the big, strong guy look stupid." My voice was cooler than I'd intended but it seemed to do the trick.

"Of course not. What the hell do you take me for?"

"Well, then. We have it all resolved. It's not your ego. You did everything to help. Mom's alive and healthy because of you. You're normal just like all of us who were tricked, and Illyria is dead for her troubles."

He stared at me.

"So is that all wrapped up now?"

He didn't move.

"I'll take that as a 'yes'. No more moping. No more woe-is-me?"

He nodded.

"Good. If you're done feeling sorry for yourself, we now need to figure out how we're going to tackle this case."

He raised an eyebrow but didn't respond. Instead, he patted Lily's hand where it had sat encircling his arm all through the conversation.

"Right." He took a breath. "Let's catch this bastard."

CHAPTER 17

I KNEW EVEN BEFORE I slipped my key into the lock that Mom and Grams were home.

Both watched me with strained expressions as I came in and tossed my bag under the coat rack behind the door.

"What did I do now?" I said.

"Kids." Mom smirked as she played with the crumbs on her plate. "Everything's always about you."

I went over to her, grabbed the plate, placed it on the coffee table, and then sank against her.

She squeezed me tight and sighed.

Tilting my head up, I studied her closely. "This new guy in your life, he giving you a hard time?" I narrowed my eyes. "I know where he lives. I could break a few bones for you."

Grams snorted and Mom smiled. "I'll let you know if it ever comes to that." Although she spoke to me, I got the feeling she wasn't really with us, her mind was off somewhere, probably concentrating on the High Council and their shenanigans.

"So. Anything I need to know?"

Mom shook her head. "Not a peep from the council, though your father and his friends have a good idea of who the mole is."

"Mole? *Ooh*." I wriggled my eyebrows. "Sounds very cloak-and-dagger."

"It is," Grams said. "The bastards are out to ruin our families." She sat back, studying my face as if she just realized something. "You know this will affect you too, right?"

I shrugged. "Not as if I care about being alpha."

Mom shook her head. "Honey, I don't think you should be so blasé about this."

"But why should it bother me?" I asked, genuinely confused. "If Dad doesn't stay an alpha, Iain will take his place. I don't think I'll even be considered as a possible successor."

Grams leaned forward. "This is where I will have to agree with your mother. You can deny it, because you've never liked the idea of leading, but it's your blood you're talking about."

I snorted. "Half-blood, you mean?" I asked, belatedly glancing at Mom's face. "No offense."

Mom laughed. "None at all. You're the half-breed, not me."

"Mom." I cried, feigning hurt, then let out a sputtering laugh which totally spoiled the effect. Then I sobered. "I know you're worried about me—me and Logan—and I understand, but it's not a problem."

"How is it not a problem?" asked Mom, the warmth in her voice dropping a few degrees. "What are you planning?"

They both stared me down and I shifted in my seat.

"Kailin Odel, you aren't going to leave that boy, are you?"

I didn't respond.

Leaving Logan had been my intention all along, but I hadn't faced it head on until now. Says a lot for one's subconscious.

"You are." Mom did not look impressed. "Now it makes total sense why you've been so calm about all this. Cutting and running as soon as the going gets hot?"

I wanted to say 'look who's talking', wanted to say she'd done the same thing to us, but from the look in her eyes she knew exactly what was going through my mind.

So I didn't say a word. I knew what she'd sacrificed and why. She'd left to keep us safe. Us. Not herself.

I sighed, leaning my head against the back of the couch and staring up at the ceiling. "I haven't really thought about it too much. After that first high council meeting, with all the threats of expulsion for fraternizing with non-walkers, not to mention everything Logan has going on that's way less important than my problems, I guess I'd already half decided."

Grams pursed her lips. "So all this nonsense about not wanting to be an alpha has been posturing?"

"Not always." I had finally admitted it. "It hasn't been a lie for most of my life. It's how I felt. But recently, things have happened that changed me, changed my perspective. We'd all trusted Uncle Niko, but his behavior, his experiments, his lack of care for his family, his experimentation on Mom—he killed that trust. Then Greer. We'd never gotten along, never seen eye-to-eye, but she'd had her own demons to deal with, her own horrors. And in the end, she was my sister who died admitting she really did love me."

The silence in the room was a living breathing thing, holding the women of my family in suspense as they waited for me to break it.

"All those incidents made me realize that as much as I've been running from my responsibilities as alpha, I keep on doing things that make me responsible for others."

I gave a short laugh. "Did you know that Anjelo and Lily have both declared me their Alpha?"

Grams raised her eyebrows but didn't look shocked.

"Not entirely surprising," said Mom. "Both work with you, trust you, care about you."

I nodded. "Yeah. They certainly have contributed to my troubles."

"And where does Logan fit in?"

I shrugged. "Maybe he doesn't."

"Does he know he might not fit, and why?"

I shook my head. "He's struggling with his own issues. The last thing I want is for him to be bothered by my problems."

Mom laughed. "Really? This is how you think relationships work?" She sounded annoyed. "You finally accept that you are an alpha, that you can handle responsibility, and then you go and do something like this?"

Like what? "What? What did I just do?"

"You're finding reasons to bail on your relationship." Grams sounded as unimpressed as Mom. "Is there another man?"

I thought of Justin, but I hadn't given him much thought since Greer's funeral. I shook my head. "Nope. Nobody else."

"You sure?" asked Mom, her dark eyes piercing.

"What do you know?" I asked, finally suspicious.

"Justin came to see your father."

She *had* to be kidding. "And that was enough for you to think he was in the picture?"

"It was when he came to ask for your hand in marriage."

"For *Ailuros'* sake, Mom," I snapped, losing all patience. "That was premature of him. One conversation weeks ago and suddenly he pops the question? And to Dad not me?"

"When did you talk?"

"Greer's funeral."

Grams shook her head. "That boy certainly has bad timing,"

Mom smiled. "I know you had feelings for him."

"A teenage crush, Mom." I said, and stopped short. "How did you know about it?"

Mom opened her mouth, then closed it, her eyes flicking to Grams.

"Should have known," I grumbled, glaring at Grams. "What else did you tell her?"

Grams lifted her chin. "Whatever she needed to know."

I turned to Mom. "Do you have *any* idea how lucky you are to have a mother-in-law like her?" I jabbed a thumb in Grams' direction.

The two women shared a warm smile, but neither said a word. They didn't need to. Amid all the frustration and worry they shared a moment of happiness and I was there to witness it.

"So, can you get Dad to tell Justin to back off?" I asked, changing the subject.

"Already done."

"Huh?"

"When I heard, I told your father what I thought."

I laughed. "I'm guessing Justin was stupid enough to say I had no knowledge of his offer."

Mom nodded.

Idiot. "He has zero skills."

Mom nodded. "So you're sure you aren't interested in him."

I gave a swift jerk of my head. "I'm sure." I stared off into nothing for a moment, thinking about the kiss, thinking about the years I'd spent head-over-heels for him. "Another place, another time. Maybe. If Logan wasn't in the picture. Sadly, I only have eyes for one guy."

"Hah. I knew it," said Mom, pointing her finger at me. "Then what's all this about leaving him?"

The same things she'd walked away from Dad over, I supposed.

"I just want to protect him from all this drama. And . . . if I stay with him I can't be alpha. Then, if my people need me, I won't be able to help them."

"So you'd sacrifice your relationship for the possibility of your people needing you."

I groaned. "Mom you're making my head hurt."

She chuckled. "There is only one way to sort this out."

"What's that?"

"By ensuring the High Council doesn't win. Our future *is*

integration, even if it means just integration within the para-normal community for now."

Mom leaned forward. "We've been inter-marrying for centuries. It's always been accepted, even if it hasn't been publicly acknowledged or encouraged. When I happened along it was accepted and people just lived with it. With paranormals, the genes aren't watered down. They're amplified by each other."

Amplified genes. "Is that why I have both walker ability and tracking power?"

Mom nodded. "Omega managed to do some in-depth studies into gene-sharing. I guess the facility had its benefits."

I gritted my teeth. "Don't even joke about it." Just the thought of what Mom had been through in that facility made my heart hurt. "I still can't understand how Uncle Niko allowed it to happen."

"He didn't just allow it," Mom said. "He performed any proce-dure himself. Said he didn't trust the other scientists, that they'd likely hurt me in the process. And he always made me comfort-able. Sedated me if something was going to cause pain, never left me badly hurt."

"Stop it." I glared at her. "I can't believe you're making excuses for him." Even now she wasn't sharing exactly what had happened.

"I'm just being honest, Kai," Mom said. "Perhaps he had no choice. Perhaps he had to do it, so he treated me well. Whatever he did, he never caused me pain or discomfort. And he always seemed sorry."

"*Seemed.*"

My tone was hard, and even when I realized that Grams was sitting across from us listening to us talk about her son, I didn't apologize for my attitude.

He might have been my Uncle, but he'd hurt us all. And even though Mom's words had struck me deeply—was there a possibility that Uncle Niko had done those awful deeds under duress? —I wasn't ready to give him a pass.

"I know it upsets you to talk about him, honey."

"I heard what he said about me," I said softly. "When they captured me, drugged me. He stood at my bedside and spoke about me to Greer so impartially, as if having an alpha in his clutches was a strategic benefit to his research, never mind that the alpha happened to be his own flesh and blood."

"He spoke to Greer?"

"Yes, they were the only two people in the room."

Mom and Grams exchanged a long look. "Then," Mom said, "have you considered that his comments to Greer would have been an act?"

I didn't understand. "Why would he have been acting?"

"Because Greer was aligned with Brand and maybe even Widd'en?" Mom spoke softly, kindly, as if she knew that reminding me of my sister's relationship with Brand, a notorious drug-peddler and walker of questionable sanity who believed himself free to feed on humans, would hurt.

And that Greer's loyalty to the Wraith Lord would still be a raw wound. Widd'en had been intent on taking over the human world, and I'd spent my time killing wraiths who'd been taking over innocent humans. Little had I known that I'd merely been putting out brush fires, and that the firestarter himself had gotten my sister and uncle under his control.

"You want me to consider that Uncle Niko was being manipulated the entire time?"

"Maybe not the whole time. In the beginning maybe he was the instigator. But I suspect things got quickly out of hand."

I remained silent, absorbing her theory. It was odd having my inner confusion turned into words, and by Mom of all people.

Then Grams broke the silence. "Forget the past for now. Let's talk about the present. Where have you been?"

Reality check. "You're not going to like it."

"Do tell," said Mom and they both leaned forward.

I told them about promises and massacres—both bloody—and of mind-melds and assassinations—both sickening. And when I finally finished, I waited.

"What the hell were you thinking?" demanded Mom, her face pale.

Grams made no comment and I knew why.

I faced Mom. "I needed to save Greer. The seal was the only way to reach the Graylands."

Mom shifted her gaze from my face to Grams. "That reminds me. I still have to deal with you for giving Kai my seal in the first place."

I bristled. "It's not Grams' fault, Mom."

"Grams can defend herself thank you very much," said Grams, a pleasant smile on her face. She seemed totally unaffected and not in the least bit guilty. She definitely didn't need my help in her defense.

Mom ignored both of us. "And a blood promise? Do you even know how serious that is?"

"I do now," I said drily. "I have to kill someone. And the fact that he's someone I want to kill definitely makes this the easiest blood promise to fulfill."

Mom sat back, troubled, her forehead creased, her skin pale, and I waited for the explosion.

"So what do you need from me, Kai?"

My eyes snapped to Grams' face across the coffee table. "What do you mean?" I was very aware of Mom, so still beside me.

Grams smiled serenely. "You clearly need information before you can take the next step. I'm assuming you have your young man already probing Omega for information."

I nodded, unable to resist her smile. My young man indeed. "So you want to do some probing of your own?" I asked.

"It wouldn't hurt. I personally haven't heard anything but we usually don't know things that don't pertain to us directly, or when they're classified."

"I think knowing about the existence of a man who kills paranormals a dozen at a time affects all of us directly, classified or not. I'd think there'd be a worldwide warning issued so we're all on the lookout for the danger."

Grams shrugged. "I can't even begin to assume what Omega would want to do about such a situation. They have their protocols. We have ours. And right now we need to know what's going on."

"Won't you be endangering your position?" I asked, suddenly afraid for Grams. "What if someone catches you?"

"There isn't a damn thing stopping me from looking for information except where I need a high-level security clearance. I have a few ways of getting around security."

"Grams, you devious devil you." I grinned and Mom did too. She'd sat there so long without saying a word, but if she could still manage to crack a smile then maybe she wasn't too pissed off with me.

Grams nodded then shifted forward on the couch, patted her knees, and shoved to her feet. "There's no time like the present," she said, striding to the coat-rack to grab her bag. "I'll be back soon."

"Can't you access the mainframe from here?" asked Mom. "Going in in person may get you in more trouble if it sets off any alarms."

"Actually, being here would be worse," I said slowly. "It would be more compromising since both you and I are here."

"Good point," they said together.

"Have you returned to Sentinel yet?" I asked Mom.

She gave a small shake of her head. "Not yet. They've insisted I take some time to recuperate. I'm meant to head in for debriefing and testing next week."

"Perhaps you should start tomorrow?" suggested Grams. "I'm

beginning to think it would be best to have more of us on the inside."

Her pointed look at me was sharp enough to draw blood. "What? You want me to come on board now? Won't that look suspicious?" I still hadn't told them about the Elite Corps offer.

Grams shrugged again. "No more suspicious than *not* joining all this will make you look."

"What's suspicious about me refusing to join?" I asked. "My relationship with Logan?"

Mom put her hand on my forearm. "Your associations will always be judged, honey. If you decide to join Sentinel now, getting inside with the purpose of infiltration is no better reason."

"In that case there's no better time to join Omega," I said softly.

They both stared at me in silence. For once I'd managed to shut the both of them up with one sentence.

Always a first time for everything.

$\mathcal{I}$'D BEEN TO LOGAN'S HOTEL only a few times in the last couple weeks, purely because I didn't like hanging around in a place owned by Omega.

I'd been surprised that Omega provided so well for their out-of-town agents, even going so far as to offer private living arrangements. Of course, where Logan and Jess were concerned, it seemed that they were now permanently attached to the Chicago branch.

Nobody had even hinted that they would be transferred yet, so the current assumption was they were in for the long haul.

Now, with my mind focused on the death of an innocent, I needed to be around Logan more than anything. Just being with him always had the side-effect of making me feel safe, even if it was for one night. And if he wasn't home, just being in his space might lend me some calm.

Omega had taken over an entire floor in the once grand and beautiful Blackstone Renaissance hotel. Its split-leveled lobby and dark paneled pillars still lent an air of majesty to the place despite the slightly aged air.

The city had taken over the property when its last owners had fled to greener pastures, and now, the place barely saw a visiting tycoon let alone a president.

Tracking across the white marble floor, I admired the contrast of the little black squares, paying little attention as the scowling concierge gave me a curt nod. If he smiled, I'd never know considering his mustache was long enough to cover his mouth.

Upstairs, I entered the silent hotel room and left my bag and jacket on the floor beside the door. If he wasn't home they would give him advanced warning of someone in his space. I'd rather let him know I was here than risk having him fry me to a crisp thinking I was an intruder.

I headed past the dark doorway to the bathroom on my right, to the bedroom and caught a glimpse of Logan's sleeping form. He was sprawled on the bed, sheets tangled around his body. He hadn't heard me enter. Granted, I was panther-quiet but he looked to be so deep in his dreams that any noise I'd made on entering would have gone unheard.

He struggled, shifting from side to side, his face scrunched up, frustration and sorrow furrowing deep into his brow. His skin was covered with a light sheen of perspiration and I could feel the heat rolling off him from where I stood so many feet away.

I kept still, watching, unsure if I should disturb him, or stay as far away as possible. Being barbecued didn't appeal to me.

I deliberated for a few seconds then decided to run a bath. The sound of water would wake him in a less dramatic fashion.

Or at least I hoped it would.

I turned on my heel and headed to the bathroom door.

"Hey, beautiful." His voice drifted toward me, a sleepy croak that made me smile.

Relieved, I turned back and headed to his side. "Hey. You were dreaming again."

He shifted over, making space for me to sit. "Yeah. More and more each day."

I sank onto the mattress beside him. "Late night?"

He nodded, rubbing his hand across his face. "Yeah. Got back from Japan five hours ago." He sighed deeply. "Onmoraki demons are the darnedest creatures to banish."

The mere name of the demon made me shudder. "Crap. I disturbed you."

When I began to move away he grabbed me around the waist and pulled me gently over his body so I landed on the other side of the mattress. "You are welcome to disturb me anytime. Not even a half human, half bird demon can keep me from you."

"*Mhhm*," I murmured as he nuzzled my neck. "Good to know."

Laughter rumbled through his chest and the sound vibrated against my ear as I cuddled close.

We stayed like that for a while, with Logan tracing his fingers across the top of my neck. Right then, lying within his arms, I couldn't imagine being anywhere without him. How had I even considered leaving him out of my future? The High Council be damned.

"What's bothering you?" he murmured.

"My problems are the least of your worries." I lifted my head. The strain of the dream was still painted across his features. "You were dreaming again."

He smiled. "I'm always dreaming."

"The same girl?" I pressed, knowing he'd be reluctant to respond. He always was because he always put everyone else before himself. This time it was all about him and I refused to let him hide.

"Yeah."

"Did you speak to Jess?"

"Not yet." He cleared his throat.

I sighed. "I really wish we could find something concrete to go on."

"Me too."

He sounded sincere but I knew him well enough by now not to take what he said at face value.

Had he spoken to Jess, but just didn't want to worry me about what she'd told him? The Titan had already provided me with a couple of major revelations but I wondered if she'd even share them with Logan should he rustle up the nerve to ask her.

Jess had admitted she was here to look after him because he was special. But did that have anything to do with these dreams? I intended to find out. Sometimes men were so pigheaded they needed female guidance, gentle or not, to get their act together.

"How did it go with Kira?" he asked as he turned on his side and propped his head on his hand.

"One of Kira's daughters was killed not too long ago. She wants me to find and kill the SOB."

Logan scowled. "Nice. What happened?"

"I saw it for myself. A large room, a pool table, a bunch of paranormal kids all gathered and killed by someone who wasn't a paranormal using a power that seemed to be ethereal. Add to the mix the strange fact that the killer's face was blurred and unrecognizable and you have a more than terrifying case."

Logan's face whitened and he shoved up into a sitting position. "There was a pool table?"

"Yes." I asked getting to my knees. "What about it?"

He rubbed his hand over his face. "Couple of days ago I attended a scene. The place was a mess, like a hurricane had erupted within the room. Splintered wood lying around. I figure it was the remains of a pool table."

He'd walked the murder scene. "Did you see the bodies?"

He nodded and then took a huge breath. "I didn't get the memo that one of the kids was Kira's."

"Not just *one* of Kira's."

"What do you mean?" he asked, his dark eyes hooded now.

"She was Kira's *daughter*. Flesh-and-blood child."

"Shit."

"Yeah."

"That's bad."

"Yeah."

"Makes sense now why she'd call in her marker."

"Yeah."

"Having vocabulary issues?" he grinned, despite his tension.

"Yeah." I sank to the bed again. "I'm done already and I haven't even started."

"Tell me what you need and I'll help you."

I narrowed my eyes. "You mean tell Omega?"

"I work for Omega but who knows how much longer that will last. Either way, if you don't want me to talk about it, I won't."

I nodded. "Okay." His word was enough for me. "The guy was professional. Calculated. Organized. It looked like he'd been with them long enough to be familiar to them, to not look like a threat. He took them by surprise. They never knew what hit them."

"So he infiltrated them with ease. Definitely a pro. And he took them out with ease. More professional. But what I don't understand is why?" Logan got more comfortable on the bed and linked his fingers, his brow furrowed. "Is it a vendetta? Or an organized elimination drive?"

"I'd bet on the latter."

"What gives you that idea?" Logan asked. "We haven't received any news of other incidents."

"Maybe not on the North American continent."

I gave him a quick rundown of Gaia and Sini's presence and information. And the more I spoke, the darker his face grew.

"This is not good at all."

"Yeah."

He grinned at me. "Okay, so let me get into the system, see what I can find. You think you can get more information on the other deaths?"

I nodded. "I'll speak to Nerina. Check if she knows anything."

"Have they been helpful?"

"Very. They aren't holding back. The girl's death affected them all. And it's not only the DeathTalkers who are grieving for her." Logan's head jerked up. "Anjelo was her friend."

"Crap."

"Ditto."

"He okay?"

"I think so. He's pretty determined to help so he's channeling his grief in a constructive way. The same can't be said for her mother. Kira was like a stone. Rock-hard, as if nothing affected her. Then suddenly she blew."

"Understandable."

"Ditto." I sighed. "Okay. I'd better get moving. I need to speak to a few people, then speak to Nerina. I hate that Tara isn't around, though. Not that it matters. I have no idea what type of weapons I need anyway."

"Identify the foe," Logan said. "Then arm yourself accordingly."

"Easy for you to say. While I'm identifying I might get my head exploded because I wasn't prepared."

"So could I. If you say this killer is after paranormals that would be me."

"We all have to watch our backs."

Logan nodded and swung his feet to the floor. "Right. Let's catch the bastard."

I burst out laughing.

CHAPTER 19

I WAS STANDING IN MY apartment trying to decide what to do next when someone knocked on my door.

For the first time in a long while, all I wanted to do was to dive into the bed and hide under the covers. Unfortunately, hiding under the covers wouldn't get rid of my visitor. So I did the adult thing and opened the door.

Nerina gave me a weak smile and I waved her inside. My stomach did a somersault, and I was grateful I hadn't had breakfast. What else had she come to tell me? Who else had died?

"Has something happened?" I asked, unable to keep the ripple of fear from my voice.

Nerina looked sad. "There has been another incident. Lady Kira has sent me here so I can keep you informed. She believes you need to know exactly what happened. She also believes that any knowledge we can provide may help you find and stop the killer."

I nodded and guided her to the dining room table and into a chair. I stood there for a moment, wondering if I should offer her something to eat or drink. In the end, I just sat down beside her.

"Tell me," I said.

She sighed and lifted her gray eyes to mine. "This one won't be easy." Then she let out a ragged laugh. "What am I saying? As if the first massacre was easy."

"It's okay." I covered her trembling hands with mine, pressing down gently to help stop the shaking. "I know what you mean."

How was Kira treating the people around her? Not with tender care. In her grief, the woman was likely amplifying her awfulness.

"How is Lady Kira?" I asked, feeling as if I should at least inquire. It was the respectful thing to do.

Nerina gave me a bleak smile. "Worse than usual."

I raised an eyebrow, surprised at her openness. "That's as expected. Grief does terrible things to people."

Worse, it does terrible things to terrible people.

Nerina bobbed her head, the movement making her hood slither off her head. She didn't seem to care, not bothering as the fabric drifted away to reveal her gray hair, and fall around her shoulders in a silky pile.

I gave her hand one final squeeze before moving away.

DeathTalkers, despite their humanity, became something *other* after their Turn. They lost their human scent, and even their skin took on a cool, almost bloodless feel. Spending a lot of time in the Graylands ate away at their humanity, the place being devoid of all life. There were rumors of ancient DeathTalkers who walked the path of the dead for thousands of years. Some were said to still exist in a state of half-life.

At last, Nerina cleared her throat. "I'm here at your service, Kailin. I will remain with you to assist in whatever way you require."

This I *wasn't* expecting. I forced a smile. "You don't really need to, you know. I can handle it."

Nerina smiled too, a little self-deprecatingly. "I'm sure I'll probably end up in your way, but I'm here on the strictest of orders."

"Ah, I see."

I did see. Kira had sent Nerina to keep an eye on us.

Her face fell. "Please don't be offended."

"Of course not. I understand your position. And you're more than welcome to stick with us." I grinned. "We have nothing to hide."

Nerina shook her head. "I'm not here to spy on you. Despite my orders, I will only relay the information that you wish me to. Lady Kira does not need to know how you tie your shoelaces, or what you have for dinner." She gave a conspiratorial nod.

I trusted her. A little. But I was still aware that her loyalty didn't lie with me. In any case, we really didn't have anything to hide.

"All right," I said. "I'll tell you where we are so far, but there are a few things we can't reveal simply because they are only leads. Nothing certain."

"That's fine," she agreed. "You give me the formal version and I'll pass that on."

I nodded, launching into a brief description of nothing.

After I finished, Nerina considered what I'd told her in silence. "Perhaps I can broaden the picture for you."

"I'm sure you can. Will you do another mind-meld?"

She nodded. "Come."

We got to our feet and she led the way to the sofa where she waited as I lay down with my head on a pile of cushions and straightened my clothes.

Then she knelt beside me as our sofa was barely wide enough to seat two comfortably, and only one lying down. Less than one. My legs stuck awkwardly off the other end of the sofa.

My stomach felt a little strange, churning in anticipation of the mind meld. My last experience hadn't been fun.

"No special juice this time?" I asked.

Nerina laughed. "Unfortunately, no. But having already had

the experience once before, your body should be able to adjust very quickly."

I settled back down as Nerina held my hand gently within hers.

"Just remember, keep calm. Relax. Nothing that's happening *around* you is happening *to* you."

I took a deep breath and waited as the strength began to slowly leave my body. Although Nerina would be near to guide me, I still anticipated disliking the whole experience.

I did as she'd instructed me to do the previous time, leaned on her energy which pulsed beside me, a constant comfort.

Lights danced beneath my lids, much brighter than in the last vision.

I opened my eyes slowly, bringing my hand up to shield them from the bright sun beating down on my head.

Strangely enough, I felt no heat against my skin and even the air I inhaled was not warm at all. A good reminder this was just a vision. I wouldn't experience injury or death if it came.

But someone had.

I floated, weightless, and when I looked down in search of solid ground I found it a few inches below me. On it were the upturned toes of a pair of dusty, dark feet.

I shifted my view and saw that the feet belonged to an ancient woman whose blank white eyes stared up at the bright blue sky.

I'd found the source of my vision.

The land around me stretched into the distance, dusty and dry, dotted by desiccated, skeletal trees that had probably last produced leaves hundreds of years ago. In the distance, a small collection of grass huts huddled together against the heat, while a little boy wielded a pale stick at an emaciated cow, herding the animal back to the tiny village.

No, not a stick. A slim rod of silver light.

Something shifted beside me and a man in dark military clothes moved past, his dusty boots making a deadly hollow sound against the dry ground, a holstered black pistol slapping against his upper thigh.

I tensed. Watched helplessly as the boy skipped along, unaware of the danger that followed him. There was nothing I could do as the soldier closed in on the child, drew the weapon, aimed, and squeezed the trigger.

A blast of light spewed from the barrel, reaching out toward the boy and knocking him over almost instantly. The little body jerked and fell forward arms and legs in an ungainly sprawl.

The soldier continued past the cow, ignoring both child and animal as he headed for the huts.

This killing was entirely different from the last. This was no complex infiltration via friendship. Here was simple execution by a stranger.

Unable to move, tied to the spirit of the old woman, I was forced to watch from afar as the man went from hut to hut sending blinding flashes of light spewing through one doorway after another.

A few times I saw responding flashes of light—perhaps the people of the village trying to fight back—but they were soon overpowered. Then it was over, and the lone gunman started back toward me.

A shout sounded to my right but I couldn't see what was happening until the woman's spirit saw. I waited, heart in my mouth. Then two men ran toward the village, deep ochre skirts draped around their waists, their faces tattooed, colored necklaces swaying frantically around their necks.

This was a Masai tribe who had paranormal powers.

A Masai tribe who had just been massacred.

The soldier pulled a second weapon from behind his back and ran, sending bursts of bright lightning straight at the tribesmen. The Masai warriors gave as good as they got, sending their own streaks of silver energy bolts straight at the soldier. They would have won, their power was strong enough, but two more black-clad soldiers joined the first.

The three soldiers bore down on the approaching warriors firing non-stop. I swallowed hard, studying the guns. They weren't the normal, run-of-the-mill weapons, and the ammunition used wasn't of human origin. The killers were using paranormal ammunition.

Although the warriors had managed to fight off one man with their powerful air magic, they were defenseless in the face of this new assault. They died as the rest of their people had died and their murderers set fire to the village.

Smoke billowed around us and I blinked automatically before realizing that the acrid air had no effect on me. I hovered over the old woman's body while the entire village died, gutted that I'd been unable to help. It felt wrong. It *was* wrong.

My attention moved back to the men, now huddled together as one pulled out a sat phone.

He placed it against his ear and said, "Victor here. Mission complete."

The air buzzed and Victor nodded. "Yes, sir. Right away, sir."

He put the phone back into his pocket, slid his pistol into the holster at his thigh, and made a circling motion with his finger in the air above his head. They moved out and my view shifted to watch them disappear along the horizon.

I could still feel Nerina's presence beside me, and though it was a comfort, it did nothing to make me feel better. I needed to go back. Find this ammunition.

My mind immediately went to Tara, and then disappointment surged through me. I had no way of contacting her, so whatever information we needed regarding this paranormal ammo we would have to get it somewhere else.

More moments passed. I was beginning to wonder what I was still doing there when I heard the sound of feet slapping the ground.

A young girl sank to the sand beside the corpse of the old woman, her head bent forward so I couldn't see her face.

She wailed in anguish and threw her hands out over the body. Then she held shaking fingers over the woman's chest. Soon light shimmered, flowing from her fingertips, and sinking into the corpse.

The light burned so bright I wanted to shield my eyes, but I didn't dare in case I missed something. But, as I watched, tears pricked my eyes. The magic wasn't working.

The girl began to cry in earnest, rocking back and forth beside the body, wailing out her grief. The sound floated on the hot, thick air and faded away into the silent plain.

I felt my insides tighten, and knew Nerina was taking me back. But as I drifted away, the girl looked up. Her gaze followed me, those eyes glowing brightly, swirling light shimmering, disappearing only when she blinked.

She stared at me, eyes wide, surprised.

Then she blinked once more, her eyelids lowered. Before they lifted again I was gone.

CHAPTER 20

I MANAGED A HEAVY-LIDDED blink, then dragged my eyes open. Nerina had transported me to the African desert, and yet I hadn't been submitted to the intense heat of the blistering sun, nor had I taken scorching breaths of midday air.

I knew this.

It didn't matter.

I exhaled, forcibly expelling the air from my lungs, frantic for a breath of fresh cool air, as if the heat had parched my very soul.

A part of me recognized the desire to erase the hot air was really a symbol for the desire to erase the awful experience. I'd watched helplessly as a boy had been gunned down, as a village was decimated, and as an old woman died in the arms of a grieving child.

I hated just being a bystander. More than anything I hated that I'd gotten there after the fact, a mere observer, rather than be of any help.

My body convulsed in a shudder and soft fingers wrapped around mine, a comforting squeeze I didn't even realize I'd needed.

"How are you feeling?" Nerina asked, her voice soft and concerned. Her face without its usual cowl was unshadowed, and for the first time I saw color in her pale milky eyes. A honey brown that reminded me too much of the child I'd left alone in the desert, the one whose keening had struck my heart.

I cleared my throat, the sound rattling around as I slowly pushed into a sitting position. My head throbbed, a dull, insistent pounding and I suspected the trip had taken its toll on me, especially since I'd gone in without the special magic juice.

"I'm fine." I forced the words out. "Just tell me what the hell that was." My voice cracked in my too-dry throat and I hacked a cough. Clearly my body hadn't gotten the message that the vision wasn't real.

Nerina's mouth twisted into a sad bow. "I know how you feel. The first time I experienced that vision it took me hours to recover. The only difference between us and paranormals like yourself is that we experience every emotion as well as the impact of the immediate environment."

I nodded, wincing at the throbbing in my head. "Yeah, I definitely noticed that. As hot as it was, I didn't feel the heat in the air. Or the sunshine. At the time it made sense, since I wasn't actually there, but now I feel really strange. As if my body doesn't believe what my mind already knows."

Nerina nodded as she removed her hands and straightened. She folded her fingers in her lap. "It's because you are not a DeathTalker. The vision we experienced was through the eyes of the old woman. Just for the record, for a short while after death, the recently deceased do experience environmental impact, so she would have still felt sunshine, and the heat of the day. She would have still been able to smell the dusty air and smell the blood."

I opened my mouth to say I still found the DeathTalker's ability fascinating, when a knock on the door interrupted me and then a key scraped into the lock.

I drew on a tiny bit of my panther nose and confirmed that Anjelo and Lily had arrived.

Anjelo smiled as he held the door open for Lily, then shut the door behind him and handed her the key. Then he saw us.

"What the hell happened to you?" he asked, brow creased.

A hiss of breath escaped my throat and I let my head drop back against the sofa. "You came just in time. Nerina was showing me what happened in Africa."

The pair took seats on the opposite sofa, both bore worried expressions while they waited.

I gave them a rundown, from African sunshine to Masai warriors with interesting powers. Anjelo's head moved almost imperceptibly left to right, the tiny action telling me he was still uneasy about me being in danger.

When neither said anything, I shifted my gaze to Nerina. "So, in essence we have a paranormal Masai tribe massacred by a team of unknown soldiers."

Nerina nodded. "The villagers were caught unawares. The surviving child told Sini everything. Her grandmother had taught her to run and hide in the reeds if anything bad ever happened. The poor child was hysterical, convinced she should have stayed behind, that she could have saved her people."

I shook my head. "From what I saw, that wouldn't have been possible. The soldiers were well armed, looked very well organized. But, what I don't understand is why send three soldiers to a tiny village in Africa, and send one man to kill a dozen teens in the US?"

Nerina inclined her head. "We wondered the same thing."

"Maybe they were learning," suggested Anjelo.

I nodded. "Which incident happened first?" I asked Nerina.

"The African village."

"I thought so." My head still throbbed but at least the pain was now receding. Pity the pain in my heart had nowhere to go. "My guess is they realized killing paranormals was easier than they'd expected. No need for three killers."

A somber silence fell upon the room. An image flashed in my mind, the vision returning so suddenly that I had to swallow a gasp. The killer all dressed in black standing a few feet in front of me, his hands reaching out, the burst of paranormal energy from the muzzle—

Paranormal ammunition.

I frowned.

"What's wrong, Kai?" asked Lily, shifting restlessly.

But I wasn't yet ready to discuss it with them. First, there was someone I needed to speak to. I raised my hips off the sofa and dug into my jeans pocket for my cell phone.

Grams answered on the third ring. "Hey, honey. I'm on my way home. Be there in ten."

"Er . . ." I hesitated.

"Is something wrong?"

Suddenly, I realized I shouldn't be discussing this particular piece of information on an open and unsecured line.

Grams seem to get the message. "It'll have to wait until I come home," she said, casually. There was something else too, a hint of excitement. "In ten." And she cut the call.

"What is it?" asked Anjelo, his face tight with impatience.

"I wanted to wait to hear what Grams had to say first. She'll be here any minute so I guess it doesn't really matter."

I pushed to my feet and shoved the phone back in my pocket, suddenly restless, needing to pace. "The group is organized. They definitely have a military feel to them."

Anjelo shrugged. "Anyone can buy military gear. Anyone can look military if they want to."

"Exactly what I was thinking. But one thing stood out. One thing that made me wonder what the connection was between these men and either Omega or Sentinel."

"What?" Angelo and Lily spoke together.

"The weapons they used were normal, standard issue, probably Glocks. But the ammunition they used belongs to an entirely different spectrum."

I turned to Nerina. "Did you notice the guns?"

She met my eyes, her expression confused. "I am not sure what you mean."

"The markings on the weapons. Are they familiar?"

Nerina shook her head, looking frustrated.

I shoved my fingers through my hair. "When I first came to Chicago, Storm sent me to Tara when I needed weapons. Working with Tara taught me a few things about weapons manufacturers, more especially paranormal ones. Every paranormal weapons creator is incredibly proud of what they create."

"And every weapons manufacturer marks his, or her, weapons with their signature," said Anjelo quietly.

"Exactly."

"So, the killers are using weapons created by a paranormal weapons manufacturer."

"Right."

He scowled. "And there are only a limited number of good paranormal weapons creators and most of them are either attached to, or contracted to, both Sentinel and Omega."

"So it's possible one of those two organizations have something to do with these killings." Lily's voice shook a little.

It was odd to hear her give an opinion when Anjelo was around. Back before he'd disappeared into the wraith world, Lily had preferred not to talk when Anjelo and I were together. She hadn't liked me. But now that she'd graduated from unofficial hater to official side-kick it seemed she'd thrown off her shell. And probably burned it along the way.

Go, Lily.

I nodded, still pacing. "And we all know which organization we'd put our money on."

I pulled out my phone again and dialed Logan, then listened to it ringing over and over again. It didn't even go to voicemail.

Before I could think of the numerous reasons Logan couldn't answer, the apartment door opened and Grams breezed inside. She hung her handbag on the coat rack and came to me.

Though excitement lit up her eyes, the emotion was tempered by a glint of concern. And something deeper.

I stopped pacing. "What's happened?"

"Sealed files. That's what." She slapped a small chip-drive into my palm. "I think I might have tripped a couple of alarms so I got the hell outta Dodge. We need to have a look at this as soon as possible, but first tell me why you called."

I gave her a quick rundown ending with my thoughts on paranormal ammunitions.

She blew out a breath. "That makes a hell of a lot of sense."

"What do you mean?"

"When—"

Someone began to hammer on the front door.

I frowned and sniffed, my panther nose pricking to attention. "I don't know who they are, but I smell tension."

"Sentinel Military Police," a male voice bellowed over the banging. "Open up."

As if we had a choice.

I marched to the door and flung it open. "Damage my property and I'm sending Sentinel the repair bill."

The officer stalked past me and stopped in front of Grams. "Ivy Odel, your presence is required at headquarters immediately."

"And this needed a dramatic entrance?" Grams stayed cool, but her voice was edged with steel.

"Your presence is required in order to answer questions regarding your recent access of Top Secret files."

"Really? I wasn't aware there were restrictions on my clearance."

The officer paused. "That is noted. I suggest you take it up with the High Council today."

Grams sighed. "Very well. Let me get my purse."

The officer gave a curt nod, watched Grams take her purse from the coat rack, and then shepherded her out the door.

As she crossed the threshold she looked over her shoulder. "I won't be long, darlings. But if you can't wait, start without me."

When the door closed behind them I dropped into the nearest chair.

"Shit," I said.

What else was there to say?

CHAPTER 21

SENTINEL HAD TAKEN GRAMS AND I hadn't done a thing to stop them.

I clenched my fists and felt the thumb drive bite into my skin. I opened my hand.

"What's that?" asked Nerina.

I held up the drive. "Grams must have suspected they would come for her. Just as well she gave it to me first thing."

Anjelo grinned, as proud of Grams as if she was his own grandparent. "Grandma Ivy is one smart lady."

"True." I bounced the chip on my palm and then went to my room to grab my laptop.

As I returned to the dining room and headed to the table Lily laughed.

"What?" I asked

"You actually have a laptop?"

"Of course I do. I'm a woman of the times."

"So you say," said Anjelo with a smirk.

"What do you mean?" I said, slightly offended. "I use computers all the time."

"Sure. Especially when you're traipsing around the Graylands or the wraith world."

"Or the highlands of Scotland."

I knew what they meant. After Clancy had died I'd tried to maintain my job at the Rehab Center, but after being poisoned, then scouring the Graylands in search of Greer, then being suckered by Illyria I'd been a little pre-occupied. Life hadn't slowed down any since then, either.

"How much computer time do you guys put in, anyway?"

"A whole lot more than you—considering *we* are actually getting an education."

"An education which *I* already have. Just so you don't forget." I tapped in my password, opened a directory, and inserted the drive. Moments later, a slew of files cascaded onto the screen.

Nerina slid closer as I clicked on a folder. "An education isn't always as important as it's made out to be. Wasn't there a famous computer company owner who hadn't finished university?"

I raised my eyebrows, impressed. I kept forgetting that Death-Talkers were human to begin with.

As I tapped on the next file Anjelo grunted. "Text from Storm," he said lifting his phone. "He's asked around and none of the kids have reported anyone suspicious, or even anyone new in the area."

I let out a breath. "Dead end, then."

"Yeah. He said he'll keep looking. He sounded very strange when I told him. Like it was a big deal."

I scowled, my attention no longer on the laptop. "Isn't it?"

Seeing that Nerina and Lily were also glaring at him Anjelo raised his hands in defense. "Hey. No. That's not what I mean."

"Then what did you mean," asked Lily, her tone icy.

Whoa.

"I meant that Storm took it in stride. Like it hadn't shocked him at all."

I mulled it over. "So he wasn't surprised."

"Yep. I mean nope. He wasn't surprised. Shocked. Upset. But not surprised." Anjelo leaned back and folded his arms. "Why would that be?"

Not everyone knew that Storm was Immortal. "He's not your run-of-the-mill guy."

Anjelo shrugged. "Must have something to do with all the time he's been spending with Jess."

"Maybe." My mind was busy, dancing between worry over Grams and the fact that the files she'd given me all seemed to be empty. Had she taken the wrong ones or were they protected in some way?

Then what Anjelo had just said clicked in my head. "Storm and Jess?"

He nodded. "Not romantically. I don't think. Just very . . . busy . . . And very serious."

"Interesting," I murmured.

Jess's sudden association with Storm pushed her up my list of people to talk to. If Storm wasn't surprised about the massacres then it was possible Jess knew something.

No one said anything as I returned my attention to accessing the data. At last one file opened. Letters and numbers filled the screen.

"What's this?" I asked, flipping the laptop around for Anjelo to see.

He glanced at the screen and snorted. "How the hell should I know? I don't read code." Judging by the look on his face reading code was in the same category as wearing a dress.

"Lily?" I asked.

She shook her head. So did Nerina.

"Then we're all outta luck," Anjelo said. "Anyone know a coder?"

I had to smile. "As a matter of fact, I do know someone."

"Who's that?" he asked.

"My friend Baz. He's a hacker."

"You know a hacker?" asked Anjelo.

"Yeah. Cassie and I dropped him off at Storm's yesterday."

"Oh, the English kid." Anjelo nodded. "He's not much of a talker."

I smiled and removed the drive. "Can you get him to decode this for me?"

"You think that's a good idea?" Lily asked frowning. "Shouldn't you keep a copy at least? Or have him come decode it here, or somewhere safer?"

"Good thinking. I'll figure it out." I tapped the drive into my palm while I tried to decide what was best. At last I sighed and slipped it into my pocket. "You two do some nosing around with the other kids. Ask about anything unusual."

"But Storm—"

I cut Lily off with a wave of my hand. "Yeah, but I'd rather not put all my eggs in one basket. The more sources of information we have the better."

Lily nodded, and as she got to her feet, Anjelo rose with her. They seemed to work fluidly, moving together as if they still belonged. And I hoped for Lily's sake that they really did.

They were good for each other.

As they headed for the door.

I scented Logan on the stairs outside. Hurrying to see the pair out, I greeted him at the door. We huddled for a moment, everyone saying helloes and goodbye, with Anjelo's awkward greeting a little painful to see. He still had problems with Logan and I had to figure that one out as soon as I had time.

Waving them off, I dragged Logan inside.

"So?" I asked as Nerina looked on expectantly.

Logan's expression was dark. "It's not good."

I sank onto the nearest seat at the dining table. "Is anything good right now?"

Logan remained standing, his face tight. In the last few days he seemed to have aged a decade.

"Sit down," I told him. "Tell us what you found."

He hesitated. Then he pulled another chair out from under the dining table and sat.

"I scanned the scene report," he said. "It's been tampered with. No entries to suggest a massacre. The incident now reads like a paranormal accident. The energy detectors measured pretty high amounts of paranormal Air energy, which suggests an air mage was involved, but the conclusion is accidental death. The file is now closed."

I couldn't believe it. "And they didn't get a DeathTalker in?"

"You saw the scene," he said. "There wasn't much left to talk to."

"Such things do not matter to a DeathTalker."

Both Logan and I swung our attention to Nerina.

"When a DeathTalker dies," she said, "the spirit of that person can roam the normal plane for a certain time. For millennia, this ability has allowed us to communicate with the living, to pass on crucial information, family secrets. In Mika's case, her spirit found its way back to our estate and contacted her mother."

I shuddered. "That must have been awful for Kira."

"It was," she said sadly. "Lady Kira may not be the kindest of people but she is respected. Seeing her grief now has made it all the more clear to us how much of her emotion she hides. But Mika's arrival alerted us to the fact that she'd been killed and as soon as she showed us her vision, Lady Kira and I traveled to the scene to verify it."

"Verify?"

"Lady Kira could not completely trust the word of her daughter even in death. They had a lot of history." Nerina sighed and twisted her fingers. "The scene confirmed what Mika had said. Confirmed, too, that there was little left of her body. So we left."

"Kira didn't want to claim her child?"

Nerina shook her head.

I sat back, not understanding. "There are urns in your castle containing the remains of long-dead high-priestesses, but Kira's own flesh and blood isn't important enough to take home?"

My voice had taken on a dangerously critical edge.

Nerina's lips curved but it wasn't a happy smile. "Lady Kira does what she must. She felt that it would endanger the rest of the order if we came forward to claim the body."

"She wanted to avoid the scandal," I said, my voice hard. "She knew any media attention would focus on her relationship—or lack of a relationship—with Mika and would have been bad for her reputation."

And suddenly I no longer wanted to discuss Kira. Her daughter was more important.

I turned back to Logan. "I want to see the scene for myself."

Logan sat back, his brow creasing. "I'm not sure we can do that. Both Sentinel and Omega have people watching the place."

"I can get in and out and they'll never know I was there."

Skepticism gleamed in his eyes. "Turning into a panther doesn't always make you safe. It can make you vulnerable."

I scowled. "I'm fully capable of protecting myself, panther or otherwise."

"I'm well aware of that," he said. "But there are armed agents guarding scene. Not even your panther can survive being shot by modern weaponry."

He had a point. "But I still need to see the scene myself. I might just pick up on something you all missed."

Logan nodded. "Fine. We haven't used a walker at the scene. Your sense of smell may provide more information."

I got to my feet and dusted off the seat of my jeans. "I'm ready. Call Saleem."

Logan frowned. "I don't want to get him involved."

"He's already involved," I said, starting to lose patience. "And I can just imagine what he'll say when he finds out you went without asking him to help you." I raised an eyebrow. "Or would you rather *I* asked?"

In answer, Logan drew out his phone.

While he called Saleem I talked to Nerina. "Will you be able to get there on your own?"

DeathTalkers can move within the ether, going from place to place wherever they are needed. I'd also heard they used the Graylands to travel.

Nerina nodded. "I know where the place is. I shall meet you there." She drew her hood back over her head. "But first, I should report to the Lady Kira."

I made a face. "Just be careful what you tell her. A lot of what we have is just speculation. We don't want to get her hopes up."

Nerina nodded, her expression determined, as if she was building up the strength to face the grieving woman. "I will tell her only what is necessary. Don't worry, Kailin. We are both on the same team."

I smiled and nodded. Watched as she disappeared into a tiny hurricane of gray shadow and then disintegrated into nothing.

And wondered which team Nerina would support when it came to a fight.

CHAPTER 22

WITH NERINA GONE, I TURNED to Logan, ready to depart. And saw the expression of concern on his face. I smiled and he took me in his arms. There, in the privacy of the empty apartment he let himself go. What started as a simple hug built fast into a passionate kiss. I'd missed him so much and the depth of my need for him built as our lips met in blazing heat.

Finally he pulled away. Squeezed my butt. "Saleem's on his way, you know."

About five feet away someone cleared their throat. "Already here."

We both turned to the *djinn*, and found him grinning, his dark eyes sparkling. It always amazed me how he found the time for humor in the middle of all the mayhem that defined his life.

He clapped her hands together then rubbed them vigorously. "Now where are we headed on this clandestine mission?"

I gave him the address and told him to take us a block away. Appearing inside the room while it was occupied would be a bad move.

The shift through the planes was as disorienting as always,

and my stomach turned. I was a big bad alpha panther and I got ether-sick. How embarrassing.

And just as suddenly as we'd left we returned to the human plane, the ground beneath my feet solidifying as the quiet street slowly came into view.

Cicero was a small city, west of Chicago, which had at one time been a bustling city. Not anymore. Now, most of the buildings were abandoned as citizens sought better opportunities in other more lucrative cities.

But the city, like Chicago, hadn't been entirely abandoned. Although Chicago still had a city council to maintain services, facilities, and run numerous businesses, Cicero had no council, and provided nothing to its citizens. The people who remained had to live without power and water, and so the city's atmosphere had sunk into something akin to a squatter camp.

Along its southern edge ran what had once been a popular nightspot. Its restaurants and bars now stood abandoned and bare, with glass frontages smashed, and doors hanging open to dust, dirt, and animals.

As we moved down the street I allowed my panther to filter through my senses. Sounds of scurrying. Sniffing. The stench of garbage, old fat. And desperation.

Logan led us to the nearest corner, paused, and then peered around it into the street on the right. From that position we should be able to see right inside the destroyed room, the energy blast having destroyed a good portion of the front wall.

He pulled back quickly. "We have Sentinel on guard duty on this side of the sidewalk, and Omega throwing their weight around on the other side of the street."

"Why are both organizations watching the place?" I asked.

"They don't trust each other right now," said Saleem softly, giving Logan's enigmatic face a glance.

"With good reason," I said, my tone dry and little too hard.

Saleem grinned. I wasn't the only person on this sidewalk who didn't feel friendly toward Omega.

"So. You spiriting us inside the building?" I asked him.

Saleem nodded and held out a hand. Then he looked at Logan. "Coming?'

Logan nodded and grasped his arm.

When we rematerialized, it was inside a dim hallway that stretched ahead of us into darkness. A door loomed a few feet from us. We'd solidified outside the bar where the kids had been killed, and somehow the murky dark that occupied the threshold to that awful place seemed to be filled with ominous shadows.

I took a step closer and inhaled a sharp breath. Logan placed a supportive palm on the small of my back, leaving it there for a few comforting seconds.

And then we entered the darkness.

CHAPTER 23

MY NOSE TWITCHED, THE PANTHER scenting the coppery tang of blood. Although dried and old, the life essences in the children's blood called to me and I stepped deeper into the room.

Logan held out a hand, barring me from moving forward. When I glanced at him he pointed down. A little yellow flag lay beside a dark spot on the gray concrete floor.

Blood.

Stupid. I should have known to be careful at a crime scene. Instead, I'd barreled inside like an idiot oblivious to the evidence I could destroy by carelessness.

Get it together, Odel.

I sank into a crouch and stared at the dark spot as Saleem stepped around me to do his own search. The blood had dried to a red-brown, so much like the ochre sand of the African village that I had to suppress a shudder.

I drew on my senses and focused, giving my panther more access to my human body. My nostrils flared as I huffed in more of the scents around me, and I smelled the blood itself.

My ability to smell blood remains went only so far as to identify it as blood with a particular unique odor. And yet, now, as I stared at the reddish blotch, and inhaled the scent of the DNA, an image floated before me.

I blinked and jerked back slightly, thankfully not too far that I fell over on my butt.

"What is it?" whispered Saleem as he too hunkered down beside me.

I stared blankly at his dark face for a moment, unsure what it was that had just happened to me.

"You okay?" he pressed, his brow furrowed in concern.

I cleared my throat. "I've always been able to smell blood, then identify the owner at a later stage by recognition. Like a bloodhound. But now, for some reason I can *see* an image of someone when I smell that drop of blood."

Saleem frowned. "Could be a coincidence?"

I shrugged. And looked back at the drop on the floor, seeing again the blurred image of a girl.

"How about we test it?" I glanced back up at Saleem as he spoke. "Keep studying the room, and when you get to the next blood smear, see if that also has the same result for you?"

I nodded and got to my feet, feeling the wobble in my legs match the strange tumble within my gut. What the hell was going on with me?

I scanned the room, my eyes falling on Logan who'd wandered over to the far wall beside a huge pile of debris.

A scent, out of place amongst the odors of the kids who'd been regulars within the room, caught my nose. A stronger, feral, more adult note. My nostrils twitched as I scented the air again, studying the notes. Again I blinked when the image of a man came into view.

His humanity was clear from the odor, but there was something strange about it. Something I couldn't quite fathom. His face brought back the images I'd seen of the silver-eyed killer from Mika's memories. I frowned, unsure if I should trust the instinct that was saying I'd caught the scent of the killer. Or wonder if this was just me projecting my memories of Mika's vision into the scent.

I cleared my throat and decided to try a different tactic.

I headed over to Logan, coming to a halt beside him, I asked, "So can you describe what it looked like when you saw it? I'm assuming they've cleaned up the place a little."

From where I stood, I could see smatterings of dark patches marring the concrete and the bare walls behind Logan. More blood, but I wasn't yet ready to tackle those stains.

Logan nodded and passed me his phone. The screen showed clearly the initial damage, hiding little of the horror of the scene. There were scraps of clothing and pieces of flesh from the victims littering the floor.

I suppressed a shudder at the horror of it all. Inhaling sharply, I looked closer and began to compare the image with what the room looked like now. They'd removed the bodies, and swept the debris, both concrete and wood, all to one side of the room.

I studied the patterns of where the children had ended up and the bloodstains that now remained. Then I gave the tablet back to Logan, hoping that if he saw the tremor in my hand, he would ignore it.

He did.

I inhaled again and walked closer to another streak of blood that marked the rutted concrete floor. The ground too bore the marks of the impact of the explosive force used to kill the kids.

I crouched down and studied the patch of blood, lowering my nose closer to the surface. I felt self-conscious knowing my panther nose took a partial physical form and that my human face would look decidedly feline. Neither Saleem nor Logan would say anything but the fact they'd see me in partial animal form made me uncomfortable.

Again, the scent of the blood penetrated deep into my nasal passages and I inhaled and concentrated.

Then I hissed with shock.

A face hovered in front of me. A face I knew. A girl, all blue hair and metal jewelry. The pool player from my vision.

This was her blood.

I surged to my feet still staring down at the blood. "This belonged to a paranormal girl. Around seventeen. She was dressed punk style, lots of metal, a dog-collar. And she was an air Mage. She played pool with her ability to manipulate air energy."

When I looked up, both Logan and Saleem were staring at me, their eyes wide and white.

"Did you go full-psychic on us all of a sudden?" asked Logan.

I gave a dry laugh. "I wish. Nerina showed me what Mika saw. When I smelled this blood, I saw the face of that girl again. She seemed to be the leader because she was the one who called the group together. The killer convinced her to do that. Apparently he wanted to tell them something important—or that's what it sounded like."

Logan's jaw went tight. "Must have been bloody important for such a large group to gather."

I shrugged. "Or the girl commanded the respect of her group. Think about it. All Storm has to do is send out word and dozens gather."

Saleem made a face. "Sometimes people obey because they're too scared not to."

"Good point," I said, giving a reluctant nod. "For the record, I didn't get that impression from the behavior of the people in the room before the massacre."

"So they trusted her," said Logan softly as he scanned the devastated room.

I nodded, tempted to lean against the only clean space on the concrete wall.

"And then they died for it." Saleem's words hung in the air as he shifted away from me toward a concrete pillar.

I opened my mouth to respond, but didn't get the chance. A

bullet plunged into the wall an inch from my ear, sending small shards of concrete and plaster flying into my face.

I felt the sting as the sharp edges of debris cut into my skin, but I ignored the slight pain and dropped to the ground in a crouch.

Logan grabbed my arm and tugged me closer. "You okay?" His voice was harsh as he ducked below the line of a barrage of gunfire that peppered the back wall.

Something warm and wet slid down my left cheek. Logan swiped his hand over my skin, glared at his blood-stained palm, and then gripped my chin hard while he inspected the damage.

I tugged out of his grasp—I hated being babied—and another bullet whizzed past my ear, so close the heat of the metal warmed my skin as it passed me. I grunted and ducked lower, checking on Saleem as I did so.

He was missing a chunk of his shoulder-length hair and his face was set and grim. "Who the hell is shooting?" he snarled. "And why?"

Another round of gunfire. A dull thud high in my chest. I looked down. Red liquid flowed out from a hole in my leather jacket.

I'd been shot.

"YOU'RE HIT." LOGAN STARED AT the gory bloodstain spreading from under the palm of my hand and down the front of my shirt, his expression shocked and angry.

Why did people always get angry at me when I got shot?

"You think?" I snarled, keeping the pressure on the wound. My body's initial shock had worn off. Now the pain was starting and my panther wasn't happy.

Before Logan could respond the air beside me shimmered cloudy and gray and Nerina materialized.

Her eyes went wide as gunfire peppered the wall above her and she dropped beside me with a sharp gasp.

"What is going on?" she squeaked.

"Kai's getting shot," snapped Logan.

I didn't bother to respond. "What took you so long?"

She gave an apologetic shrug. "Lady Kira was listing her requirements. She wants you to—"

Seriously?

"Not now, Nerina. I'm busy."

Nerina's gasp told me she had finally noticed the gaping hole in my chest.

"You've been shot."

"Exactly what I was just saying," said Logan dryly. He popped his head up to peer over the broken wall. Another burst of gunfire had him ducking down fast.

"We need to stop the bleeding," said Saleem. "Walkers heal fast but blood loss is still not good."

To her credit Nerina didn't miss a beat. She gathered her skirts together and tore a wide strip of fabric off the bottom. "It's a good thing we're required to wear such voluminous skirts." A couple of seconds later and she held a solid pad of material. "Let me see it."

I lifted my hand. "You don't need to use that," I said, shaking my head. "The bullet will come out on its own soon. It wasn't very deep. See?"

Nerina just stared at my chest, her expression strained. I sucked in a painful breath and realized that somewhere in the last little while my pain had increased, not dissipated. Now agony blazed within my flesh.

Nerina leaned closer and pulled the shirt fabric away from my broken skin. I blinked and tried to focus on what she was looking at. Along with blood there was a light blue liquid leaking out of the wound.

"Now that's not something you see every day," I said and caught my breath.

"This is nothing to joke about."

I peered over the rubble at him and raised my eyebrows. "Well, if you saw this for yourself you'd know what I mean."

Logan glanced over his shoulder at Saleem. "Cover me."

The djinn gave him a brief nod and he elbowed over toward me, keeping low to the ground.

Rocks fell and dust rose in the air around us as Logan reached my side. Nerina moved to give him space.

"What in God's name is that?" he asked, his voice breaking on a harsh cough as he sucked in dust.

Nerina lifted her hand. Blue liquid gleamed on the tip of her forefinger. She squinted at it. "It looks like some kind of liquid metal."

"Like Mercury?" I felt strangely adrift, as if I was experiencing everything from a distance. Even the agony had grown a dull edge.

"Very much like it. And it glows. So I'd guess it's poisonous too," she said, her face dark with worry. "Kai, you need medical help. This isn't a good. We have no idea what they shot you with."

Logan touched my arm and then my face. "Nerina is right. We have to get you out of here." He raised his voice. "Saleem, take Kai out of here while I hold them off."

But Saleem had an odd look on his face and the moment I saw his grayed, furrowed forehead I knew that something was terribly wrong.

"Saleem?"

He gave me a rueful smile and glanced down at his stomach. His navy shirt was stained dark, and glistening with blood as he leaned back against the rubble. "Don't worry. I'm not dead yet. But . . . I am grounded. Normally, I'd be able to take you with me even if we're both injured, but for some reason I'm too weak."

"It's that liquid. I'm sure it's some kind of poison." Nerina kept her voice low. At least *she* was thinking straight.

"Something that affects paranormals." I gazed up at the unpainted ceiling. "Now, who would have a weapon that could injure us like this? That can kill paranormals with a single blast of energy?"

"I have no idea, but I'm damn well going to find out." Logan crouched over me. "Saleem, can you leave on your own?"

He thought about it for a second. "I believe I could. I have just enough energy for myself."

"Then do it," I said. "And stay off Omega's radar until you're healed."

Saleem nodded, saluted with a blood-stained finger to his forehead and disappeared into nothing.

I inhaled, the sound harsh and ragged, and I glanced again at my wound. But, I didn't have time to pay attention to myself. Not with Logan a sitting duck behind the rubble and Nerina a target if she stayed. "You need to get out of here, Nerina."

Logan nodded agreement. "Yes, Nerina, Go now. Kai and I can figure out what to do next."

But she was shaking her head. "I'm not going anywhere. I can leave whenever I want. I can move from place to place within seconds. I'm safe here. And I can help."

Logan didn't blink, clearly unimpressed as he studied her face, then returned his attention to the hole in the wall. "How?"

But even as she'd described her ability, I'd had a thought. "Could you get behind the gunmen without them knowing. Maybe shift over there, grab a weapon and come back here?"

Her eyebrows lifted and then she began to smile. "What a brilliant idea." She pushed into a crouch. "I'll be back."

"I hope so," I muttered as she shimmered away.

A shout rose from across the road, followed almost instantly by another yell, and then Nerina was back carrying a short rifle fitted with a scope in each hand.

"Well done."

"It was all I could manage on the first trip." She handed one rifle to Logan, the other to me.

I grinned. "Did you get an idea of where they are?"

She nodded. "Yes. I had one false start. They are further back than I expected. They're hiding behind a vehicle on the other side of the street. A navy Chevrolet."

Logan grunted. "That's the Omega team's car."

"Do you think they're the ones shooting at us?"

"Maybe they think we're intruders?" suggested Nerina, her usually ashen skin now flushed.

"That's a possibility."

"What about the Sentinel vehicle?" I said, frowning and hoping there wouldn't be more bodies for us to find outside.

Logan shook his head. "I can't see anyone inside the car. Maybe they're slumped down out of sight."

"Nerina, could you do another recon?" I asked her softly. "Check the Sentinel car and come straight back."

She nodded, disappeared, materialized again within seconds. Her mouth opened slowly, as if she struggled to say the words.

I saved her the trouble. "They're dead, aren't they?"

CHAPTER 25

ERINA SWALLOWED HARD BEFORE GIVING a jerk of her head, which I interpreted as a nod.

"Did you see anything else the first time you went to take the guns?"

Nerina squinted and studied the ceiling for a few seconds while she thought. "No. Actually I didn't."

I sighed and pushed up into a sitting position. "Then it's probably Omega agents who are shooting at us, which means Omega is part of this whole conspiracy." I glanced over at Logan, who was now watching me, his eyes dark with worry. "But that doesn't explain why they're shooting at you too. You're Omega. They know you."

He shrugged. "Not everyone in Omega knows who I am. Maybe they do think we're intruders."

We *were* intruders.

"So it's okay if an Omega team takes out a Sentinel team and then shoots with intent to kill at anything else that moves?"

My voice held a note of accusation but it was how I saw it and I couldn't seem to hold back. When Logan turned my way again I was glad to see that he was pissed off. With Omega, I hoped, and not with me for daring to say something against his agency.

I suppressed a sigh and forged on. "So how do we get out of this alive?"

"I can take more of their weapons away," Nerina said.

I shook my head. "Too dangerous. You've hit them twice. They'll be ready for you now."

Her face fell.

"But there is a way you can help," said Logan, although he clearly didn't like what he was about to suggest.

Nerina's expression brightened.

"Give us a distraction," he said. "Go to the other end of the street, cause some kind of disturbance, get them focused on you. Then we'll try to get out of here."

She nodded. "Good plan."

I thought so too. "Just don't do anything stupid."

She grinned. "I won't. I'll make them come after me—or at least look in my direction."

I nodded and she disappeared. "We've created an adrenaline junkie," I said as Logan hauled me up. "Kira's going to kick my ass."

"Forget Kira. *I'm* going to kick your ass if you don't get it moving."

It was hard moving in a crouch. The fire burning into my flesh was way worse than the wraith obsidian poison I'd encountered not so long ago.

I gritted my teeth as Logan and I crawled across the ground to the door. The passage outside led directly onto the street, its glass windows shattered by the original incident.

If we stepped into the corridor now we'd be in full view of the shooters. But from where we sat on the threshold we were unable to see outside. Both positions were dangerous. I pulled a compact from my bag and flipped it open.

"What are you doing?" Logan asked as I slid the mirror along the floor, slowly positioning it so we could see the street.

"Nice," he said, nodding his approval.

I pushed the compact further along, got a glimpse of the navy Chevy, a person's head beside the front end of the car, the thin line of a rifle, a flash of long red hair—and the compact shattered, sending splinters of wood into Logan's face and fragments of mirror into my fingers and palm.

I yanked my hand away. "Shit! That was close. She's a good shot."

"Do you always have to be so blasé about endangering your life?" Logan glared darkly.

"What else do you expect me to do? Cry? Shiver and shake in the corner? I'm alive, so I appreciate the brush with death and move on."

Logan stared at me for a second, his eyebrows slowly lowering. "Okay," he said. "Okay."

I snorted softly. "Come on, Nerina," I whispered. "Do your thing,"

Logan wiped splinters from his cheek and shifted closer, muscles as tense as mine, ready to spring up and run the moment we were all clear.

It didn't take long. A yell ripped through the air. Feet and bodies shuffled and scraped.

Logan popped his head around the corner, checked our exit, and hauled me to my feet. "The Sentinel vehicle. Now."

I ran with him, ignoring the pain and lightheadedness. Logan shielded me all the way out the front door and diagonally across the sidewalk toward the silent Sentinel vehicle.

Just as we dropped behind the vehicle, the back tires blew and bullets peppered the metal. The car sank to the ground—tires hissing as they deflated. At least we no longer had to worry about our legs being shot out from under us.

Stupid move on their part.

Nerina materialized beside me. "Sorry, that's all I could do. They sent one man my way and I had to get out."

"Better safe than dead," said Logan, his finger tight on the trigger of the paranormal gun.

"I hope you aren't planning on using that?" I snapped. "We don't need to kill more paranormals."

Logan glared at me. "They're shooting at *us*. To kill *us*. And you're worried about *their* lives?" He shook his head and turned away. "They know what they're getting into. Whatever the deal is, these guys are prepared to die doing it."

He had a point. Judging by Nerina's expression, she agreed with him.

Warfare was one thing when your target wasn't human. A whole other ballgame when you're trying to kill your own people.

I blinked.

Silence settled on the street and I pressed against the metal of the car door. Leaning closer to Logan, I whispered, "Now what?"

He continued to watch the street. "We're going nowhere until we can elude this team. Which means unless they run out of ammo or we manage to kill every last one, we're stuck here."

"What if they decide to circle around and advance on us?" I asked.

"Then we're dead."

My response was cut off by a thunderous explosion.

CHAPTER 26

THE EXPLOSION SENT THE THREE of us sprawling on the sidewalk and tossed the vehicle into the air. It hit the ground, rolled a couple of times, and rocked to a halt ten feet further down the street.

Bullets zinged past us as Logan grabbed my arm and dragged me to the now mangled car, using it as a shield. But if they'd tossed the car once they were likely to do it again.

Logan grunted, but kept his eyes trained on the car across the street. "I can see movement. They could be reloading, regrouping, or even calling in backup."

I sighed and began to shuck off my jacket. "I can't believe I'm doing this again so soon."

"What are you talking about?" His voice was muffled, and he didn't look my way.

I handed my jacket to Nerina and began to pull my shoes off my feet.

"Do you really need to go full shift?" she asked softly.

I ignored Logan's "What?" and nodded at her. "It'll give me more power." And I couldn't stomach the thought of a half-shift.

It brought back memories of Brand, and his behavior while he'd been half transformed.

"A half-transformation will give you power too." Nerina's tone was hard. "There's no reason to strip, shift, and put your panther in such a vulnerable position. However powerful she is, the feline form itself isn't all that robust. One well-placed bullet *will* end you."

I opened my mouth, then shut it with a snap. She was right. Hunting demons while in panther form made sense, but an attack out in the open would be stupid while in animal form.

I sighed and pulled my shoes back on. "Fine. Just keep the jacket. I don't want to ruin it."

She nodded and held the leather close while I pulled my panther to the surface.

The bones in my hands and face burned as those parts of my human body gave way to the feline. Slowly ears, eyes, nose, and fingers all shifted, but only so much that they would provide me with added strength and power. I didn't give my panther full control. She didn't like that and bucked against my hold, frustrated.

I ignored her, pretended Logan wasn't watching.

I had to get over my self-consciousness when it came to a half-transformation. Even with Nerina, I'd kept my face averted not wanting to catch an expression of distaste should she not be able to handle what the half-transformation did to my features.

Ugh. More deep revelations. Kai, you really have perfect timing.

"Shit," said Logan as he lowered himself back to the concrete.

"What's wrong," asked Nerina.

I glanced over and found him staring off into nothing. Then he turned my way and his eyes were dark, the skin pale and tight at their corners.

"I think I recognized one of them." He had an almost desperate look on his face.

I frowned. "You think? Or you're sure? Maybe he just looks like someone you know."

Logan paused, his jaw tightening. Then he looked off into nothing again and cleared his throat. "I hope you're right." He turned and focused his attention back on the shooters across the street. "I really hope you're right."

We couldn't sit here forever being shot at. And who knew when they would decide to explode the car again.

"Cover me," I told Logan and dashed around the far end of the car.

Logan opened fire and the Omega agents responded. As I rounded the car I kept an eye on them, especially the redhead who was closer to me.

Walker speed made me light on my feet and super-fast. When I got to the redhead's side, she hardly had time turn those deep green eyes my way before I hit her. Her head bounced against the ground as I grabbed her gun and flung the weapon in Logan's direction. It hit the blacktop with a clatter and scraped across the hard surface.

She groaned and lifted her head, her eyes going wide at the sight of my face. Then she passed out, blood glinting at her temple. Its scent wafted toward me, and something about her blood smelled odd, just a note that didn't fit.

I shook my head. Probably oversensitive with all the mayhem around me.

But there wasn't time to analyze. I sank to the floor just in time. One of the other agents scrambled closer to me, a gun pointed straight at my bleeding shoulder. His hands trembled, probably in fear of my partially transformed face.

Deciding to use that fear to my advantage I took a deep breath and allowed the panther inside me to growl. The rumble from my throat, coating the air around us.

The agent's eyes widened. His skin paled. His hands began to shake. I breathed in his scent. He was so young.

I took a step closer to him.

He stayed where he was, perspiration popping on his fore-head. He looked like he was about to faint.

I snatched the gun out of his hand leaving him standing there, mouth open, eyes wide, his breath coming in terrified whoops.

I growled again and tilted my head as if considering.

He ran. At the corner of the street he glanced over his shoulder. Then he rounded the bend and disappeared.

Two down, two to go—and one of those two was approaching me from the other side of the car, all in black except for his face. He smelled human and carried the same strange odor as the redhead. He wasn't bleeding so maybe the scent wasn't only in the blood. Drugs?

A shadow flickered in my peripheral vision as the fourth agent ran for his life. Guess he didn't believe in leaving no man behind.

My opponent however, faced me down, strangely unafraid of me. His eyes narrowed, anger flaring in his eyes.

I tensed.

And moved closer to him, the other agent's gun weighing my hand down, reminding me that I too had a weapon. I raised it and aimed it at him. From the calm expression on his face, I wondered if the weird ammunition in the gun would have no effect on him.

My eyes never left his.

The slight twitch in his cheek was enough of a warning that he was about to shoot. As I pulled the trigger, I darted to the left just as his barrel exploded, sending a bullet straight toward me. Had I not moved, it would have embedded itself beside the other one in my shoulder.

The agent grunted. He probably thought he was a crack shot. And maybe he was. I was just faster than most of his prey.

The only problem now was that my bullet had gone wide, and now I had to kill him if I expected to survive.

I didn't want to kill him. But when he raised the gun again, and pointed it straight at my head I had no choice left.

I sprang forward, claws extended sharp and ready to rip flesh, sever veins and arteries.

A shot rang out.

The agent's eyes popped wide. Blood gushed from a hole in his throat. The muzzle of his gun tilted down as his grip loosened on the weapon. The gun hit the ground first. The man followed, crumbling at the knees.

I didn't move. My body felt numb.

In the end, I would have killed him.

Thanks to Logan, I hadn't needed to.

HE STREET ECHOED WITH ITS emptiness.

The redhead groaned, as she regained consciousness at my feet. She scrambled onto wobbly legs and grabbed for the pistol from her hip holster, but came up empty.

Nerina stood beside the agent, her face impassive, the missing gun dangling from her fingers.

The agent snapped her blazing eyes to the DeathTalker, and her lip curled. And I found myself fascinated by the fact that her eyes were almost the same green as mine. Similar, and yet so different.

"They'll come looking for you." Her voice was deep, and cracked as she coughed.

I shrugged. "Let them come. I have witnesses." I gave a cold smile. "*I* didn't kill anyone."

The agent glanced around me, her eyes going a shade darker as she registered the corpse of her partner. Logan had left him where he'd fallen, probably in order to do a quick recon of the area. The last thing we needed was to be fired upon by someone else.

She gave a nod in her partner's direction. "What about him? He looks dead."

"Wasn't me." I watched her, saw her jaw tighten ever so slightly. "The game's up. Who do you work for?"

She let out a harsh laugh. The sound ending with her bent over, her body spasmed by a succession of ragged coughs. She sounded like a dying chain smoker. At last she wheezed to a halt and straightened, her smile knowing, confident.

"I'm not saying shit."

"We have ways to make you talk," I said, trying to sound serious. It must have worked because Nerina's eyebrows rose.

But the redhead snorted. "We know who you are, Hunter. Despite your long list of kills you're no murderer."

She knew more about me than I knew about her, and I didn't like the way the scales were tipping.

"Even so," I said. "I'm not afraid to do what I have to. I will get the information that I need."

"Not from me." She sounded too cocky.

"I wouldn't be too sure about that." But something felt *off*.

Her skin turned pallid and gleamed with sweat. Her hands balled into tight fists and the whites of her eyes turned pink. Then red.

"Shit," I yelled, leaping the three feet between us.

But I was too late. She'd held out long enough to make it impossible to save her.

I caught her by the waist as she fell. Lowered her to the ground. Checked her neck for a pulse. It was there, but my panther hearing told me it was too slow. And slower. Slower still.

I grabbed her chin, opened her mouth.

Sighed.

Sat back on my heels. "Damn it."

"What is it?" asked Nerina walking closer.

"Can you not tell?" I asked, unable keep the snap from my

tone. "She's dead, I would have thought you'd be an expert in the field."

Nerina smiled, despite my attitude. "I specialize in what comes after death."

She sank down beside the dead girl, and looked as I pointed at the exposed tongue. "See how it's all blue and shriveled."

Nerina nodded. The mangled mess had once been pink and flushed with blood. Now it looked like a piece of dead meat infected by a rabid fungus.

"Poison," said Logan. He'd come up so quietly that I twitched at the sound of his voice. He touched my shoulder in silent apology. "Some of the Omega agents use a deadly poison when they go out on sensitive missions," he said. "I've only ever heard of an agent using it once in all the time that I've worked for Omega."

"What kind of poison?" I asked, appalled and yet fascinated.

"It's a poison extracted from the Devil's Spike plant." When I raised an eyebrow at the unfamiliar name he said, "It's a succulent from the Faelands."

"Of course, it is," I said dryly, wishing more than ever that Tara was around to answer my growing list of questions.

I sighed and placed my hands on my hips. When in doubt act like you're cool, stand like you're in charge, and bullshit like you know what you're doing. "So we have two dead agents."

"Maybe," Logan said. "I'll have to check the database. I don't recognize these two."

"No reason why you should," I said, studying the bodies.

"True. I don't know all the agents on the Chicago team."

"That's not what I meant." I leaned closer to the mangled agent and took a second sniff. "Unless Omega Chicago routinely uses humans on their missions, I'd say these two are not Omega. Or not directly Omega."

I didn't mention the odd smell of their blood. Not until I was sure what I was talking about.

Logan grunted, taking his tablet out to get a photograph of

the girl. I'd already heard him snap a few off of the other agent. "This makes no sense."

"And yet strangely it makes a lot of sense." Nerina scanned the area around us as she spoke.

"I take it your friend made a run for it in the drama?" I asked Logan.

Logan withered me with a look. "He's not my friend."

Touched a nerve, did I? "But you know him?"

He gave a terse shake of his head, his jaw tightening as he stared at the redhead's corpse. "He'd seemed familiar at first. It can't be him, though. If it is, then Omega could be behind all of this."

I understood his difficulty. He'd been with Omega since he was twelve and came into his power. The organization was practically his family. Imagining they could be involved in mass paranormals slayings, was probably too much to handle.

I'd been devastated to find out that my own uncle, Niko, had been a mass murderer—even if he'd been more than a little nuts and explained away his experiments as in the interests of science.

I moved toward Logan, even though I suspected he wouldn't welcome comfort.

"We don't know anything for certain," I said. "These people could be from an entirely different agency, or just a bunch of whackjobs. Your friend could be a mole, or even have defected from Omega. Or you might have seen his doppelgänger. And this," I waved my hand to indicate the destruction around us, "could all just be a setup. Someone trying to make Omega look bad."

Logan smiled thinly. "Bit of a reach, don't you think?

I shook my head. "Not really. The point is, we don't know anything for certain."

Logan grunted, then reached for the rifle that lay beside the dead agent. He unclipped the magazine and glared at the ammo.

Rows of bullets, half glass casing filled with neon blue liquid, half silver base.

"That's a double whammy right there."

I nodded. Silver for Fae, whatever the liquid was for the rest of the paranormals. I cleared my throat. "Well, I'd guess whatever the poison is, that it's meant for the younger crowd."

"Why is that?" Nerina frowned.

I tapped my chest. "Because I'm feeling better already. The poison is powerful yes, and it could probably bring down a kid instantly, but against me, it's only temporary. So maybe whatever this ammo is, it isn't aimed at adults, or perhaps it isn't designed to attack walkers."

Logan nodded. "Good point."

"Yeah, that just makes things all the more complicated. And all this was a waste of time."

"Not entirely," said Nerina, her lips twisting in a smirk.

"You got something?" I asked.

"Not yet," she said, "but I will soon." She pointed at the body of the male agent, and took the few steps toward him.

I looked around. "Let's get both of them under cover. The street looks clear now, but with all the noise we've made I don't think we have much time left before both agencies send in reinforcements. Maybe we should just leave them and go."

"We *should* go," Logan said. "But these two could give us valuable information. We'll have to take the chance." Logan glanced at the body. "Grab his legs, Kai."

I did as requested and we took the body back inside the ruined pool room, placed it on the floor then headed back out again.

I followed closely, helped him bring the redhead inside as well.

When we set the dead girl down Nerina was already kneeling beside the young man.

Logan grunted. "I'll be outside. Someone needs to keep watch." Then he was gone.

Did that mean he didn't like watching DeathTalkers at work? Who would, considering what they did? But I stayed, to keep Nerina company and to hear what the two had to say.

Nerina settled onto her knees and laid her hands on the male agent's chest. I was surprised at how young he looked. Not much older than the guy who'd run away.

The worry we now had was that the two surviving members of this team would bring backup, and that they knew who we were.

The redhead had mentioned the Hunter. Had they been aware that I was coming? Or was I just that famous?

$\mathcal{I}$ CONCENTRATED AS NERINA LEANED forward and opened her mouth. A stream of gray smoke poured out. The cloud rose and swirled before turning and diving into the mouth of the dead man.

She bent closer so that her lips hovered over the agent's mouth and drew the gray smoke back into her lungs. As weird as it looked, it made a kind of sense.

Then she sat back, her face was serene and expressionless, and when she opened her mouth again it was the dead man who spoke.

"Where am I?" he asked.

Neither man's body nor Nerina moved, so and I was forced to answer. "You're on your way to the Graylands."

As the words left my mouth, I realized how harsh that may sound especially to someone so recently dead.

"Oh," he said.

My words hadn't frightened him. "You're not going to panic?"

"Why should I?" he said. "I knew this was likely to happen."

Resignation, not fear. "You expected to die?"

"Not expected. More like I knew it was a hazard of the job."

"And what job are we talking, exactly?" I asked.

"I work for Division Seven."

"What is Division Seven? Government?"

"Yeah. Off the books."

I'd bet it was. "What does Division Seven have to do with Omega?"

There was a pause. "What's Omega?"

Okay.

"What's your name?"

"Daniel Chou." He didn't say more so I left it at that.

"Who was the fourth agent? Not the young one who ran, the older man."

"Oh," Daniel said. "That's Blake. He's on loan from another agency. Inter-divisional cooperation or something like that." His voice faltered, becoming hollow as if echoing through a long dark tunnel.

"Blake?"

Daniel nodded. "*Agent* Blake. He's an odd one but he keeps to himself." He fell silent for a moment. "He ran?"

"Yes, he did."

"So much for interdivisional cooperation." Daniel sighed and even the sigh seemed to be getting fainter.

I had to hurry. "So what does this off-the-books division of yours do, exactly."

"We eliminate paranormals."

What could I say in response to that? It was very much cut-and-tried. "On whose orders?"

"That's need to know."

"Well, I need to know, and you're dead so nobody will care that you told."

He shook his head. "I'd tell you if I could. But our section leader just passed on the orders. Orders come from above. We followed them. We didn't need to know who gave them."

I didn't understand this attitude. If I was ever told that I didn't need to know where an order came from I'd make finding out my first priority. "And those guns?"

"Don't start me on those things," he said. "I hate them. Way worse than using normal bullets for humans." He paused. Seemed to struggle to speak. When he began again his voice had grown fainter. "Like using hand grenades to kill a herd of deer. Cruel and unnecessary."

This interrogation wasn't going to last much longer. "So what exactly were you doing here? We thought you were Omega agents."

"We were supposed to watch the site. Eliminate any intruders. Eliminate any paranormals."

He seemed to accept the existence of paranormals easily for a human. But there wasn't any time to get into why. He was probably trained well.

"Who killed the Sentinel watch?"

"Blake."

"Why?"

Daniel shrugged. "Don't know. We asked but . . ."

"Need to know?"

"You got it." Then he paused, his voice tinny now, fading. "Sorry I couldn't be much help."

"Sorry we shot you," I said, feeling a little stupid even as I said it.

"We did our jobs. Mission complete."

"You mean 'mission successful'?"

"Mission complete," he repeated, his resignation clear even as his voice faded to nothing.

Nerina shuddered, lifted her head, and opened her mouth. The smoky gray tendrils wafted from her lips, rising, roiling in the air until they gathered together as if compelled by some invisible force, and swooped to the boy's mouth.

The smoke plunged between his lips and disappeared, leaving Nerina shuddering. She bent over, sucking in great gulps of air.

"You good?" I asked, a little worried.

She nodded. "I'm fine. He seemed . . . okay with his death."

"Too okay if you ask me."

"Yes. I agree."

Footsteps crunched outside on the concrete floor of the hallway and Logan came in.

"Anything?" he asked, even as he scanned the room and the hole in the external wall for potential threats.

"Not much." I said softly. "Agent Daniel Chou, Division Seven. Off-the-books government agency. He was a drone who did what he was told, never asked questions, never knew where his orders came from. But he'd never heard of Omega, and your friend was on inter-departmental loan and his name is Blake."

"Blake, my ass," muttered Logan through gritted teeth.

Nerina cleared her throat. "We should speak to the second agent before her time passes."

Nerina was right, but I wished we had more time for her to recover. She looked tired and strained. Saying so, however, would hurt her feelings—or her pride—so I stepped aside so she could access the redhead.

Logan remained at the threshold, gun in hand, his attention focused on the door and the hole in the wall.

Nerina sank beside the woman's body and performed her smoke exhalation/inhalation procedure. Despite having just witnessed it I found the process just as fascinating the second time, and just as gross.

When the DeathTalker finally lifted her head, her face was expressionless. And, unlike Daniel, this one wasn't talking.

"Can you hear me?" I asked.

Nerina's body stiffened. Then her lips stretched. It wasn't a nice smile. And she remained silent.

I glanced over at Logan to find he'd moved so he could cover Nerina as well as the other threats. And he was right. Something was definitely wrong with her.

"Can you hear me?" I repeated. "What's your name?"

"You think you're so smart," she sneered. "But *we* are smarter."

Nerina began to shiver. The pale whites of her eyes began to go black and a cough ripped through her like a dull scream.

"Let her go, Nerina," I yelled, hoping she would hear me and pull free from whatever hold this dead girl had on her.

Nerina's shivers changed to shaking and then to convulsions, as though a terrible fight was taking place within her. I leaped over the redhead's body and grabbed Nerina's shoulders, supporting her through the convulsions, praying she wouldn't break bones, wouldn't die.

"Nerina," I shouted. "Logan?"

I looked up at him, terrified now that we wouldn't get Nerina back. That we'd lose her.

He was looking at the redhead. His face darkened. And I saw it too. The dead woman smiled.

The bitch *smiled*.

Logan didn't wait, didn't flinch. He chambered a bullet and shot her straight in the heart.

The sound of the shot thundered in my ears and Nerina again convulsed in my arms. Once. A second time, weaker. A third time, weaker still. Then she stopped moving, her skin paler, her eyes wide open.

I sucked in a shuddering breath. Nerina's eyes were slowly returning to normal, her skin beginning to warm to its usual simple paleness instead of a porcelain death-face.

I grabbed my jacket from the pile of rubble beside her and folded it before dropping it on the ground. Then I lowered her to a lying position, her head on the jacket.

Just in time. She gave one last, massive shiver. It lifted her head inches off the jacket and then dropped it back so hard that it bounced.

I winced. How would I explain a DeathTalker with a cracked skull to Kira?

"I'm fine." Nerina took a deep breath. "I'm feeling better now."

As she inhaled again, the air beside us shimmered and Jess arrived. "Cassandra Monteith let me know you needed transport back home."

I blinked and shared a worried look with Logan, wondering what he'd say about his superior officer now knowing he was investigating a case off the books.

But he didn't miss a beat. "We'd better get moving," said Logan. "We've been here long enough. Their backup will be arriving shortly." Logan kept his eye on the doorway.

I put an arm around Nerina and Jess helped her to her knees, then to her feet.

"I'm fine," she said again. "I can manage to walk myself."

I glared at her, refusing to let go. "You don't look fine to me. The last thing I'm going to do is to let you kill yourself on my watch. I like my head on my shoulders, thank you very much."

Logan snorted and Nerina laughed, too.

"So, Lady Kira scares the shit out of me. I admit it."

Nerina patted my shoulder. "I really am all right. You will be able to get out of here faster without me." She took a step away. "I can't take you with me, but I can get myself to your apartment safely enough."

I nodded. "If you're sure."

"She's sure," said Logan. "Go now, Nerina."

"You don't have to tell me twice," she said, and disappeared in a cloud of gray smoke.

Jess didn't say a word, just held out her hands. Logan and I took a hand and Jess took us home.

CHAPTER 29

JESS LEFT US ON THE landing outside my apartment and left after a quiet word with Logan that I pretended not to hear.

When we walked into the apartment, Grams and Mom were sitting in the lounge having a heart-to-heart with Nerina. Thankfully, she looked fine, alive and well.

I was safe from Kira.

The women of my family had plied the DeathTalker with tea and cookies, and seemed to have had much success, judging from the satiated smile on Nerina's face.

I dragged my feet as I stumbled into the room, dropping my bag on the floor as Logan closed the door behind me. My limbs trembled and though Logan attempted to grab my waist for support, I shifted away and sank into the nearest chair, exhausted, both mentally and physically. I leaned forward, and unzipped my boots. Too late, I realized the impending danger of keeling over. I blinked and swallowed hard before flinging the boots at the coat rack behind the door.

One landed at least a foot from its destination and Logan shook his head. He toed the errant boot back to its partner and frowned as his phone began to buzz loudly. He tugged the device from his pocket, but by the time he answered I'd already lost my concentration. I closed my eyes, squeezed them tight, then opened them again.

Everything was blurry.

"Kai, honey. You look awful," said Grams, rising from the couch. She didn't even ask, just went into the kitchen and put on a kettle. My grandmother's answer to everything was a nice hot cup of tea.

And at that point I couldn't think of anything better.

Wait a goddamned minute. Hadn't someone taken Grams away? Like arrested her or something?

Nerina got up from the sofa and glided toward me. Funny how she seemed to float on the air, her gray skirt flowing in an invisible breeze.

Get a grip, Kai.

I glanced up at Mom who was close on Nerina's heels. Before I knew what was happening, my mother knelt beside me and opened the buttons of my blouse to inspect my bared chest.

Not that anyone here hadn't already seen said chest before, bared or otherwise.

Despite the trickle of gleaming neon-blue liquid that escaped the wound, the single bullet hole beside my sternum had already begun to knit together. The bleeding had stopped a while ago, thankfully. I didn't need to hear Grams nag about blood on the polished wood floor.

Mom surged to her feet. "Stay right there," she said, pointing sternly at me as she hurried off to my bedroom. I heard her rummaging inside the secret space behind my closet where we kept our guns and ammunition and an assortment of other weaponry.

"If you insist," I said, unable to hide the fatigue from my voice. The poison, though not fatal, seemed to be having some sort of effect on me. I never felt this tired.

Mom returned, holding a tube which looked like something she could have stolen from one of Uncle Niko's chemistry labs. She came to stand beside me and placed the tube against my chest, holding it close to my skin as the liquid dripped slowly into the container.

As she worked, I turned to Logan. "The djinn?"

He gave me a nod. "Sleeping on the couch." I shifted my gaze over Mom's shoulder and was satisfied to see his sleeping form draped across our sofa.

At last, when Mom had gathered enough of the neon liquid, she lifted it to the light and stared at it.

Grams clicked her tongue from the kitchen. "Staring at that damn stuff isn't going to help you figure out what it is. I'll get that to the lab as soon as possible. You hold down the fort."

I laughed softly, more a giggle than anything else.

"What's so funny," asked Mom, coming to sit beside me. She used the side of my shirt to wipe away the dried blood from my wound.

"You holding down the fort."

Mom frowned.

"When you're AWOL it's hard to hold down any forts."

Mom grinned. "Very true." Her eyes glittered. "But, now that I'm back I can, can't I?"

I gave a nod, finding my head very heavy. Strange.

"Have fun," I said, with a drunken wave.

Then I began to slide down the chair as my body went totally numb.

The last thing I recalled was Logan grabbing a hold me before I slammed face first into the wood floor.

I WOKE, sitting bolt upright in the silent bedroom. Sunlight streamed into the room and I could hear the clink of cutlery against plates outside my door. I shoved the blankets aside, ignored the decidedly heavenly feel to my room, with all the golden sunlight and white sheets, and padded to the door.

When I swung the door open, all conversation stopped and I was pleased, surprised and taken aback at the scene at our dining table. Saleem was gone, and my parents, and Grams were eating Sunday lunch with Logan.

Well, knock me down with a feather, why don't you.

I blinked, opened my mouth, then closed it again.

"Honey?" Dad pushed his chair away and dropped his napkin on the table. Here too, the sunshine streamed into the room, making everything bright and a little unreal. When I felt Dad come to a stop in front of me I had to accept that I wasn't dreaming the whole scene. "You okay? You up to having lunch?"

I nodded, then rubbed my eyes. "How long have I been out?"

"Just overnight." He smiled, placing a hand on my back and guiding me to the table. "We let you sleep in."

"Now you change your mind?" I teased as I sat in the vacant seat beside him.

The tight lines at Logan's eyes told me that he found the whole meal a strain.

I glanced across at Logan where he sat bracketed by Mom and Grams. Poor guy. I hated to think of what he'd been through in my absence. Iain was one thing, Grams and Mom alone with him was a totally different form of torture.

Dad cleared his throat. "What do you mean?"

I had to force my thoughts back to his question. "All our lives you've insisted that sleeping in was a form of inherent laziness, and now you say it's okay?" I asked as Grams placed a plate of eggs and bacon in front of me. Logan forked a sausage onto my plate and I caught Mom giving him a glance that was on the 'oh so cute' side.

"It's a scientific truth, Kai. The one thing one finds most in common in successful people is that they are early risers."

"Is that a fact?' asked Mom, a knowing grin on her lips as she focused her attention on him. She propped her elbows on the table and threaded her fingers in front of her. Seeing her fiddle made me more aware than ever that I'd missed out on years of learning her habits and mannerisms.

I chewed eggs and bacon as I watched Dad shift his gaze to his wife and I was struck by the tenderness in his eyes. The man who'd keep himself distant from us, who I'd thought cold and unfeeling, seemed to overflow with love for his wife. Or was it his estranged wife now? Or lover?

My head hurt.

"Yes, that is a fact," he said firmly.

"Then explain to us how it's possible for *you* to be so successful when *you* aren't an early riser?" She smiled pleasantly.

Tea appeared at my right hand and a piece of warm toast hovered in front of me. Everyone was taking care of me. I could so get used to this.

Dad grunted, then threw Mom a sharp warning look.

"Mom, we all know Dad never sleeps in." I frowned as I stabbed a piece of bacon.

"Another secret to successful men," said Grams with a short laugh. "Secrets."

"Not you too," said Dad leaning back against his seat as if that small distance gave him some safety from this onslaught.

"Grams, are you saying Corin Odel is a slacker?" I asked giving Dad a glance.

"I should know. Mothers know these things about their children." Grams popped a piece of sausage in her mouth and chewed around the grin that remained emblazoned on her face. She was enjoying this way too much.

"Mother," said Dad, the warning clear in her voice.

That set everyone laughing.

"Dad, just accept it. Your secret is out." I snorted. "And your scientific facts are BS."

He laughed ruefully. "I guess it is, then."

I ate, listening to the banter around me, feeling at home and relaxed for the first time in a while.

At some point Grams' cellphone buzzed and she picked it up. Seconds later she cleared her throat. "I do hate to destroy the happiness and light at the table but there has been news."

Everyone looked at her, waiting, dread darkening the bright midday sunbeams that danced around us.

"Sentinel's just informed us that there's been another killing. This time a cluster of goblins in the Alaskan forest."

I'd never met a goblin before. Said a lot about my upbringing though, considering I'd never know my own mother was human until I'd walked headlong into the fact not that long ago.

Mom made a strangled noise in her throat. "Why the hell would they want to attack the goblins? They've lived in peace for centuries. And they keep to themselves. Why target them?"

"Target practice," said Logan quietly.

Nobody argued.

Goblins could be vicious when attacked, but they weren't fighters. They hated any exercise that didn't further their own personal goals of a happy carefree life. Hence Alaska and other far-flung countries were usually populated generously with goblins.

Logan shook his head. "What better way to test paranormal weaponry than to use targets who have zero evasion tactics, and even less defensive capabilities. And who like living as far from civilization as possible. Easy targets and nobody will notice. Best of both worlds."

I shook my head. "All this, everything that's happened to date, all the murders . . . They all seemed so random, so unconnected. What reason could there be for randomness-"

"Unless the randomness was deliberate." Logan finished my sentence, nodding to himself. His gaze was focused angrily at his plate as if Grams' bone china dinner plate was one of the killers.

"They've been testing whatever ammunition and techniques they have on different paranormals, different parts of the world. But maintaining a distance from civilization."

"Makes sense," said Mom, looking angry.

Before I could say anything, a knock sounded at the door. Grams' eyebrows rose and I knew she already knew the identity of our visitor.

Mom got up to answer and when the visitor proved to be Jess, I wasn't surprised.

She walked in, her movements graceful, and as should be expected from a Titan. She inclined her head in greeting as she stopped beside the table.

Both Logan and Grams rose, and Grams said, "Would you-"

Jess lifted a hand regally and everything stilled.

I blinked.

Logan and Grams were standing way too still. I stared at them, and blinked again.

A glance back at Jess confirmed that the Titan and I were the only ones still able to move.

My jaw dropped.

She'd frozen them.

CHAPTER 30

I'D HEARD OF THE TITAN'S ability to freeze time and always thought it was some kind of magical mumbo-jumbo. Apparently it wasn't.

I stood for a few interminable seconds, almost as frozen as my family. A small part of me wondered, in shock, if they'd come out of that state even aware that they'd been paused in the first place.

Then I was just angry.

"Why did you do that?"

I hadn't even bothered to greet her, but I didn't care about being rude. She'd just frozen the people closest to me; I doubted she'd expect me to bow at her feet.

"Because we need to talk."

My gaze flickered between Mom and Logan, to Grams, her mouth half-open, lips frozen in mid-speech. To Dad. If I wasn't so annoyed, the whole scene would be hilarious.

"Do not worry about them. They are all perfectly fine."

I shoved my chair back, ignoring the angry screech of the legs against the wood floor. I even managed to not glance at Grams to see if she was glaring at me in admonition.

I stepped away from my seat and, walking around Dad, came

to stand in front of the Titan. I moved slowly, deliberately. I wanted to convey that I wasn't afraid of her, or intimidated by her. But something told me she already knew what was in my heart.

That I was more than a little terrified.

"What do you want to talk about?" I asked, tightening my throat muscles so my voice wouldn't shake.

"We have a problem."

You don't say.

"Which one?" Right now, we had a whole bunch of them.

"The killings."

The most annoying thing about Jess was that she was stingy with information. She only gave me bits and pieces, and only then when things got dangerous.

I folded my arms and waited.

Jess sighed and began to pace. It was uncommon for a Titan to display such human emotion. Interesting.

"I have been with Omega for a long time and nothing like this has ever cropped up on my radar." She made a disgusted sound. "I am beginning to sound too much like these . . . agents."

She said 'agents' like it was a dirty word. Even more interesting. "So Omega had something to do with the massacres?"

"I cannot be certain. We suspect it may be the case but we have no definitive proof."

"Who is *we?*"

"I cannot tell you." Jess tipped her chin. "I can only tell you what will assist you in your investigation. I do not have the authority to divulge anything beyond that."

I raised an eyebrow, the action drawing an indulgent smile from her.

"I am sorry, Kailin. I am doing everything possible to help, without stepping over the boundaries placed on me. I have orders, and I am fulfilling them to the best of my ability. But something has gone very, very wrong."

"Omega agents have been involved with killings. Logan told me about Agent Blake at the massacre site. And then there is the paranormal ammunition. It even knocked *you* down. Perhaps it didn't kill you but it was certainly powerful enough to incapacitate you for a time. That is a concern.

"More killings are happening daily, and we are frustrated that we cannot trace the source. The perpetrators are smart, and ruthless."

That was for sure. "Why are they doing this?"

"At this point, we cannot be certain, but from the nature of the killings and from studying some of the scenes, I believe the person behind it all has something against paranormals."

"You don't need to be a genius to figure that one out," I snapped—and then wished I could stuff the words back down my throat.

Titans were many things but they weren't patient and they didn't like disrespect. It was one thing to think rude thoughts. It was quite another to say them aloud. With some Titans it was asking for a death sentence. I'd also heard stories of people losing their tongues, or their minds, and sometimes both.

"Stop being so melodramatic, Kailin."

I stared at her stunned. "You—"

"Read your mind?" she asked, her eyes narrowing. "Of course, I read your mind. You have absolutely no shields. I can hear every thought you have. Titans, Immortals, and Angels all have the ability to hear the thoughts of other beings."

"Can you hear each other's thoughts?"

"Thankfully, no." She seemed relieved.

"So, if you can hear our thoughts, why can't you just read everyone's minds and find the culprit."

"Because they seem to have help from someone. Someone who knows how to bypass my ability."

"Then Omega knows who you are?"

"Strangely enough, no. Whoever this is, either knows who I

am or they suspect an Immortal has infiltrated. Or they are just being paranoid and careful. In any case, it is bad for me because the culprits are either magically blocked, or they are manipulated in such a way that they have no idea that what they are doing is wrong."

I nodded. "And if they didn't think they were committing a crime they wouldn't be thinking like a guilty person."

"Precisely." Jess was still pacing. "Everyone I have read is going about their business. Nobody has walked past me with fear or guilt or awareness on their minds."

"That just proves whoever is behind this is very smart."

"And very powerful." Miss State-the-obvious.

"Any ideas?"

"Possibly an Elder, an Ancient or one of the Immortals." Jess looked worried.

"Why would you think that?"

"Just the breadth of knowledge that they seem to possess, the ability to manipulate people so skillfully. The ability to evade Sentinel's investigations."

"So Sentinel has been aware of this?" I asked.

"Since it began." She fell silent.

"When did the killings start?" I asked. Something told me I wasn't going to like the answer."

"About a year ago," she said with a sigh. "I have been keeping an eye on the attacks, reporting back. We have been monitoring the situation and trying to implement ways to stop it. But we have been frustrated at every turn."

"Almost as if they know you're coming?"

She nodded, frustration lining her face in deep grooves.

I knew the feeling. I was still stunned from learning that the killings weren't a new thing.

"We did not think it prudent at the time to educate the Races," Jess said before I could ask why they hadn't shared. "Only when the murders began to increase in frequency and number, did we realize the severity of its escalation would make wide-spread awareness unavoidable."

I narrowed my eyes and watched her. She spoke so impartially, with so little emotion, that I almost understood how they could have ignored the murders for so long.

"You do not understand," Jess said, her tone steely. "We did not ignore the murders. We believed they were separate incidents. Unfortunately, we were wrong. It soon became clear that we were not dealing with either separate incidents or a serial murder spree."

My voice was dead when I finally said the words.

"We're dealing with attempted genocide."

"Yes."

Jess sighed, her shoulders drooping. I'd never seen a dejected Titan before. But then I'd never talked about paranormal genocide before either.

But she'd known, so why would she be reacting this badly? Unless...

"Did your High Council know this was going to happen?" I asked. The Immortal High Council was the most powerful council across the Planes, the Fae excluded. Fae were a whole other story altogether.

Another breath. "Not exactly."

I waited. No sense in pushing her.

"We knew something was going to happen," she said after a moment. "Sometimes Oracles are highly specific. At other times they are more confusing than informative."

"That I know," I said dryly.

Jess gave a soft laugh. "These predictions were specific enough that we knew the timeframes. We have been watching. But we still did not recognize it immediately." She began to pace again. "The problem has been, that for every step we make that gets us closer to the killer, we seem to take two steps back. It is as you said. Perhaps we have a mole."

"Or maybe the killer is a Titan?" I suggested, knowing I put my life in her hands as I did so. Titans were known for their fury. Maybe my mouth would get me killed after all.

Jess's face paled, but she met my eyes. "I am beginning to wonder that myself."

I inhaled slowly so she wouldn't know I was taking a huge freaking sigh of relief.

"What can I do to help?" I asked. She'd come here for a reason, after all.

Jess inclined her head, a regal thank you. "If you would help me fill in the blanks, it would be most helpful."

She wanted information. But that would mean I'd need to tell her everything that we found out. If she was part of the problem then I'd be giving information straight to the killers.

Wait. What? Did I really think Jess was capable of murder?'

The Titan laughed, the sound soft, yet musical as it danced around me. "My dear, you must know that I do not need permission to obtain information from you. I much prefer that we both worked together on this. I dislike having to probe the minds of the unwilling." She made a face. "I usually emerge feeling . . . tainted."

"Uh . . . Yeah." I wasn't sure what to say. "I'll help, of course. Anything to end this horror."

I was being truthful. I'd even help the perpetrators if it meant being the instrument of their downfall.

Jess paused and stopped in front of me. "I thank you, Ni'amh."

I blinked. "I haven't been called Ni'amh in a while" I sighed. "I wish I knew more about that, too. And about what's going on with Logan."

Jess smiled. "To show my gratitude I have a gift for you."

"A gift?" I parroted, wondering why she'd be gifting me anything right now.

"If you encounter any other Titans, your suspicions, along with what we've just discussed, will be available for them to read if they so wished. Therefore, I will give you a shield, a permanent block on all your thoughts against anyone who has the ability to read minds. The only time the power will fade is when I remove the block."

I nodded, unsure how to thank her.

She just reached out and placed her fingers on the side of my head, her thumb against my temple, the rest of her fingers spread against my skull. She closed her eyes. "Be still."

I held still, not moving a muscle. Jess's eyes remained closed as the pressure of her fingers against my skull increased. A tingling spread into my brain. Before I could worry about the cold lightning sparking inside my head, Jess let go and stepped back.

"It is done," she said with a satisfied gleam in her eye.

"Thank you," I said. "I never imagined I'd need such protection."

"That, my dear, is my job. Do not worry. You will get your information."

I smiled.

"But not yet."

I frowned, suddenly very unimpressed.

"I apologize, but I must get back—and I have frozen your family long enough. Unless they remain so for months or years it is not wise to keep someone in stasis beyond fifteen minutes."

Months? *Years*? Not a chance. "Oh, then we'd better wake them up now."

Jess smiled and turned to face the table. "I will be in touch shortly. You will have your information as promised."

She waited only for me to take my seat again and then, with a wave of her hand she freed everyone from the trance.

"—like some tea?" Grams said.

Grams and her tea.

Jess shook her head. "Sadly, I am only here to collect my

agent." She shifted her gaze to Logan who got to his feet and reached for his plate.

And got a smack on the back of his hand from Grams for his troubles.

"Don't even think about it, young man," she said. "You go do your job. We'll take care of the dishes."

I was about to comment that dishes weren't solely a woman's domain, and that she was an agent just as much as he was, when Grams crooked her finger at Dad. "You. In the kitchen. With me."

Dad's strangled response was enough to make laughter bubble up inside me. I turned it into a cough and averted my eyes, glad when Logan signaled with a lift of his brows that he wanted to talk privately.

I went to his side. "What's the plan?"

He lowered his voice. "I have to leave. We need to be on site in Alaska." I nodded. "You want to come with me to see for yourself."

I shook my head. "I would, but I have to do something first. And we'd need Nerina, of course." I frowned and looked around the apartment. "Where did she go?"

"Back to the estate. Said she'd return soon." He glanced at Jess over his shoulder. "Can you call Nerina?"

She nodded.

"I'll be back," he said as he headed for the door.

"Famous last words?" I asked, unable to hide my amusement.

His laughter was still wrapped around my heart long after he'd left.

CHAPTER 31

I ENTERED STORM'S BUILDING WITH my stomach feeling like a giant ball had taken residence there.

What the hell was I doing? What the hell was I even thinking?

But ever since Jess had come by, I'd been fixated on the only Immortal I knew. Storm.

Even the *thought* that he could be involved in something as heinous as genocide seemed wrong.

I knocked on Storm's office door, and didn't have to wait long before his deep voice rolled out, bidding me to enter. I turned the knob and went in.

Storm was sitting bent over at his desk, studying something, afternoon light from the window behind him glinting off his golden hair.

It didn't surprise me that he was able to tame so many of the young children that came to his guardianship. He was kind, strong, solid, and handsome. All in all, an arresting man.

And here I was, suspicious, worried that he might be guilty of all these horrible murders. Or at least know something about them.

He looked up and smiled, his bright blue eyes gleaming. Nothing about him shouted, "Suspicious!"

He sat back in his chair and his smile broadened. "He's doing fine."

I blinked, then realized Storm was referring to Baz, our new vampire.

"I'm glad," I said, instinctively forcing my mind to think worried thoughts about Baz. "I was worried,"

Then I remembered Jess had given me the mind shield. At least I didn't have to be concerned about Storm reading my thoughts and knowing immediately why I was there.

"So has anything else happened?" I asked, watching his face. He shook his head, looking a little unsure as to what I meant. "Any disappearances on your end?" I made the question clearer. "Any suspicious deaths?"

Another shake. "Not that I know of. I'd tell you if I did."

I wasn't so sure about that anymore.

"I know you would." I forced a bright smile on my face. "I just came by to check on Baz. Is he around?"

"He's in the mountains. We sent him on a training mission."

I tried to imagine Baz on a training mission and grinned. "He's a geek. Is it a geek retreat?"

Storm returned my grin, relaxed and easy. "Exactly that. I'll tell him you came by."

"Thanks. I'll call in again next time I'm passing." I felt the weight of flash-drive in my pocket. I'd have to find another way to get the device to him. I was done here, that much was clear.

I hesitated then turned to leave and the door opened.

Niki came in, neutral smile on her face as she saw me. She glanced past me at Storm.

"Yes?" he said.

"The team has returned from the site. They didn't find a killer. We have managed to identify the dead though." Her eyes widened.

I looked at Storm. "What is she talking about?" I asked, a hint of annoyance in my voice. He *had* lied to me. Not that I was going to say so in front of the girl, though.

"Oh. You didn't tell Kai?" asked Niki softly, her face a little fearful that she'd made a mistake and yet she did look curious too.

Storm's face tightened, his blue eyes darkened. "I intended to tell you only when things were verified. Now that they are, yes, unfortunately we do have something to report."

I waited, understanding that he'd been forced to tell me only because Niki had revealed the information in front of me.

"That's okay. I'm glad to save you a call. Any help in this case is progress—although more death is the last thing we want."

Storm nodded then jabbed a few keys on his keyboard. "I've emailed you the crime scene pictures. Details from this recon will be sent as soon as I have them."

"Great." And I'd chase him for them if necessary. "Where did it happen?"

"The train station." Members of City Deep haunted the abandoned lines of the old Union Station. I nodded. I'd been to many a City Deep meeting there. "Were the victims young?"

Storm nodded and Niki gave a watery sniff.

I glanced over at her. "Did you know them?"

"One of them," she said. "He helped me out when I first arrived."

I reached out and touched her arm. "I'm so sorry."

She nodded and then looked past me to Storm. "Do you need anything else?"

"Just the debrief notes when they return," said Storm.

Niki nodded and exited the room quietly.

I faced Storm, analyzing his expression. He looked tired, strained. Affected. Maybe I was on the wrong track entirely. Maybe he was innocent after all and I was chasing a dead lead. But, I had to make sure. I'd deal with the guilt if I was wrong.

I was about to leave for the second time when I remembered I'd also meant to ask about my sidekicks. "By the way, any idea where Anjelo and Lily are? I haven't heard from them in a little while."

In fact, it had now been almost a day since I'd last spoken to either of them. I was tempted to pull out my phone and check my messages, despite my gut telling me that there would be nothing to see.

Storm got to his feet to walk me out, ever the gentleman. "Unfortunately, no. They both took off yesterday afternoon. In fact, they said it had something to do with helping you out." He shrugged. "I knew they'd return when they were able, so I didn't worry. But now ... I am worried."

So was I. The last thing we needed was for the two kids to be in any kind of danger, especially with the killer lurking around knocking off paranormals left, right, and center.

"I'm sure they're okay," I said. And hoped I was right.

"I'm sure you're right," Storm told me. "Anjelo knows the streets very well. They'll be fine."

I nodded, barely hearing him. It was easy for him to say, but the two teens were family.

Of course I worried about them.

$\mathcal{I}$ ARRIVED IN THE ALASKAN forest surrounded by members of Logan's Omega team. Despite being accompanied by agents potentially aligned with the bad guys, I still felt safe. Probably because I knew most of them.

When I materialized within the trees, in Saleem's grasp, I found we were on the edge of a clearing that held an enormous log cabin.

Three stories high, the mansion was huge enough to fit a clan.

I felt comforted that Saleem had finally shown up, but the tension in his face warned me that his presence was likely temporary.

As I followed Saleem's silent gesture, I understood that it probably *had* housed a clan. Its male occupants lay strewn across the lawn, staring with blank eyes at the afternoon sky. One of the older men was lying broken across the threshold as if he'd tried to stop the intruders using his own body as a shield.

Nothing external would alert a human eye to the fact that they were goblins. Yes, they had the obligatory pointed ears; glamored so only those humans with the Sight could see them. And they were made of stockier stature than a human, but goblin glamor was inbuilt and so strong that it would take days after death before their magical wards would fade and reveal their true form.

When I entered I knew why he'd protected the house to the death. There were families here. A woman and her child lay on the floor near the door staring up at the wood ceiling, their blood pooling on the floor from a single wound to each of their chests.

Who were these bastards?

I tried to breathe through my fury, blink through the tears that filmed my eyes. They'd killed a defenseless innocent baby no more than two years old.

In the rooms beyond we found more death. And even more. After a while all I wanted was to leave. I wasn't sure how much more I could take.

The children were the worst to see. The hardest to accept.

I tried to keep my concentration on the details, like the splintered door frames and the blood spatter instead of the ruined bodies. But I soon realized that focus wouldn't help. It especially wouldn't be respectful to the victims if I pretended they didn't exist.

I forced myself to concentrate on one detail at a time. The shapes of the wounds, the existence or absence of any kind of paranormal ammunition or residue—of which there were plenty —how the placement of the bodies revealed the journey the killers made through the house.

At last, we reached the attic door. It hung open and a child's shoe lay at the foot of the open ladder.

Logan looked over at me as I reached the ladder. "The techs have been up there. One body." His voice held a note of warning in it. It was going to be bad. I suspected it meant the child was young.

Logan climbed the stairs first. As I arrived at the top the air beside me began to shimmer gray and Nerina appeared, her expression apologetic.

"I came as soon as I could," she said.

I waved a hand. "You came. That's all that matters."

She nodded as she studied the attic space, her eyes falling on the little boy who lay sprawled in front of a giant silver mirror. His eyes were open, and the expression on his face was rebellious, as if whatever the intruders wanted, he'd never give. I could sense his bravery and wondered what he'd done that made him feel so resilient.

I hunched down beside him, swallowing against the lump in my throat. "He's so little."

Nerina's skirts swished beside me. "He looks about eight."

"Goblin years or human?"

"Human." Nerina sank to her knees beside me and touched the side of the boy's face. "He's been dead about two days. He may have already passed over into the Graylands, which would make it harder to access his memories."

"They'd be fading, right?"

Nerina nodded, her face a little strained. She looked angry and frustrated and I wondered if her reasons were other than the bodies littering the house. Had Kira chewed her out while she'd been at the estate? Or was she just tired and in need of rest?

I'd bet on Kira. But I didn't probe. She seemed too focused on the child as she leaned over him.

"Let me try," she said. "Anything is better than what we have right now."

"I agree," I murmured as I studied the room. Pulling on my panther sense of smell I scented the air, hoping to catch a sense of the killer. Or killers.

What I did scent was a shock in itself. So much of a shock that Logan sensed it.

He was at my side in an instant, his eyes filled with concern. "What's wrong, Kai?"

Even Nerina was looking at me, worried.

I shook my head and touched my finger to my lips. Then my

attention shifted to the large mirror leaning against the wall beside us.

I pointed the finger at the mirror, mouthing a single word.

Silver.

Logan's eyes widened as he gave me a short nod, then navigated to the other side of the mirror. I strolled the opposite end, finding my way blocked by a stack of old boxes.

Logan moved closer, then grabbed the mirror and swung it away, revealing a narrow space behind—a space containing two shivering little children who stared at us, terror in their eyes.

CHAPTER 33

ALTHOUGH I COULD SEE THEY were whimpering we couldn't hear a sound.

"Glamors?" I asked, thinking out loud.

Nerina shifted closer and moved to the little boy while I bent toward the girl. They looked no older than four, but seemed smart enough to know they ought to keep their glamors tightly wound around them.

"It's okay," I said, holding a hand out to them. "You're safe now."

It didn't seem to impact them at all. They just stared at me, as if unable to understand my words.

"The glamor isn't theirs," Nerina said. "It's been placed on them by someone with a stronger power. Probably so they wouldn't hear what was going on in the rest of the house." She waved her hand around the children. "I can try to remove it, but I can't guarantee success."

Neither Logan nor I said anything as Nerina continued her work. At last we heard the little girl's soft sobs.

"Hey, sweetie can you hear me?" I asked gently, kneeling on the wood floor.

She huddled over, peering up at me through tear-filled eyes. She sniffed but didn't answer, but I knew she'd understood my question. She was just too scared to respond.

The little boy, on the other hand wasn't afraid. "We don't want to go with you. Leave us alone."

"Please don't be scared. We are here to help you." Nerina spoke softly, and the boy, despite his bravado, hesitated, as if he really wanted to believe her.

It must have been something in Nerina's voice because the boy finally relented, his stiffened hands relaxing, the strained muscles in his neck relaxing.

The girl, seeing him giving in, moved closer toward me, and then she was in my lap, her arms tight around my neck.

When she sniffed my neck, I stiffened and she giggled in my ear. "I know what you are," she whispered. "But I won't tell."

I didn't want to scare her, but I did want to keep her talking. "So, what do you think I am?" I asked smiling at her. Out of the corner of my eye I could see Logan waving at someone behind him to cover up the body of the older boy.

"You're a cat," she whispered, a smile in her voice.

"And *you* are so very clever," I said, tapping her nose with my finger. "My name's Kai. What's yours?"

She grinned. "Alina Longford. That's my brother Alix. He's my twin."

She pointed a thumb in the boy's direction and a glance at him showed me Alix was a glowering little ball of fight. He wasn't playing nice at all, despite giving in to Nerina's coaxing, and I wondered what had happened.

At least Alina seemed relaxed and comfortable and we were desperate for information so I figured I would give it one try.

If she became upset or agitated then I'd stop.

I cleared my throat and asked, "Alina, do you think you could help me figure out what happened here?"

She gave a sad nod. "We know what happened. We saw it. And

then Nathan came to take us away. Then Papa threw the glamor and we didn't hear anything after that."

"And can you tell me what happened?"

She nodded and her smile no longer lit her face. "Two *men* came," she said, an edge to her voice that implied the men themselves were different.

"Men?" I urged softly.

She blinked, staring over my shoulder at the men moving behind me. I shifted around so she wouldn't be able to see the removal of the boy's body.

She nodded. "Human men."

Her voice, though soft, rang out in the attic and movement around us stilled.

"How do you know they were human?" I had to ask.

"I smelled them. Just like I smelled you."

"Ah, yes. Your clever nose."

She wrinkled said nose. "It's not clever. It's just a goblin nose. You know that." Her smile faded.

I laughed softly. "Yes, I do. And even if your nose isn't clever, you are still a very smart young lady." She fell silent at that and I wondered what I'd done wrong. Maybe she was tired? "Do you want to take a break? I know this must be hard for you, honey."

Alina shook her head, her dark red curls swinging around wildly. "I want you to find the men."

"Can you remember what they looked like?"

"I only saw one of them. The blond one."

Chills went up and down my spine and I glanced up at Logan. He met my eyes for a brief moment then looked away and I felt a tug of concern. Why was he evading me? Was he worried that he may have been wrong and that maybe he really did know Blake?

I refocused on Alina. "Do you recall anything else about him?"

"He was tall, and his arms were big." She lifted both her arms and blew out her cheeks to indicate bulging muscles. "Funny hair." She made pulling motions with her fingers on the top of her head.

Yes. This was pointing directly at our friend Agent Blake. He had spiky hair too.

"Anything else about what happened that you want to talk about?" I asked, leaving the question open to Alina. We'd gotten the information we'd come for— Blake was the perpetrator, which meant this incident was officially linked to the other killings.

Alina's voice was high as she spoke, breaking into my thoughts. "Do you know why their guns were so soft?"

"Soft?" I frowned. "You mean they were quiet?"

She nodded. "The shooting. We didn't hear it until they were banging down the front door. Daddy didn't have any time to save anyone. Just me and Alix." Her voice quivered. "Not even Nathan."

Her gaze drifted over her shoulder again and though she didn't look directly at the body I knew she knew that the little boy who'd saved them had been killed while doing so.

She settled against my shoulder, and I stayed where I was as the Omega team hurried around, logging evidence.

A bustling at the stairs to the attic indicated a new arrival.

An Omega agent popped his head into the attic and said, "Sentinel's here."

Logan nodded. "Send them up." He seemed to have no problems with inter-agency cooperation.

Seconds later a square head and bulky shoulders appeared at the top of the stairs and I groaned silently as Paulson climbed into the attic and headed to Logan. Even Cassie bringing up his rear didn't make me feel better.

"Paulson." Logan gave him a cool, impartial nod.

"Westin."

A brief handshake later, Paulson scanned the room and

caught sight of me. The look he gave me said, *What the hell are you doing here?*

I lifted my chin. *I belong just as much as you do.*

In the dusty silence of the attic, Logan gave Paulson a brief rundown and—on a tablet handed to him by one of the passing agents—pointed out the locations of the main evidence bags. He focused on areas where most of the paranormal ammunition had been discovered.

Logan's gazed flicked in my direction a few times, his eyes going from Paulson's stony features to mine, his expression curious and a little amused. It wasn't hard to tell that Paulson wasn't a fan of mine.

"Hey," said a subdued voice beside me.

I looked up and gave a parody of a smile at Cassie as she hunkered down beside me.

She studied the now sleeping child, whose dark red curls framed her little face.

"Survivor?" Her eyes looked bleak, even more faded than her usual pale gray, possibly a result of her being shot in the chest. But, I could do with even a hint of brightness right now.

I nodded. "One of only two." That reality stabbed my heart with its vicious blade every time my mind went to the children and what they'd experienced at the hands of 'the blond man'.

"Where'd you find them?" Paulson called from where he stood with Logan, his voice shattering what little calm I'd drawn over myself.

I glanced up and inclined my head at the mirror. "Behind that."

He slapped his hands on his hips, his posture accusing, as if I was spinning extravagant nonsense from dreams and stupidity. "How the hell did the killers not find them?"

My jaw tightened. "I'm guessing the silver hid them."

The tone of my voice dropped a few degrees, enough to

extract a hint of a smile from Logan who watched me from Paulson's side.

I continued, "And that means it's likely that the killers used some sort of detector, maybe something that can read energy waves to identify species."

"And what makes you think that?"

The challenge lashed at me, his sharp tone a whip, and at my side Cassie groaned.

Gritting my teeth, I said, "Because we all know silver acts as a protector. It's also a ward against magic so it makes sense that it would hide magical energy too. Of course, that's just my assumption. I'll leave it to you smart agent types to verify."

I lifted my chin as I watched him process the information. His face revealed how little he liked the fact that I'd come up with something smart and worthwhile.

He gave a short nod. "Very well." He turned to Logan, dismissing me instantly.

I made a face as he continued his conversation with Logan. "Chauvinistic bastard," I muttered, realizing too late that the kid was still on my lap. I breathed a sigh of relief when I looked down and found she was still fast asleep.

Cassie echoed my sigh. "Times may change, species may evolve, but men, they stay the same."

I snorted. Wasn't that the truth?

CHAPTER 34

"WE'LL BE LEAVING SOON. SALEEM will be back in a few minutes." Logan's voice broke through my concentration. He stayed a few feet away, eyes focused on his phone as he read through something, a dark scowl wrinkling his features.

I was sitting on the forest floor, in a quiet clearing about a hundred yards from the house, the early evening sun too weak to warm the icy in my heart. Nerina had left to bring Lady Kira up to speed, while Logan and Paulson oversaw the final cleanup. We'd decided it was best for the kids to get them away from the house while Sentinel and Omega wrapped things up.

Jess had left the mayhem and come to check up on us. She was sitting on a tree-stump, watching the two children who'd fallen asleep after having a small bite to eat. Thankfully, we'd found bread and cheese and smoked fish in the kitchen, and the two were satiated and resting. Not that I imagined for a second that they would come out of this experience undamaged.

It struck me how unreal it was to find beauty and peace so close to carnage and mayhem. It did not seem right.

And now it was time to leave.

The closer it had come to leaving the more agitated I'd become. My gut churned, screaming at me that I couldn't let the children end up with either of the agencies. Not when everything about the two organizations was so up in the air. Granted, Sentinel was the more reliable of the two right now, but I was hesitant to leave the children with Paulson, even though Cassie would be there to keep an eye on them.

He didn't exactly instill a great deal of trust in me, and I was pretty sure he'd end up rubbing the kids the wrong way too.

I had a plan but there was one person I had to call first.

Chloe Murdoch our mage with the magic touch.

I shifted on the stump and faced Jess. "Do you think you could call Chloe for me?"

Jess inclined her head. "Chloe would be perfect."

I cleared my throat. "Can we be certain Chloe takes the kids somewhere safe?"

"You mean other than Storm's care?" Something in her features tightened.

I shrugged. I didn't want her to think I'd begun to suspect Storm. Not yet. "I think they're a bit young for Storm."

I knew they weren't. Hadn't Mel told me she'd been placed with him at a young age? But, no. She'd been around twelve or thirteen.

Jess, however, didn't challenge me. "Where else could you send them?"

I swallowed, wondering if this would get me in trouble. "Tukats." I cleared my throat. The walker town where my father lived would be the safest place for them. "Chloe can take them there for their safety and from what Alina said they seem to be fairly comfortable with walkers so the situation wouldn't be too strange for them. You don't have to worry about anything. Anyone under my father's care is under the care of the entire colony."

"Even now?" asked Jess, an eyebrow curving gently.

"Even now," I responded, feeling a painful twinge deep inside me. Dad hadn't spoken about it and I wondered now how much support he had within the colony after the High Council's decree. I made a mental note to ask him.

"Very well. If you are certain they will be safe then Chloe can take them there." Jess disappeared.

I watched the children and listened to the birds calling in the trees, resisting the urge to transform and run free for the briefest time. Being caught buck naked by the infamous Paulson-with-no-first-name, wasn't a comforting prospect.

Jess reappeared soon with Chloe in tow, the mage shaking her head and blinking hard. "I don't think I can ever get used to those jumps."

I got to my feet and leaned in for a hug. First reason was to greet Chloe because she was just that kind of loving person. The second reason was so she could take away some of my nerves and fear too.

She held me tight. "My dear girl. Why do you hold so much inside?" She leaned away, but still didn't let go of my hands. The warmth from her fingertips swirled through mine, searching and wending its way up my hands.

I'd never known what drugs had felt like until Logan had used some super powerful concoction to knock me out once, but this throbbing, searching feeling very much resembled a drug. Quite the addictive buzz.

I tried to tug away but Chloe proved stronger than I expected. "Oh no, you don't. You need a little more, Kai. I can't believe you aren't taking care of yourself. A nervous breakdown on the job isn't going to be good for you, or for your charges."

I glanced down at the kids, for a moment terrified that she expected *me* to take care of them.

Chloe clicked her tongue. "I didn't mean them, silly. All the people you help along the way. You owe it to each one of them to bring your A game."

I nodded. "I know. I just don't have the time. Too much going on."

"*Too much going on* is not a good enough excuse." Chloe narrowed her eyes on my face. "What else is going on that I don't know about?"

"Anjelo and Lily are missing," I whispered.

"Oh?" A frown creasing her brow. "But I saw them not too long ago. They were on a mission for Storm."

Ice washed over me, a cold dread that sank into my bones. "Oh? Where did you see them and when? I was with Storm a few hours ago and he said he hadn't seen them."

"That's strange." The lines on Chloe's forehead deepened. "I just saw them. They got back from the scene of the murders."

I frowned.

"Storm said they were out doing something for me." I swallowed hard, and my head felt hot. I glanced up at Chloe. Now I was more than just frowning. My heart was thudding a mile a minute. "He said they were on a mission for me. Not him. And he said he hadn't heard from Lily and Anjelo for a while because they didn't tell him where they were going. He seemed to think *I* would know where they went."

"That is the weirdest thing I have ever heard. What is going on with Storm?" asked Chloe almost to herself. With Chloe occupied with her confusion, I pulled my hand free and stepped away.

I didn't like the thoughts that I was having. Could I trust Chloe? She worked so closely with Storm, what if he'd influenced her?

I cleared my throat. "Chloe could you take these two to my father's place?"

"You don't want me to take them back to Storm's?"

I shook my head. "I'm just a little worried about where peoples' loyalties lie. I'm not questioning your loyalty either. I just want to be one hundred percent sure that these kids are safe."

"Did they see anything? Did they see the killers?'

I hesitated, then glanced at the kids. They were stirring, with Alina blinking wide eyes against the bright sunshine.

"No. They didn't see anything." Alina blinked again and watched me. She'd heard what I'd said. "And it's probably for the best that they didn't. They're safer."

That was enough of a message to the child, and I could tell from the darkness in her eyes that she understood.

"They'll be safe with my father. He'll make sure they're taken care of until we can figure out where they can stay. They might have family who will claim them."

Chloe shook her head. "But that may not happen until we can find out who is killing the paranormals. Everyone will probably go to ground now." Then she sighed. "You are right, though. It's likely the safest option for them."

She seemed troubled and I wondered what she'd do now. Would she confront Storm or play the waiting game?

At least now I knew Anjelo and Lily were back. I needed to track them down to find out what the hell was going on. But first, the kids.

I went with Chloe to sit beside Alina and Alix—who was now also awake. He was sitting up, pouting, and rubbing his eyes. He was going to be a handful but his behavior earlier was probably just because he'd been tired and stressed. Or at least I hoped so.

"Alina, Alix. This is my friend Chloe and she's going to take you to my dad's house. It's very safe there and I'll come to see you as soon as I can. Okay?"

I asked the question giving the children the impression that they had some say on where they went. They didn't, but it didn't hurt to let them think they did.

The twins exchanged a glance and then Alina nodded. "We'll go. As long as we go straight to Kailin's dad's house." She gave a firm nod, as if that finalized everything.

Chloe grinned. "Absolutely. You can even keep my phone with

you. Kai is on speed-dial so if you need her just press the button and she'll be on the other end of the line."

Chloe glanced at me and I gave her a grateful smile.

Jess moved in and said, "Right. We need to go. I'm afraid Saleem has been sent on an errand for Omega so I will take the children to Tukats. I will be right back to take you there too, Chloe, so you can check them out and make sure they are both well."

Chloe nodded, and Jess held out her hands. The twins each took a hand without a word and the three of them disappeared from the clearing.

"Thank you for doing that," I said, feeling really bad that I had to hang a question mark beside her name. I crossed my fingers and hoped she'd prove innocent. I really hoped, if Storm had gone bad, he'd had the sense to keep Chloe out of it.

"It's my job, Kai. You know that. And don't for one minute think I don't know what you're up to."

I raised my eyebrows in innocent question. "What do you mean?"

She sighed. "I can see where the suspicions are heading. And if Storm is up to something, whatever it is he has his reasons and I am positive he's not endangering any of our kids."

Then why did he have to lie to me?

I wanted to ask the question aloud, but she was not the person to pose it to. Neither was she the person to answer it.

"I hope so, Chloe. I really, really hope so. I don't think I can handle another betrayal by someone I care about," I whispered.

Chloe nodded and would have answered had Jess not chosen that moment to arrive. The mage gave me a short wave and disappeared with Jess.

I grabbed my phone from my pocket and sent off two short texts—one to Anjelo, one to Lily—both amounting to little more than 'where in Ailuros' name are you?'.

The brush behind me crackled and Logan walked toward me. He looked drained, and haggard.

"How're things going?" I asked, worried now at the toll it was taking on him

He rubbed his hand over his face. "I'm supposed to be used to this type of thing."

"It's always harder when it's kids." My voice was emotionless only because if I allowed myself to feel right now, I'd be in his arms, a bawling mess.

"You're right. And it's for them that we need to resolve the situation as soon as possible."

I nodded.

"What did Alina say about the killers?" I met his gaze and gave a short shake of my head.

"Agent Blake, huh?" Logan grunted. He wasn't happy.

"You do know who he is, don't you?" He'd mentioned someone from his past the last time he spoke about him, but nothing since then.

Logan looked at me, his struggle clear in his expression. When he shook his head and said, "I'm pretty sure he's not the man I remembered," I wondered why he thought he could hide his feelings from me. "And if he is, then . . . "

"Then what?"

"Then I'll have to do something about it."

CHAPTER 35

I LEFT THE ALASKAN BUSH angry.

But I held it in, more so because I wasn't willing to expose my stupid mood to the people around me.

Because it *was* stupid.

There were a number of good reasons why Logan wouldn't tell me something important, not least being he could get himself in serious trouble if he spilled sensitive information.

If he was going to tell me anything, he'd do so in his own time. No amount of pushing would speed up that process.

Logan sent me off with Saleem, who had the grace to look chagrined before he transported me to my apartment.

When we materialized inside, Saleem paused to study my face.

"What?" I asked, defensively.

"Something's wrong."

"Right," I snapped.

"I understand." His smile was rueful. "He gets like that sometimes when he thinks he's at fault about something."

"What the devil could be *his* fault in a situation like this?" I asked, then paused watching Saleem's blank expression. "Does it have something to do with the ever-elusive Blake?"

Saleem blinked. "Perhaps."

I wasn't in the mood for teasing. "Don't *perhaps* me, Djinn. I'm worried. What are we going to do about him?"

Saleem sighed. "You have a one-track mind."

"You bet your ass." I said sharply. "Logan's hiding something from me and I want to know what that is."

"What if you don't need to know?"

I'd strangle the next person who said those words to me. "As long as it has something to do with this case then I *need to know*."

"Point taken."

"I'm meant to kill this bastard," I said. My blood promise was ever present in my mind.

"Have you considered," Saleem said carefully, "that *the blood promise* could be Logan's problem?"

I frowned. "I hadn't thought of that."

Logan could be keeping certain information to himself either to protect me or to protect the perpetrator. "If that's the case, then he'd better be doing it to protect me, because if he's protecting the killer then I'm not sure how I'll handle it."

"Whatever he does he *will* have his reasons."

Sage advice from the djinn. "He can have his reasons. I don't mind them—as long as his reasons don't stop me from keeping my blood promise. I know he's not happy that I agreed to it."

Saleem's eyes filled with compassion. "Do you really think Logan would put you in danger by thwarting your attempts to honor your promise?"

I stopped. Thought about it. "I guess not." I sighed. "Please tell me why this is so goddamned hard."

"Because we care," he said immediately. "If we don't care then we're not as emotionally invested as we'd like to think."

"More wise words, djinn?"

He shrugged, then grinned. "I have my moments."

I grinned back at him. He could always diffuse a situation with one of his well-timed grins.

"So, how are you by the way. You look pretty cheery for a guy who looked like he was at Death's Door just a day ago."

Saleem glared at me. "Hey, I do get to recover as fast of as the walker, don't I?"

I laughed. "But seriously, you good?"

"I'm good," he assured "But I won't be if I don't get back. We have debrief."

"They won't want me there, will they?" *Please say no.*

"I don't think so. Nobody has indicated they want your side of the story. If they do, they'll come for you."

"That's guaranteed I'll sleep easy," I said with a snort.

He lifted an inquiring brow. "Why would you worry about such a thing? Omega wants you on board. Even with all the mess that's going on, they've been at Logan to bring you in."

"Have they now?" I asked, folding my arms. "Funny. Logan hasn't mentioned it once."

Saleem shook his head, his dark hair shifting against his shoulders. "Of course, he wouldn't. He doesn't want you to feel pressure. And there are other reasons."

"I know," was all I said.

We both knew Omega's respectability in my eyes was in serious question. There were also my current issues with the Walker High Council and my alpha status—although Omega wasn't interested in my alpha status.

When my phone beeped and I reached for it Saleem took the opportunity to escape. *Coward.*

The message was from Anjelo. I called him immediately.

"Where are you?"

The *damn it* in my tone must have been obvious. "I'm sorry," he said. "Look, some weird shit is happening. We need to talk."

"Where?"

"The usual place."

Which meant O'Hagan's. And also meant I needed to be more than worried if Anjelo was going all 'secret codeword' on me.

"See you there in half an hour," I said.

He responded with a grunt and ended the call leaving me staring at my phone.

My *ringing* phone.

This time it was Dad's face on the video calling app.

"Hey Dad," I said taking in the strained and tired look on his face. I hoped it was just a bad camera phone.

"I have your two little packages here." He smiled when he said it, which was a good sign.

Yeah, I'd take anything I could get right now.

"How are they doing?"

"They're both fine, and the reason for this call. You have one very strong-minded girl there."

I felt a glow of pride, as if Alina were my own child. Which was weird because I wasn't a maternal kind of person.

Alina's face appeared on the screen, with Alix showing in the top right-hand corner, peering at the screen with his forehead scrunched. He still looked angry, but markedly less so. It was more than I could have asked for.

Alina waved at me. "Hey, Kai."

"Hi, kiddo. How you doing?"

She nodded. "Your daddy is nice. I like him."

I grinned. "I like him too."

She giggled.

"How's Alix?" I asked, pretending I couldn't see him.

Alina stabbed a thumb in his direction. "He's here. He's fine. He ate a lot."

"That's a good thing right?" I asked.

Alina's face fell. "Mom doesn't like it when Alix eats too much. She'll be mad." She hung her head.

"Alina, listen to me." The little goblin girl looked up at me. "I know for a fact that your Mom wouldn't mind at all. She will totally understand."

"You think so?"

"I know so."

"How do you know?"

I paused considering a white lie. Decided against it. "Because I know how people feel when they pass on to the afterworld."

"How do you know that?" Her eyes widened, a little suspicious, like a child on the verge of assuming the adult was lying to her.

I sighed. "Because when I spoke to my sister after she passed into the Graylands, she told me that all a person's anger and negativity just fades away."

"Oh." The child paused, thinking. "You sister died too?"

"Yes, honey." I gave a twist of a smile. "Not too long ago."

"I'm so sorry." She said it softly, then looked up, probably at Dad sitting beside her. "I'm sorry," she said to him, her face uplifted, her eyes moist. It was the sweetest, most saddest thing I'd seen in a long, long time.

More surprising was Dad's reaction. He bent and kissed the little girl on her forehead. "I'm sorry too, Alina. Maybe we can help each other through this terrible time?"

The girl smiled and in the background, Alix watched, anger gone, eyes wide at the revelation that they shared a deep loss with their new guardian.

It was a good start. We ended the call with promises from me that I'd come by and check up on them.

Then I headed out to see Anjelo.

As I hurried down the stairs, my panther senses picked up odd sounds from the floor below. My panther wasn't always switched on, but she did remain in the background, always accessible if something strange happened.

The surreptitious scrape of a heel drew me up short. From where I stood I had a good view over the railing and along the

Birdcage to the floor below. They edged around the elevator well, descending all the way to the basement level. From my position I caught shadows where there shouldn't be any. Someone was creeping up the stairs.

Nobody I knew would creep up my stairs that way. Nobody I trusted at any rate. I stilled, considering what I should do next.

I drew on my panther senses and a whiff of the air confirmed three men, the smell of metal said they were armed.

I didn't stand a chance.

That meant the roof, because I'd prefer to not have my apartment ripped apart. This guy looked like he was here to make life difficult for me.

I tip-toed back up the stairs, past my door to my floor, and up the next flight. At the top of the landing, a single door led to the rooftop. Outside would be concrete floors dotted with air-conditioning vents and fans. A dilapidated old bird coop roosted in the center of the rooftop, the result of a long-dead resident's hobby.

Decades ago, when the droughts dried up what used to be arable land, many residents had found the pigeons and other birdlife, a good source of protein.

Life hadn't changed that drastically over the last few decades —we just had fewer birds, less farming, less city maintenance.

And fewer jobs.

Let's not forget *fewer jobs*.

I kept my breathing low as I slowly pushed open the door to the roof, then blinked at the bright light.

And at the man standing there, waiting for me.

Agent Blake.

CHAPTER 36

THE MEN AT THE BOTTOM of the stairs had stopped their journey upward. They'd been herding me upstairs. And here I thought using the rooftop was the safe choice.

I'd run from them because even I wasn't stupid enough to take on three armed men.

But, I'd just played straight into Blake's hands.

I let the door swing shut and backed away, my heels skidding on the gravel.

I skirted metal duct, keeping an eye on Blake when he swung his weapon at me. As I threw myself onto the floor I caught sight of the sun reflecting on the neon blue flecks marking the barrel. A previous bullet had sprayed poison on exit.

"I've been looking for you, Walker."

Lame.

"You've found me. Now what?" I asked coldly, frustrated that I couldn't see him. His henchmen would be on their way soon, too.

"Now, I kill you."

"You're very confident."

"Easy to be confident when you know you'll win the fight."

More lame.

"How about you fight and let's see what happens?" I suggested, keeping a tight grip on my bag. I couldn't reach inside for my own weapon so the bag itself would have to do.

He pulled the trigger and I ducked. The bullet whizzed past my ear and slammed into the door behind me.

I hit the ground. Rolled over before coming to a stop behind an air vent. Blake circled, sending more bullets my way.

He rounded the vent, plugging a dozen bullets into the ground and into the vent. Bullets hit, concrete chips flew at me, burning a path down to my chin. I ignored the sting, digging into my bag for a gun.

I swiped at my cheek and ducked around the vent, drawing my pistol free and sending a few shots in his direction.

He just followed, spraying me with more bullets.

I waited until I heard him release and reload, and sprang forward, emptying my weapon, aiming at his head.

Blake moved faster, his next bullet slamming into the top of my gun, sending it flying from my fingers.

Shit!

I ducked low, letting my claws flow to the tips of my fingernails, sharp and deadly, forced to use what Ailuros had given.

Ready, I waited until he had to reload again, then ran full tilt at him. I slammed into his chest, putting the full force of my panther into the leap. He tripped over, his feet slipping on the ground, and hit the concrete full force.

Only, he was ready for me, and moved straight into a roll, tipping the balance between us and wedging me between his knees on the ground. With his hand on my neck.

A walker's neck wasn't an easy thing to break. An alpha's neck even harder. Blake growled and pocketed his weapon before concentrating the force of both his hands on my throat. His fingers grew tighter, cold now, like ice stabbing into my throat.

I gasped, stabbed my claws into his sides and rolled out from under him as he yowled and grabbed at his waist.

His vest was thick, but the sticky wetness on three of my claws confirmed he'd suffered at least three injuries. I'd hit home.

He sprang at me again, even as I rolled away, planting a knee to my back. He bent close, his arm going tight around my neck. He gripped his wrist with his other hand and began to squeeze hard, driving his freezing arm against my throat. I coughed, and struggled for air, and almost reached out to pull his fingers from my throat when I realized my claws were still in full form. Rather than impale myself on my own claws I decided to use them on my assailant.

To his own detriment he'd gotten too close.

I swiped hard at his face, the sharp edges of my claws hitting skin and scraping bone as my hand moved in a backward grasp. He yelled out, fell back onto the concrete and rolled away. Within seconds he was on his feet again, holding his ripped face together with his hand.

His other hand hung limply at his side.

My strike had caught him first on his bicep and then his lower jaw and cheekbone, three deep slices and one shallow scrape.

As I righted myself, Blake began to back away. There was no fear in his eyes though. He was just making a calculated decision to retreat while he still had his life in his hands.

Not to mention his face.

But I wasn't planning on letting him escape. I launched into a run, my panther giving me a boost.

I slammed into him, knocking him flat, swinging my claws across his throat to finish the job.

But my claws met with nothing.

A shadow shimmered beside Blake and in the next instant he disappeared.

Someone had jumped him to safety.

I HELD ONE OF GRAMS' old handkerchiefs to my face as I half-limped half-walked to O'Hagan's.

The tiny cuts made by the flying chips of concrete would heal soon enough, along with the sprained ankle that I'd only noticed after Blake had escaped.

His henchmen hadn't come to his rescue, neither had they come to kill me, so that made me think there was more going on than I knew.

And he'd been saved at the last minute.

Someone powerful was protecting him, and I wasn't going to sit around waiting to find out who.

The doorbell tinkled as I pushed into the bar. Its aroma of alcohol and fried bar food smelled familiar and comforting. No wonder it had become my go-to place when I needed down-time. I hoped the sense of comfort would last a while longer.

I slid into the booth where Anjelo sat hunched over.

Alone

Something in my gut twisted, a premonitory twinge. "Where's Lily?"

He was silent but when I kicked him under the table he raised his eyes to mine.

"She's missing."

I felt dizzy. *Deja vu* dizzy.

"What?" I failed to keep my voice down.

Anjelo didn't seem to care much. "I don't know how it happened. One moment she was there, then the next she was gone."

"'There' *where?*" I leaned forward. "Storm said you were both out doing something for me."

Anjelo's eyes widened, and anger flared in their depths. Anger and disbelief. "That's a lie. Storm sent us to investigate the disappearance of the two City Deep kids."

"Storm said there were murders, but he was certain that you two were investigating something for me." I frowned thinking about the files he'd sent—and about the ones he hadn't. Two files on two of his missing teens. None of the follow-up information he'd promised.

"Storm told you that?" Anjelo couldn't have looked more stunned if I'd slapped him across the face.

I nodded. "Something is rotten in the state of City Deep."

"Yes," he said. "It is."

"Tell me."

Anjelo took a moment. "Storm sent us to check out the two missing kids; Emma and Simon. They're both mages. One's an air mage, the other a fire. Em's still in training but she'll never be very powerful. We call her our Power Puff girl."

Funny. Sad. "How did they go missing?"

Anjelo shrugged. "Storm just said they were gone and Lily and I went to look for them."

When he stopped talking I knew he was trying to process the fact that Storm had lied to us all. No time for that now. "And?"

"We tracked them to the train station, up one of the older abandoned tunnels."

I nodded. "How were they killed?"

His mouth went tight. "Bullet to the chest. One each."

"Neon blue residue?"

Anjelo blinked. "How did you know?"

"It's been cropping up all over the place. Someone knows how to kill paranormals and turned the knowledge into a versatile weapon."

"Shit," he said, his expression dark.

"So tell me what happened to Lily?" He didn't respond immediately. "Come on Anjelo, talk to me."

"We were investigating the scene and she disappeared."

"Just like that?"

He nodded.

"You looked for her?" Of course he did.

"Scanned the whole area three times. There wasn't a sign of her anywhere."

"Did you shift?" He nodded again. "Couldn't get her scent?"

"Nothing."

This wasn't the first time Anjelo had lost Lily. I was amazed he wasn't falling apart. "Okay, Lily's gone. Tell me about the kids."

"Kai!" Anjelo was genuinely horrified.

I laughed. "Anjelo, she's been abducted before. Tortured horrifically, and she survived. She's strong."

"So *you* say."

"Yes, I do. And I also say we need to think logically if we're going to get her back. So tell me about the kids that were killed. How long have they been dead?"

"About two days, from the state of decay." He wasn't happy, and sounded it.

"Do you know where the bodies are now? Maybe we can get Nerina to speak to the spirits of the kids?"

"That's going to be a little difficult," he snapped. "The bodies disappeared when Lily did."

Crap. "So they took the bodies to stop the kids' spirits from communicating and giving us information. Why take Lily?" Wrong place, wrong time?

"Because she was there when they came for the bodies," he said. "And now we have no idea where she is or what they're doing to her, and Em's spirit can't help us—"

"Not true," I said. "I know one way to speak to the kids."

His uncomprehending melted slowly into understanding. Then into disbelief. "Kai, you can't go to the Graylands again."

There was more than a hint of horror in his voice but his heart wasn't in the objection. Because of Lily.

"It might be our only chance to find out who took her," I said. "It could be the only way to track her. And to save her."

CHAPTER 37

I HELD THE PORTAL KEY in my hand, and felt the cool bite of the iron disk against my flesh. The disk gleamed, midnight moonlight dancing off the carved lettering, giving the key, and the clear night an eerie feel.

The late fall temperature had dropped to near discomfort. All across the lake's glassy surface mist rose from the water like ghostly fingers.

I stood, the toes of my boots on the edge of the dilapidated wooden dock, taking in deep breaths of frigid night air, readying for the jump.

I'd done it before, but the idea of being sucked through that tiny donut hole in the center of the portal key made my stomach turn no matter how much magic was involved.

"Kai, you don't have to do this," said Anjelo from behind me, his sports jacket rustling loudly in the silent night.

Though his words said one thing, his tone said something else entirely. He knew how important it was that I made this trip to the dead lands. If anything, he needed me to go more than I did.

To my left, Nerina was somber as her skirts flapped, a sudden brisk wind rippling their material over her curvaceous legs.

"I will be with you, Kai," she said. "Although, I'm not sure I can do much more than be a voice in your head while you are there." Her pale face was corpselike, draped with the shadows of the night.

I shook my head. "Thanks, but you don't need to worry about me. I've done this before."

Which I had. Without any help.

"Nevertheless." Her tone was firm, edged with a hint of persistence. "I will be with you. You just never know."

I moved to face her. Was she accompanying me, in whatever insubstantial form, because Kira had commanded it?

She obviously saw the suspicion in my eyes because she inclined her head sadly. "However, if you really don't want me with you I shall remain here and await your return."

I was suddenly ashamed of my own stubbornness. "I'm sorry. It's not that I don't trust you." And it wasn't.

Her pale eyes lit for a few seconds. "I know." It was slowly becoming easier to identify her tiny facial and behavioral nuances. "It's Lady Kira you don't trust. And that's understand-able. Shall I stay here and wait for word from you? If at any time you need me, I will come."

I frowned. I'd never called her myself. She'd always been summoned by Jess, or called on by an agent of either Sentinel or Omega. "And how will you do that? Did the dead lands get cell service while I wasn't watching?"

Nerina smiled and shifted, her hand appearing almost magi-cally from the folds of her voluminous sleeves. When she opened her long slender fingers a small metal disk lay in the center of her palm.

It was a smaller version of the portal key I held in my own hand. Smaller, and gleaming bronze, not iron.

I put the larger portal key into my jacket pocket then took the bronze disk from Nerina. I weighed it in my palm, turning it over to study the inscriptions that shone in the white light of the moon.

Nerina leaned closer. "This is a key much like your portal key. But think of it as a telegraph-machine, able to transcend the veil between the worlds."

"How do I use it?" I asked, still turning the coin-like disk over in my hand.

She took the disk from me. Pointed a pale finger at one of the seven symbols carved on the surface. "This one that looks like the half moon. Place your thumb on it and say my name. Then trace the pad of your thumb along all seven symbols in a clockwise fashion. Repeat the action three times, then say my name again. The key will call to me, and I will hear it."

This was all very strange. "How can you hear it?"

"Do you recall the ceremony in which your portal key was created?"

I nodded.

"Your blood was used to generate the final spelling to ensure that the key was coded to you, and you alone. My blood has been used to generate the power of this key in much the same way. DeathTalkers use keys like this to communicate with close family members and other important people in their lives."

It made sense now. I gave a wry smile. "Is this how Kira communicates with you?"

"Yes," she said simply, and handed back the key. Clearly she was at Kira's beck and call, and now I knew how.

I nodded slowly, staring at the shining metal in my palm.

I wasn't about to lie. I was touched. Nerina was giving me more than a way of contacting her. She was giving me her trust. She'd backed off even though she'd probably been given express instructions by Kira to stick with me at all times. That was huge.

I looked up at her and smiled, my gratitude genuine. "Thank you, Nerina," I said. "I'm honored."

Maybe it was the strange shadows cast by the clouds as they

skittered across the face of the moon, but I could have sworn she blushed.

I'd come prepared for a hunt—wearing jeans, leather jacket, and boots, all black, and well-used and comfortable for running, fighting and killing. I slid Nerina's key into my jeans pocket, took the portal key from my jacket. And held it tightly.

I glanced over my shoulder at Anjelo. He'd been strangely quiet but I understood his mood. "Tell my parents and Logan where I've gone," I said.

His head jerked in a parody of a nod. "Maybe we won't need to worry them. You'll be back soon."

"Anjelo," I said, warning clear in my voice. "You will tell them. They deserve to know *before* something bad happens."

"What makes you think something bad will happen?"

I glared at him.

"Then why don't you tell them now before you jump to the dead lands?" he asked, teasing now.

"Because they won't let me go if I do."

The truth echoed in the silence. Anjelo pierced me with pleading eyes. "Kai, please find her."

"Planning on it. Let's hope those kids can tell me something." I didn't say we'd be truly lucky if their spirits had remained at the scene long enough to see what happened to Lily. I didn't have to.

"I knew this was a long shot." He was already starting to sound like he'd lost hope.

"Stop it," I snapped, rounding on him so fast he almost flinched. "Don't give up before we even try."

He hung his head. "I just want her back, Kai."

I placed a palm on his cheek. Beneath the bravado lay a frightened boy, and he couldn't hide from me. "I will do everything I can to bring her back. I can't do more than that."

I paused, staring his fear down. "Be strong, Anjelo. And stay with Logan. Help him find out more about Blake. Logan isn't going to like it but I left him a message about what happened earlier today."

"*What* happened earlier?"

"I sent you an email."

"Kai." He grabbed my arm as I tried to walk off.

I sighed and turned back. "Fine. You get the Cliff-notes version. Agent Blake attacked me before I met you at O'Hagan's. I ripped his face open and he ran off."

"That's it?" he asked looking confused.

"Yeah, I might have left out the part where they were stalking me at my apartment. They were after *me,* so I don't think they'll be back."

"Kai," Anjelo admonished. "And you're only telling me this now?"

"My little tête-à-tête with the killer was over before I even spoke to you. Lily's the most important thing. Besides, I won't be in this world, so the killer won't be able to find me. Win-win."

Leaving Anjelo shaking his head I headed to the end of the boardwalk. I stood on the edge and tossed the key over the water. It hovered there, over the lake, and as it did a pillar of light began to glow.

"Kai!" Anjelo yelled.

I grinned, and jumped into the light.

The last thing I heard him say was, "Typical."

I APPEARED ON THE OUTSKIRTS of the Graylands, where every dimension had its very own reverse version. As disconcerting as the back-to-front city of Chicago was, I'd been here twice before and more or less knew my way around.

I ran with panther speed in the direction of the center of the city, past my apartment building and toward the abandoned train station.

As I entered the subway, I forgot the changes in the city and headed left instead of right. So much for experience in this backward world. I spun around and hurried toward the tracks where Anjelo had said the bodies had been found.

When I got to the scene I stopped.

No one.

I sank into a crouch and blew out a sigh. Had I come this far for nothing?

I lowered myself to the floor, scraping my boots on small stones and concrete, and sat there for a while, waiting, watching. Hoping.

More than half an hour later, I was still waiting. But no longer in silence. A thunderous headache had started drumming against my temples and I was starving. I realized suddenly that I hadn't eaten all day.

Chloe was right. I needed to take care of myself. I hadn't done that in the rush to find Lily.

Rubbing my temples, I sighed and got to my feet. I could wait a little longer, but how much longer did I have? Sooner or later the demon lord wannabes would find me, and—

"Are you okay?"

I swung around, so tired that even the soft voice managed to startle me.

Two teens stood there—the speaker, a Hispanic girl around twelve, and a boy about the same age, his Nordic look a stark contrast to her darkness. If you could call anything about them dark. The pair looked gray and hazy, ghostly in their transparency, even to the point that jeans, sweaters and sneakers were colorless.

"Please don't be scared," the girl said. "I'm Emma. This is my friend, Simon." She gestured to the boy beside her.

"Are you from City Deep?" I asked.

They both nodded solemnly.

"How long have you been here?"

"Not too long." They exchanged glances. "A few hours maybe."

I stifled a whoop of joy. "Then you might be able to help me."

Simon snorted. "How can we help you if we're dead?"

"You know you're dead?" I asked. Some people didn't.

Simon's expression turned sullen. "Do we look stupid?"

Emma elbowed him in the ribs. "Shut up, Simon. She's just trying to be considerate."

"No point is there?" he said. "We're dead."

I decided to let them fight it out.

"There's nothing she can do to change that fact, now is there?" There was a bite to Emma's tone and I figured she was dealing with her own passing on a more internal level than Simon.

I cleared my throat. "I came to see if I could help you."

"You just said you needed *our* help," snapped Simon.

I shrugged. "A little bit of mutual cooperation then."

He just watched me, eyes wide, unimpressed.

"We're trying to find the people who killed you." There was no skirting around the word *killed*, so I just said it. "And the reason I need your help is that *you* may have seen what happened to my friend."

Emma's brow creased. "What friend?"

I mentally crossed my fingers. "About this high," I indicated Lily's height where she reached my ears, "Blonde. Pretty. She's a walker."

"We don't want to get involved," said Simon.

"Say's *you*," Emma snapped at him. "I'm helping. It's not like it's going to get me killed." Her tone was sharp, annoyed, as if she'd been dealing with him for too long and had had enough.

Maybe he got the message because he had the grace to remain silent.

Emma turned back to me. "We did see her. It's Lily you're looking for, isn't it? She's one of the kids we live with. Storm takes care of us all."

She paused for a moment then looked at the floor where her body had lain in the last few moments of her life. "They took her when they came for our bodies."

"Did you get a good look at them?"

Emma nodded. "There were two men. One was a blond guy about this tall." She held her hand above her head. "I had a feeling I knew him but I just can't remember his name."

She glanced at Simon. "What do you remember?"

Simon shrugged. "Like you said. Tall. Blond. Muscular. I think. Maybe . . . blue eyes?" He squinted up at the curved roof of the tunnel as he thought. "But I can't remember a name either. Weird."

"Why weird?" I asked.

"'Cos I'm usually very good with names," he snapped. Then he studied my face. "I feel I've seen you before. Who are you?"

"Kailin. I'm Anjelo's and Lily's friend."

"Yeah." He bobbed a finger in my direction. "I remember now. Anjelo tells everyone that you're his alpha. You know that?"

I smiled. "He's a good kid. Though for the record Corin Odel is his alpha."

"But he respects you." Simon sounded as if he couldn't understand why.

I wasn't sure what response he expected. "So one of the guys who took Lily was blond. What about the other one?"

He thought back, eyes narrowed. "Light brown spiky hair, eyes like metal. Big dude."

Agent Blake.

I should have known.

I waited hoping he'd give me more. He did. "Dude had some kind of power. Like he could freeze shit."

"Water mage?" I asked. "Powerful?"

"Hell, yeah." He seemed impressed despite the fact that the paranormal had left him dead. "Some scary shit."

I nodded. So Blake was a water mage who freezes things.

And his blond companion bore a scary resemblance to our very own Storm.

$\mathcal{I}$ DIDN'T UNDERSTAND WHY NEITHER Emma nor Simon could recall the name of our Storm lookalike.

Do Immortals have the power to erase memories?

A question for Jess.

"Did the blond man kill you?" I asked feeling a little uncomfortable.

Emma shook her head. "No. He came later. We'd just started our practice and the spiky-haired guy shot us."

"What kind of things do you practice?" I asked, trying not to sound interrogative or judgmental.

She shrugged. "Stuff. Our powers mostly. The tunnels are good because we get to practice our powers without being seen."

It made sense. "Were you there long?"

Emma shook her head. "Simon thinks the man followed us. We'd only just got there when he came up behind us."

"Yeah," Simon said. "He had a gun, and this thing like a torch, with a very fat head. I think it had a screen on the other side of it because the light reflected off his face."

Observant kid.

"The machine beeped," he said. "Then he smiled at us and said 'gotcha' and shot us, *bam, bam.*" Simon mimicked the movements of the shooting with his forefinger and I could have sworn I heard gunshots reverberate around the tunnel.

If Blake was using some kind of machine to detect paranormals then the fact he'd missed the goblin kids behind the silver mirror now made sense. Silver would have hidden their presence no matter what paranormal they were.

First the African village, then the kids in Cicero, then the goblin clan, and now the two City Deep kids. It had all seemed random but only because the killers had been learning, testing their weapons and machines on mages and DeathTalkers and goblins.

They'd been methodical, determining first if the kids were paranormal, then eliminating them instantly. They'd upgraded to direct kills now.

Direct, and much more efficient.

"Did we help?" asked Emma.

"Of course, you did," I said. "You were very helpful."

"But you look worried."

I shrugged. "It's just that I want to stop the killing. I want to find the killer. And more than anything I want to find Lily."

"You won't," said Simon.

"Shut up," said Emma, sharply.

"She needs to know what she's up against."

Emma glared at him but he paid no attention.

He met my eyes earnestly. "You need to know. They are very powerful. They know everything. And the man we can't remember . . . He's more powerful than all of them."

That wasn't reassuring. "How do you know? Did you see something after they took you away?"

Simon nodded. "Flashes of stuff. And your friend—Lily—was there too."

"Did they hurt her? Is she still alive?"

Emma's gentle mouth twisted. "When we finally left the

human plane, she was still alive. She was furious and struggled hard. They hit her a few times and when she kept fighting they tried to drug her. But none of the drugs worked. So they tied her up and gagged her and put her in a room where we couldn't see her. We didn't hear her again after that."

There was a sadness in Emma's eyes that told me she thought Lily might well be dead too.

I didn't want to ask but I forced myself to. "Have you seen her here in the Graylands?"

Emma shook her head. "Not yet. Although if they've killed her it shouldn't be too long."

I was about to hand her Nerina's key and ask her to call if she saw Lily when her eyes went wide and scared. I started to turn to see what had frightened her when the sound of gunfire exploded in the tunnel.

Pain ripped through my back. The bullet's impact spun me around into the curving wall of the tunnel—and brought me face to face with the gunman.

A *human* gunman, red-faced, bright-eyed, and in the *Graylands*.

What the hell was a human doing in the dead world? How was that even possible?

"Don't hurt her," yelled Emma, shoving into the man's way.

"Get out of my way, kid." He flicked the air with the back of his hand and Emma's image wavered like smoke as it passed through her body.

But she didn't. She yelled and began to throw blobs of ghostly gray fire at him. Simon followed suit, aiming his hands at the man, pulling dust into a mini hurricane. Dirt and stones rose from the floor and joined the spinning wind, but the demon soldier swiped a hand at it and the mini vortex evaporated.

I took advantage of the kids and their distraction and edged away down the tunnel until it curved out of sight. Then I turned and ran.

I stopped only briefly to yank open the door to what I thought was a side tunnel. It was, in fact, the entrance to a staircase. I left it wide open hoping the gunman would think I'd run that way. Then I sped off down the main tunnel in the pitch black using my panther sight to guide me.

The tunnel seemed to go on forever, but eventually it came to an end and opened out into a gray day.

I was miles from the city now. I should return to the lake and jump home.

But when my head began to spin and bile burned the back of my throat, I knew I needed time to rest before I could safely make the jump. Cool liquid trickled from the wound on my back. When I touched my finger to my back it came away covered in blue fluorescent poison.

How the hell had they gotten the ammunition to the Graylands? More importantly, why?

I was beginning to suspect whoever was killing paranormals saw me as a threat to be removed. I wouldn't be safe at my own apartment.

Whoever the human soldier was, he wouldn't be alone. Humans with deadly weapons in the Graylands were infinitely more dangerous than any demon overlord. They'd check my apartment, and if they knew what they were doing they'd probably check Tara's. I'd go to Logan's hotel room to hide.

I ran, the urge to grip my shoulder almost taking me over. My heart tightened. Pain sliced through my arm and into my hand.

But I didn't slow down, even when I neared the front doors of the hotel. Here in the Graylands with everything upside down, I had to focus to remember to go left instead of right.

When I slammed through the hotel's front doors there was no doorman with a long mustache in the lobby. No staff at the desks in the reception area. There were elevators but they didn't work.

Nothing lived here, not even electricity.

So what manner of paranormal power was behind the presence of live weapons in the dead lands?

I pushed against the stairwell doors using my weight to shove them open.

I squinted up at the stairs that I had to climb and felt the stairwell tilt, the walls threaten to close in on me.

You can do it, Odel. One step at a time.

And one step at a time was all I could manage. Six floors of one-steps as my ragged breath rasped in the silence of the stairwell and the soft soles of my boots *tap-tapped* on the concrete stairs.

When I finally reached the door to the sixth floor, the gigantic orange number emblazoned on the wall blurred in front of my eyes.

I tried to swallow the cough that ripped through my chest and succeeded only enough that it came out strangled. I swayed as dizziness took hold of me, then caught the wall and rested my forehead against the cool stone.

When I grabbed hold of the handle of the fire-escape door and pulled I expected to meet the resistance of the hydraulic door, and put my weight into it. The door swung freely and I stumbled, only managing to save myself from tumbling back down the staircase by grabbing hold of the railing.

Close call, Odel.

I hobbled along the darkened passage, straining to look at the numbers on the doors through rapidly blurring eyes.

I'd been to Logan's apartment only a couple of times, but I knew how far it was from the stairs to his door.

At the door, I bent to peer at the number on the little gold plaque on the door. Everything was backward—as I'd expected.

I paused. Would my key work? I'd brought it with me from the normal world. Did I need a backward card?

I leaned against the door jamb until the wave of dizziness

passed. Then I slipped the key card into the hatch, and waited for the tiny *ping* and the green light glow.

Nothing happened.

Crap. Just like I thought.

An upside-down world needs upside down locks and keys.

Now what? Where else could I go to hide out? Someplace where I could get inside without needing a key.

I could think of two: Storm's place and my father's house. The decision was easy. I didn't have the energy to run all the way out of the city and up into the mountains.

Storm's place it was.

Frustrated and exhausted I yanked the keycard out of the slot and gave the handle an angry slam—as if it would do any good to take my fury out on an inanimate door.

The latch groaned.

The handle turned.

And the door opened.

I frowned and brought the card key closer so I could study both sides of it with my hazy vision. Looked normal to me.

Okay, then. I shoved it into my pocket and entered the room.

Gift horse, and all that.

Once inside I shut the door and attached the safety chain. It made sense now. The locks were electronic and didn't work. A bolt and safety chain was as good as it got.

I went further into the room and saw the single unit that performed the multi-functions of dresser, suitcase storage and fridge storage. Calling on my panther strength I ripped it free from its wiring and shoved it along the floor to the front door. It wouldn't stop intruders but it would reinforce the door and slow them down.

I felt bad about destroying property but I didn't think it mattered. I doubted anyone planned to use Logan's apartment in their afterlife. So much of the Graylands remained abandoned, and 'abandoned' in the Graylands was far worse than the abandoned areas of the normal human plane.

With the door as secure as I could make it I stumbled to the bed. A couple of paces away from it my legs finally gave out, and I smacked face-first into the blankets.

CHAPTER 40

I LAY THERE FOR A while, breathing through the pain and grateful that, judging by the condition of the room, the resident demons hadn't gotten to ransacking the place yet.

When I thought I'd no longer faint if I moved, I gritted my teeth and forced myself to turn over.

I used the next few minutes to check on the condition of my body. My self-scan told me what I'd already known. I'd lost a lot of blood from the wound in my back but the bleeding had slowed, if not stopped. I was filthy, sweaty, and the front of my shirt was soaked with blood. But what really annoyed me was the bullet hole in my jacket. I loved that jacket.

Damn the gunman. How the hell did a human get into the Graylands?

And alive?

I rolled into a sitting position and eased the leather off my arms. It would tax my strength but I needed to get clean—quite a feat when the Graylands had no running water.

Good thing I was a just-in-case type. There was a stash of moist towels in my backpack with my first aid kit.

I reached over and grabbed the backpack. Lifted it onto the bed. When I'd unzipped it, and rummaged my way to the bottom I found what I was after. Tiny, crinkly packages of moist towels inside sealed foil.

I pulled them all out and dumped them on the mattress. Then I unbuttoned my shirt and let it drop open.

The towels did their job. I wiped my chest and as far down my back as I could reach. Then, after buttoning up with shaking fingers, I sat there and stared at the floor, at the pile of bloody towels, and wondered why I was shivering when I felt so hot.

I prayed the wound hadn't been infected. I prayed I could find something to wear in place of the shirt. I prayed no one would find me until I'd slept long enough to regenerate and heal. As hard as it would be to place myself in such a vulnerable position I really had no choice.

I had to get better. Fast.

I was trying to find a comfortable position on the bed when I realized there was a hard lump inside the front pocket of my jeans. It took me a moment to remember what it was. Nerina's key.

Now was probably a good time to use it—before I gave in to fatigue.

The invisible pull of my body urged me to put my head down on the pillow and close my eyes. Instead, I slid my fingers into my pocket and gripped the cool, metal disk. I pulled it out and lifted it close to my eyes. When I turned it over I realized the markings were on both sides of the disk. Did that mean one side was the wrong side?

Oh well. I'd find out soon enough.

I followed Nerina's instructions feeling uncomfortable calling out her name like a besotted lover. When the ritual was complete I lay there, waiting, ears pricked for some sign that she'd heard me.

I'd expected a ghostly DeathTalker specter. I got a disembodied voice in my head.

"Kailin?"

"Nerina?" I responded, confused and relieved at the same time.

She huffed out a breath. "Of course it is. I'd almost given up on hearing from you. What's happened?"

How did she know? "It's barely been a couple hours. What makes you think something's happened?"

"Stop playing games, Kailin. I know you well enough by now to recognize when you're in pain."

"Oh," was all I could muster. She knew me that well, huh? "Okay, then. I got shot."

"Shot?" The shock in the DeathTalker's voice was clear. "How did you get shot in the Graylands?"

I wanted an answer to that question, too. "There is at least one human with live ammo here in the Graylands."

Her silence lasted so long I wondered if we'd lost the connection. Then she said, "Humans. Living ones?"

"Yup."

"And live rounds?"

"Yup."

"That," she muttered, "is not good at all."

"Yup."

She sighed. "How badly are you hurt?"

"Bullet in the back," I said. "Through and through. I haven't bled out yet though."

"Thank goodness for small mercies." She hesitated. "Maybe it's best if you came home."

"No," I said, my voice breaking on a yawn. "Not yet. I need to find the guy who attacked me and figure out what is going on here. Whoever these people are, they are breaking ancient rules."

"They are," she said. "But policing those laws is not your job."

I paused, considering her statement. "I can't see anyone else taking a stand." Which was true. "Think about it, Nerina. If people can break the 'no-humans-in-the-Graylands' rule without being called to account, then what other rules will they break—are they already breaking? The inter-plane restrictions are there for a reason."

There were many planes of existence, each controlled by various paranormal species—no one knew how many there were.

The Graylands had its replica of the human plane but it *wasn't* the human plane and living humans didn't belong there.

She didn't answer so I continued. "Besides, I owe it to all the people who may potentially be in danger to investigate what the hell is going on here."

The sound of her continued silence reverberated in my head.

"You may think this isn't my problem, but it is. Do you really think these intruders have nothing to do with your Mika's death?"

Again, silence was my answer, but I plowed on.

"My arriving here and being shot by a *human* is too much of a coincidence, especially considering that the attacks on the para-normals back home seem to be the handiwork of humans, too."

"I do not disagree that they may be connected."

At least she was talking to me again. "My gut tells me they are. Whoever these people are, they're here to cover their tracks. The gunman found me with the kids. He knew where they'd be, and he wasn't shy about shooting to kill either. Those kids are in danger."

Nerina laughed softly. "They're dead, Kai. What danger could they possibly be in?"

This time I laughed, in spite of the pain contracting within my shoulder. "I've seen the dangers the dead face here. The wannabe demon overlords fighting each other for control. The demons aren't afraid to take advantage of ghosts who are passing through or those who haven't passed on yet. As for the dead who don't pass on—the ones filled with anger and hatred—there is a potential for violence there that we don't want tapped. Especially since a few of those ghosts are strong enough to traverse the veil."

"We're aware of the overlords," Nerina said slowly. "But we understood that they'd been deposed."

"Deposed?" I thought about it. "Sounds organized and political."

"Well, maybe it's my interpretation." Something rustled in my head, like paper being moved around. "Yes. We've information that a group of resident dead rose up against the demon overlords and pushed them out of the Graylands."

"Really?" I said, incredulous. "That must have taken some kind of organization."

"We believe it happened soon after your last visit."

I stiffened. "Was the revolt led by a Jeremy Ryan?"

"Yes." Then Nerina paused. "But we don't have time to talk about that now. Come home and recover. You can go back as soon as you feel better."

But I knew I couldn't walk out now. "I can't leave. Not yet." Jeremy needed to be warned. Or at the very least I had to see what I could do to help him out if he was aware of the danger.

I'd failed once to save him when I'd found his flayed corpse dumped in the street. He'd remained in the deadlands, refusing to pass through until he'd helped rid the Graylands of the demon factions who wanted to claim the in-between lands for their own.

A wave of dizziness rushed through my head, and though I was flat on my back I felt the room tilt and my body begin to fall. "But I will rest for a bit. I need my strength."

"And if you don't feel better after you rest?" she snapped.

"Then I will come straight home. I'm not stupid, Nerina. I know how to take care of myself."

She snorted. "I have no doubt that you can take care of yourself. It's the 'stupid' part that worries me."

My eyelids had grown heavy through our conversation and had shut themselves without me realizing it. Even my body felt heavy and crushed to the mattress. Maybe I *should* go home to rest and then return better prepared for the human ammunition, and with backup.

Then I blinked and Emma's face floated in front of me, the hazy apparition giving me a comforting smile.

I couldn't let her down.

"Kai?" Nerina was a distant whisper and I had to concentrate on the sound.

"Yes," I rasped through a throat now dry and itchy.

"Please don't hesitate."

"Huh?"

"When the time comes to attack, don't hesitate. Kill the bastards or they will kill you."

I laughed softly. "Language much?" I was glad we were talking in my head because I was too exhausted to speak out loud.

"Just promise me you will kill first and ask questions later."

Nerina sounded so firm that I knew I wouldn't get rid of her until I agreed. So I nodded.

She let a few moments pass. "Kailin? Did you hear me?"

I suppressed a laugh. "Sorry. I nodded. Yes, I promise."

"And take care of yourself."

"I will," I said. And let my fatigue and weakness lull me into a deep and healing sleep.

CHAPTER 41

MY SLEEP WAS DEEP AND dreamless and thoroughly regenerative.

I blinked and opened my eyes slowly, appreciating the fact that my eyelids felt light and weightless. Whatever had affected me earlier, had passed through my system while I'd slept.

Had the bullets been laced with the same type of paranormal poison as the fluorescent blue liquid?

I shifted my head, searching for my alarm clock. Instead, I found myself eye-to-eye with another ghost.

I let out a small shriek of surprise, cutting it off a little too late. That sound alone would have alerted anyone outside in the hallway to my presence.

"Damn it," I muttered, glaring at the transparent figure. "What are you doing here?" That I was speaking to the ghost of Daniel Chou, the human agent Logan had killed yesterday, was not a surprise. The surprising part was that he was still in the Graylands. He should have moved on by now.

His gaze flitted across my body as if inspecting me for injuries —and lingering a little too long in certain areas. "I've got some information for you," he said.

"You didn't have much last time we talked." I didn't mean it to sound like an accusation but it did.

He shrugged. "I know more now."

Cryptic. I raised my eyebrows. "How's that?"

His shoulders slumped and I felt a little sorry for him. "I listen. I watch. One advantage of being dead is no one sees you when you hang around."

I nodded, raising myself up onto my elbows. "I guess so."

Daniel's gaze drifted back to my chest.

This ghost was a bit too much of a guy for my taste, and a bra wasn't sufficient cover. The blood had dried on the fabric of my shirt and now weighed it down so that it sank against my chest on one side. I really needed to find something else to wear. I got to my feet, relieved that my legs no longer felt like limp pasta.

"So what did you find out?" I asked, heading around the bed to the corner by the window where Logan usually kept a small go-bag.

It was exactly where I'd expected it to be and I was glad all over again that this room had remained intact. The last time I'd been in the Graylands I'd visited Tara's shop. It had been stripped of almost everything useful.

I grabbed the bag and dropped it on the bed. As I unzipped it I looked up, an eyebrow curved, waiting.

Daniel had his thumbs stuck in his pockets and his attention on my breasts. "I was still at the scene when the cleanup crew arrived. They stowed the bodies into their ambulance, then sprayed the place down."

I rifled through the clothing in the go-bag and pulled out a black tee-shirt. It was better than nothing. "Sprayed?"

"Some kind of solution that destroys DNA and other evidence."

I looked up to find him studying the lace on my bra as though it contained the secret of the universe. A lecherous ghost? Who knew?

I frowned, torn between clothes and information. If I went into the bathroom to change he might leave before telling me what he knew—or follow me. If I stayed here . . . It was a simple decision really.

"You mean evidence of the ammunition that kills paranormals," I said.

"Yeah. That spray destroys the molecules and makes them unrecognizable under a microscope." Daniel jerked his gaze up to meet my eyes. "I'm sorry about what happened. I never actually meant to hurt anyone."

I shrugged. There was no point in antagonizing him if he'd come to give me information. "You were just doing your job."

"I joined the program because paranormals killed my father."

The words spilled out of him in a rush as if he had to get rid of them before he thought better of it.

"Did they?" I pulled the tee-shirt on over my head, shimmied the fabric down over my body. "Did they really?"

He cleared his throat and looked away from my hard stare. "I thought they did. I joined for vengeance, for a cause. But after I'd made the ultimate sacrifice I found out it was all a fucking lie."

He began to pace, his gaze shifting from the floor, to my face, to the wall, and back again. Pacing ghost was preferable to lecherous ghost.

"What was a lie?"

"I'd been told he was killed at the whim of some mad paranormal freak. Asked if I wanted payback. They'd train me, give me a chance to avenge Dad. I jumped at it."

Of course he did.

His hands fisted. "Didn't even think about it. My training went well. The training missions were successful. Then my superiors suggested kicking it up a notch—and I agreed. I still can't believe I was so stupid."

Young. Grieving. Angry. Of course he was stupid. "What did

they do?" His words had been far too ominous. Enough to make the hairs on the back of my neck rise.

"They said it would be only a small change." His eyes begged me to understand.

I thought I did.

Despite the efforts of our collective paranormal organizations and years of keeping our secrets from humans, someone—the US government?—had discovered enough to start dabbling in cross-species DNA integration. This was not a good thing for anyone.

"Tell me," I said as gently as I could.

He'd been staring at the rumpled sheets on the other side of the bed. Now he looked up at me, his eyes dark and shadowed. "I can move things."

My ears began to ring. "It was *you* who tossed the car over?"

He nodded.

"But if you had that kind of power, why didn't you kill us?" He could have. He was powerful enough.

He stared at the sheets again. "I'd only moved inanimate objects before. My superior was screaming in my ear to throw something else at you. Roma—that's my partner—she didn't like that I'd been chosen for the procedure ahead of her. She was cursing at me the entire time and yelling 'Kill them'."

"And yet you didn't." I studied his face, wondering at the thoughts behind the mask he'd constructed. "Why?"

He fidgeted, his fingers flicking at the top pocket of his cargo pants. "I'd never killed anyone before. Not even on a training mission."

Which might have been why he was chosen. He was expendable if he screwed up. "But we were just paranormals."

He raised his eyes. "I'd never seen a paranormal face-to-face before. Only . . . when I saw . . . I realized what my father meant. In his bedside drawer I'd found a journal. It was empty except for four words on the first page. *We are the same.* I didn't understand until I saw you all cowering after I threw the car over. You were scared. You acted like humans. We aren't that different after all. And it made me wonder if Dad's death really was caused by paras. Or something else."

"You think you father was considered a sympathizer." It wasn't a question.

He nodded.

"And they killed him for it."

He lifted one shoulder in a shrug. "It's just a theory, but yes. Like I said before I was still at the scene when the clean-up crew came. They were pissed."

I blinked. "Why?"

"Because I *malfunctioned*." He spat the word out. "The experiment was meant to create hardened warriors that they could control. Their failure to control me meant the experiment needed to be overhauled."

Yeah. Someone's head would roll, for sure. "What about Agent Blake?"

He laughed. "He came back after you left. Shit, he was furious. Said our unit was incompetent." He laughed again. "Made me glad I was dead."

"Yeah. He has a way with cold."

"He must be more furious now considering what I did to his face this morning."

A worried frown creased his brow, "What did you do?"

"A little bit of cosmetic surgery," I said with a smile as I lifted my hand and tugged at my panther's claws. Within seconds my claws sprouted and the ghost flinched.

"Bet he's overjoyed," Daniel said dryly.

"I would have done more if he hadn't been conveniently spirited away."

I pulled my mind back on track, "Did he say anything else while he was at the scene?"

"No. Actually he didn't stick around. But when he'd gone my

superior told the big guy that Blake wasn't being as efficient as he'd expected. The big guy said—"

My ears pricked up. "Big guy?"

"Yeah. The other agency guy, he's a large dude." He made 'tall and broad' gestures. "All blond and blue-eyed like Thor or Conan or something."

Or Storm.

CHAPTER 42

S TORM.

I DIDN'T WANT IT to be Storm.

"Did they mention a name?" I held my breath.

Daniel pursed his mouth, frowned. "I don't think they know it. I don't think even Jones knows it."

Jones must be the superior. "So what did Thor say?"

Daniel snorted. "That he needed Blake, but if he became a hindrance to the mission he'd be eliminated."

"Sounds harsh." Not like the Storm I knew. It couldn't be Storm. *Please don't let it be Storm.*

"They're all harsh," He spoke quietly but with a hint of desperation. "They called us bricks. Told us only what we needed to know. Said their organization was the mortar that held us together and made us function as a whole. *Cohesively.* Bricks follow orders. Good bricks move up the wall."

Good bricks, my ass. I needed to get moving.

"I'm sorry about your dad," I said. I shrugged into my jacket as I spoke—and then another question popped into my head. "How did you know I was here?"

He grinned. "Being dead has its advantages. I flit around from place to place. And it seems I can still move stuff."

"Oh," I said. That was different.

He nodded so hard that his ghostly hair bounced against his transparent forehead. So strange. "And I can go back home whenever I want to."

Really different. "Wow."

"Yeah. The soldier here radioed my superior in Chicago. It's like I'm connected to whatever they do, so radio transmissions, emails, phone calls—all communications give me the funnies and when I head to Control, I usually find stuff is happening."

What could I say? We were now past *really different* and heading into *officially weird*. "Must be some sort of emotional connection. Because you died under their watch."

He looked doubtful. "Maybe, but it has something to do with you and your people too. Jones called for an investigation into you and Westin as soon as he got the vid feed."

Logan? Crap.

"And they sent a couple people to keep an eye on your apartments."

I had to get back. Warn Logan. "And eliminate me."

But he was already shaking his head. "Nope. No order came from our department. Or at least nothing after I died. Everything since then had been mainly watching. Even the kill orders on paranormals have stopped."

What? "Someone gave an order to stop assassinating the paranormals?"

He nodded. "Yeah. Something happened but we didn't get told what. Next thing, Jones stands us all down."

So maybe I had a little time to work.

"Thanks for trusting me," I said. "Thanks for believing we're the same."

"They hate you," he said. "So you must be okay."

Yeah. I could follow that logic.

"I had to tell you," he said, "otherwise you'll get killed too. They mean business. And they're way too dangerous to fight."

"You haven't had many dealings with paranormals, have you?" I asked, grinning as I straightened my jacket and leaned to grab my rucksack from the side of the bed.

"It doesn't matter how powerful you are. They are *more* powerful. You're no match to them no matter what ability you have." He hesitated and glanced over his shoulder as if he felt someone at his back. "They know everything about you. And they can manipulate it however they want."

I didn't blame him for seeing conspiracies everywhere. "I don't think the government cares much about our day-to-day lives."

His fists balled and frustration etched grooves around his mouth. "Not the *government*. Whoever this Thor guy works for. *They* are the ones you should be afraid of. And *him*. "

"And why should he scare us?" Other than the possibility he could be an Immortal, a Titan, or something far worse.

His eyes snapped. "Because he scares the US government, that's why."

I could follow that logic too.

"Okay," I said frowning. "All I can do is be more careful from now on. We can't stop looking for the killer. If it's Blake, or even your Thor friend, we will get him."

"You won't," he whispered. "You'll lose. You don't know it all yet."

This conversation had gone on for far too long. "The only thing I'm going to lose is my patience," I said through gritted teeth. "I'm out of time. *What* don't I know yet?"

He hesitated, obviously torn, then decided to spill. "There's a plane—well, not just one, lots of them. Those ones farmers use to drop pesticides over their crops. The big guy is running the show. There's a connection between the planes and what's happening to the paranormals. That's all I know."

"That's a whole lot more than I had, Daniel," I said. Much, *much* more. "Thank you—and I mean that. Thanks."

"Your people are in danger—and I mean *that*. Whatever Thor's people have planned, it's something big." He stared at my face, shaking his head. "You aren't going to listen to me, are you?"

"You know me so well," I said dryly, then heaved my rucksack onto my shoulder. "Thanks for the information. I'll pass it on to my superiors. Is there any way that we can contact you in the future, just in case?"

He paused for a moment looking at the ceiling as if the answer lay somewhere in the white paint. Then he smiled. "I think there might be a way. When you get back, phone someone or email someone. It can be a chat room message or a text message. Mention my name."

"Just your name."

He nodded. "Use something that can't be tapped, like a secure line somewhere. I think I will be able to hear any type of use of my name along those communication lines. It was my name and the mention of Division Seven that got my attention when I arrived here."

"You should've been working with the CIA," I told him. "Thanks." He'd turned out to be more helpful than anyone else so far.

For a couple seconds he looked serious. "They were actually my first choice. But after Dad was killed . . . "

Regret and grief. They filled the brief silence—and were two emotions I didn't want to face.

"Their loss," I told him, and meant it. "You've helped me a lot."

"I only hope that I won't live to regret it." His snort of laughter edged into the hysterical. "Live. What a joke."

Unwilling to watch his descent into a grief I couldn't fix I moved toward the door.

He beat me to it. "Let me help you with that."

I moved aside as he pointed at the dresser with a transparent hand. Then he beckoned it with three crooked fingers and it floated down the little passage toward him, passing inches in front of me as it went.

I was amazed. It wasn't every day I met a human who wasn't paranormal but had paranormal powers. And in all my years as a walker, I'd never heard of a half-human half-paranormal telekinetic dead man.

He lowered the dresser and turned to me. "I'll stay with you until you leave the Graylands. Just in case."

I squinted at him. "I don't plan to leave yet."

His face fell, his expression filling with fear. "But I can't leave you alone here. Not with them looking for you."

"Who's looking for me?" I asked stiffening.

He gave me the kind of look Grams gave me when I was being particularly dense. "The people who shot you, of course. Do you think they'd let you hang around here, especially when you survived an attempt to kill you?" Then he shook his head as if he couldn't believe my choice. "I told you about the planes. They are planning something bad. Shouldn't you be going back and warning everyone? You should be trying to stop them. Or at the very least be prepared."

Okay, he was actually making sense. My fingers tightened on the strap on my shoulder. "You're probably right." I ignored his smile of relief. I had to find out more about this plane and what it was that they planned to drop from the aircrafts. "I'll go back, but if I find you've been leading me on a wild goose chase I'll be happy to come back and deal with you."

He nodded and raised his hands in front of his chest. "I understand. But you have nothing to worry about. I only want to help you."

"Thank you," I said giving the room behind him one last scan. "I only hope we can find out more about this plan in time."

"I'll keep an ear out. I'll let you know if I hear anything."

"How will you contact me?"

"I'll text you."

My inside man was a half-human, half-paranormal, telekinetic ghost. Who could text.

Life got weirder every day.

CHAPTER 43

I LEFT THE GRAYLANDS, MY mind filled with thoughts of what Daniel had just told me. It wasn't that I doubted his truthfulness, it was just that I found it hard to believe someone would go to such lengths to rid the world of paranormals.

My body was still weak from the bullet's poison, and running in walker mode had been a total stress on my energy levels. By the time I made it to the lake and jumped through the seal I was lightheaded. When I landed on the wooden dock I tripped and almost fell face first onto the platform.

I arrived as weak tendrils of sunlight danced on the lake. I got to my feet, pretended my muscles weren't wobbly, and stepped off the dock and onto solid ground.

At the top of the shallow rise I found Anjelo pacing back and forth, his hands on his hips.

"Took you long enough," he rasped.

I studied him from head to toe. He looked like he hadn't slept since I'd left. The skin on his face sagged, making him look years older than he really was, and he wore the Tweed peaked cap I thought he'd gotten rid of ages ago. It hid his spiky blond hair—

which was probably a good thing. Anjelo in this mood was a typical super-focused teenager. Bathing was not on the top of his priorities.

He'd lost Lily once already. Clearly he wasn't holding up well the second time around.

"Sorry about that. I got shot again." There was no sharpness in my tone. I understood completely what he was going through. "Let's go," I said as I continued walking past. "We have work to do."

"Did you find anything useful?" he asked, desperation edging his every word.

"I have an idea of who might have her," I said. "But until we know for sure we need to step carefully."

Anjelo rocked to a standstill. "Who is it?"

I stopped and placed a hand on his shoulder, wincing as the wound pulled a little.

"I found the two kids," I said. "They gave me an idea of who—and more particularly, why."

His eyes blazed. "I don't care why. Who is it?"

"But I can't say because I'm not sure. The person they described sounds like the one I suspect, but I'm not going to accuse without proof. That would have severe repercussions."

"You're not going to tell me?" Anjelo's voice was hard.

I raised an eyebrow. "And have you go straight to him and either destroy his reputation if I'm wrong or get yourself killed if I'm right? I don't think so."

He made a strange, strangled sound and looked up at me with bleak, resigned eyes. "Tell me you have a plan."

"I have a plan," I deadpanned, and took his snort as a positive thing.

"Yeah? What?"

"Get back to my apartment. Speak to Logan and Grandma Ivy about the ramblings of a well-informed ghost. Stop the creep who's trying to kill us. And, when I'm done, Anjelo, heads will roll."

"And Lily?"

I hardened my heart, because if I felt sorry for him I would waste time telling everything right here, right now. "Not until we're back at the apartment. The longer we wait, the more chance there is that Lily will get hurt."

We shifted into walker speed and raced back to my apartment, pausing only when we neared the building and were both hidden in shadows. To an onlooker, it would appear that the thick darkness had spewed out two people. I hoped we wouldn't have our pictures spread across some tabloid front page under the heading of *time-travelers* or something equally weird.

When we entered the building, we slowed to a stop and I urged my panther senses into full strength. I scented the air, listened for footsteps and heartbeats. Nothing.

No scents overlaid those of my attackers, not even those of Mom and Grams. Neither had returned home since I'd left. I wished they were there. I needed to get the word out. Now I'd have to waste time waiting.

Together Anjelo and I climbed the stairs to my apartment. Once inside I dropped my bag on the table and sank into the closest chair. Tired. Dizzy. I sucked in a deep breath.

Anjelo who'd begun his pacing the moment we entered, stopped. "What's wrong?" He came to crouch beside me.

"Just the after-effects of the bullet wound."

"What bullet wound?"

"The one in my back. Remember? I told you I was shot."

"Shit. Kai, I didn't realize you were injured." He looked crestfallen, upset with himself with his lack of consideration.

"Don't worry about it. I'm tired, that's all. I'll shower and clean up, but first I need to send out a few messages." I grabbed my phone from my pocket and was about to tap out messages to various friends and family when I froze.

"Kai?" Anjelo had been watching me.

"I just realized that everything we send electronically can be traced, or tapped, or tracked. Or something."

"What makes you think that?"

I met his eyes. "The ghost who spoke to me. Daniel. He said he can get into the communications systems and find any communications in relation to whatever he is searching for."

Anjelo's eyes lit up. "Then if he wanted to he could search for Lily."

I nodded. "Yes, but the killer isn't going to be stupid enough to use her name." I tapped a nail on the dining table. "But you do have a point. Let's get ourselves sorted and then I'll contact him."

I got to my feet. "Why don't you text my parents, Grams, and Logan? It'll be safer. Tell them to meet at Dad's place."

He looked to be on the verge of panic. "What am I supposed to say?"

"Say . . . " I considered. "Say I'm calling a family meeting about the alpha situation. They'll all know it's bogus and they'll guess I want to keep this on the down-low."

Anjelo nodded, relieved. "You shower. I'll text."

Showering and washing my hair proved to be more taxing than I'd thought, but in the end, I was clean and warm. Though walkers generate their own comfortable level of body heat it didn't stop us from losing most of it while we were in the Graylands.

After my shower, I dressed in jeans, a white tee and a wool-lined leather jacket. I'd get the one I wore in the Graylands cleaned before I decided what to do about the hole in it.

I followed the stench of burned toast to the kitchen where Anjelo was scraping carbon off his snack. Grateful that he didn't offer me any I wandered into the living room and dropped down onto the sofa. It was hard not to hear him crunching the dry whole-grain. It was harder not to think about Lily.

I didn't want to think about Lily. I couldn't help her, and

wherever she was and whatever she was going through was outside of my control. Things outside of my control made me anxious. When I got anxious I was liable to do something stupid.

When someone knocked on the door Anjelo jogged over to answer. I stayed where I was, inhaling Logan's spicy scent as he waited outside.

My heart ached a little as I thought about how much we'd been through and how—in spite of all the obstacles—we'd remained strong. Were we strong enough to hurdle these barriers as well? Or would we fall? Crack? Shatter?

Part of me felt as if he'd already dumped me.

That part of me wasn't reassured when he came in, either. His expression was grim enough to send a rock straight to the pit of my stomach.

But as he came closer his expression cleared.

I shoved to my feet despite my dizziness and went to him, relieved.

When his arms closed around me, however, it wasn't a hug. It was muscle memory and obligation, tension and concern. There was no warmth. No tender emotion.

His action hurt me almost more than I could handle. I wanted to pull away, to reject him as I felt rejected.

I didn't.

Instead, I forced my body to relax. It was stupid to get upset because he was upset about something that had no bearing on our personal relationship.

Lily's abduction, the murders, the possibility that Storm was our Thor, all put unrelieved stress on everyone I cared about.

I stepped back and smiled, trying to calm the tempest within my heart as I met his gaze. His lips curved up too and I found myself searching his eyes for any corresponding warmth.

There was none, and my smile faltered

Still, I took a calming breath and said, "Thanks for coming.

We need to get to my dad's place fast. I have news for everyone, and we need a plan in place like yesterday."

"You and I need to talk first," he said.

"Sure." I glanced over to where Anjelo loitered in the kitchen, looking uncomfortable. "Anjelo, go on ahead. We'll be there soon."

He nodded, evading my eyes. "Yeah. I'll be there soon. Just got something to see to first."

I frowned. What was he up to? "And what's that?"

Anjelo lifted his chin. "I just got a few things to look into, okay?" He sounded defensive, and hurt.

So I gave him the benefit of the doubt and forced a smile on my face. "Let me know if you find anything."

He gave me a short nod and sketched Logan a quick salute before heading silently out the door.

Logan waited until Anjelo's footsteps faded away before he dropped his bomb. "I can't go with you."

His words felt like rocks, hard and merciless. What the hell was up with him? "You're not coming to Tukats?"

He shook his head. "It's not a good idea."

Now I wasn't just hurt. I was furious. "Why the hell not?"

"Your family is Sentinel, remember?"

"This isn't a Sentinel problem," I said. "It's not even an Omega problem. It's everyone's problem. Every paranormal in the world is in danger, and until we catch this bastard we're counting off our days until he kills us."

I gave him a quick rundown of everything that had happened since we last spoke; Blake's attack, Lily's abduction, my tour of the Graylands, and everything the three ghosts had passed on.

I thought it best to bypass the part about getting shot again.

"There is only one person I know who fits their description and is familiar with all species of paranormals."

"Storm."

I nodded. "He's also fully capable of doing what's been done."

Logan stiffened. "What makes you think that?"

I narrowed my eyes. "Because he's an Immortal, of course. I thought you knew?"

He gave a brief nod, which could have meant, 'Yes, I know' or 'Thanks for telling me'. It was hard to tell sometimes with Logan. "You really think Storm is involved?"

I nodded. "I don't want to, but Emma described him exactly. So did Daniel, the ghost. How many people do you know fit the *tall, blond, blue-eyed, powerful, and familiar* description?"

Logan blew out a breath. "Well, there must be more than just Storm. Seriously, Kai. Do you really think a man who's been helping paranormals for years and done so much for the kids around this city and others is responsible for trying to wipe us off the face of the earth?"

I shook my head. "I don't know. I hope I'm just imagining it. I don't want it to be true. But we have to consider the possibility."

For the first time since he walked in the door Logan—*my* Logan—looked at me. Compassionate. Understanding. Tender. "Kai," he said, a world of patience in his voice, "just because the killer turned out to be someone close to you last time doesn't mean history is about to repeat itself."

"I know that." I snapped it out, but I didn't care. Right now my emotions were tangled, and he hadn't heard what I'd heard and seen what I'd seen. "I hate even thinking about it, but the kids said that the man was someone they trusted. That much they *did* recall. But the rest of their memories about him were wiped. Don't you find that odd?"

Logan nodded. "And who better to wipe their memories than someone who has close access to them?"

"Exactly." I hesitated. "He could have been planning this for years, learning our weaknesses as he works with us. Over the last few decades he's taken in almost every single species of paranormal."

Logan shook his head. "I'm still not sure I believe he's capable of murdering the very children he claims to want to protect."

He walked over to the window, staring out at the dull sky through a dusting of polluted fog. After a moment he sighed, massaged his forehead. "As much as I want to deny it," he said, "the logic is sound. Storm could be the killer. I won't strike him off the list of possible suspects. I also won't pretend to like it."

I wasn't asking him to like it. "I know how you feel. To be honest I'm a little scared to tell Grams."

He sighed. "I thought it would be a relief to clear Omega of any wrongdoing."

I folded my arms and raised an eyebrow. "Who says Omega is cleared?"

I sensed his withdrawal and moved to stand beside him. "I'm sorry," I said, looping my arm through his. "I hope you're right. I swear I do."

He said nothing, made no move to hold me. His body language shouted *don't touch me* so loudly my ears ached, but I stayed where I was.

How could I judge him for his personal demons when I had my own making me dance like a crazy person to their insane tune?

And yet, when he pulled away from me, I did judge him and my heart broke a little.

CHAPTER 44

HURT SEEPED LIKE HOT LAVA into the cracks in my heart even as I told myself I was being unfair.

From Logan's point of view Omega was the only family he'd known since his childhood. Suggesting it was guilty of such horrible crimes would make him feel defensive and, because he was Logan, responsible. I had to be mature about this.

"Okay," I said. "Let's assume you're right and Omega isn't involved. Then what about Blake? Why did he attack me? Who is he working for?"

Logan shrugged. "How would I know?"

It wasn't mature to punch someone for being an asshole. "You said you knew him."

"Knew. Past tense." Logan sighed, a deep exhalation that sounded like he'd been holding it for weeks. "A long time ago. His name isn't Blake. It's Brett Nevins. He's an air mage."

At last. Something concrete. "An air mage. That makes sense. Daniel—Daniel Chou, the agent you shot Cicero, remember?— said things got a little cold when Blake got angry."

Logan rubbed his chin. "I haven't seen him in years. He probably doesn't work for Omega anymore."

Why was I always the bearer of bad news? "Yes, he does."

"Who says?" His voice was hard, as if he was straining against the need to scream.

"Agent Chou."

Logan nodded, his eyes bleak.

"He insisted that Blake—Nevins worked for Omega, and that Chou's superior, Jones, thought Nevins was a loose cannon. The 'big-guy' mastermind wasn't happy with his performance and said so when he visited the site after we left."

Logan tightened his jaw, the action visible beneath his unshaven cheek.

I sighed. "Forget it. If you don't want to investigate, I'll find another way. But I promise you I'll find the truth and hold the people responsible accountable for their actions."

Logan continued to stare at the wood floor, his jaw muscle ticking.

Screw maturity. "Look at me, Logan." I waited until he did so and then stared him straight in the eye. An alpha stare. "I don't care how you know him. Nobody will care. But your reactions are making me wonder why *you* do. It's not like you to be so protective of Omega, especially when they've had a big fat question mark hanging over their heads since the debacle with Mom. How can I ignore that?"

He blinked but didn't speak. Then he turned his back on me to look out the window. "You're right."

About time. I folded my arms and waited.

"Your family needs you."

Right.

"I think it's best we take a break from each other."

That's— *What?*

He swung back to face me, eyes cool, jaw hard. "I've complicated your life for long enough."

I should have been shocked and upset but all I felt was a simmering anger. Logan had never backed away from me. Not once. That he would do it now, when all hell was breaking loose, meant one thing.

Somehow he'd found out about a certain marriage proposal.

"How long have you known?" I asked, my lips tight.

He didn't answer that question. "We got the message within hours of the meeting. I didn't want to talk about it because clearly it wasn't something you were prepared to discuss. But ... Justin Lake would be much better for you."

"Is that so?" What was is about men that made you want to bash some sense into them?

I watched him, knowing he'd never struck me as the jealous type. And even if Omega knew so much about me that they had files on how in love I'd once been with Justin Lake, it didn't matter.

Logan took a step back and lowered himself onto the windowsill, then spread his hands out in front of him, as if the action was his apology.

"The ruling isn't a small thing," he said. "The High Council is playing games with your families, but those games could have permanent consequences for your future."

I wanted to rant and rave but I tightened my fist, clamped my own jaw shut.

If I'd ever thought I could live the rest of my life without being an alpha I'd been kidding myself. It was who I was. Who I'd always been. Yes, I'd fought against what I'd once seen as a burden but it had only taken the experiences of the last few months to force me to wise up.

Heat flared in my cheeks and I took a shallow breath.

Control.

"You're wrong." The air vibrated with the emotion in those two words and I tightened my fists. Control. "I don't *need* to be an alpha. I *am* an alpha. There isn't a distinction."

He tilted his head, obviously waiting for me to continue. The look on his face telling me what he expected me to say. That I *needed* him. Well, I wasn't going to. I refused to use the word *need* with reference to Logan. Not when he sat there cold and hard without a sliver of his own heart showing.

Maybe it was pride. I didn't care. How had this meeting degraded from heartfelt reunion to ice-cold goodbye?

I let the silence stretch. Thin.

Logan moved, restless. "Yes. You're an alpha and I'm human. Whatever our personal difference of opinion, I'll still do what I can to figure out what Omega has to do with this situation."

Generous of him, I thought and then chastised myself for being bitchy.

I refused to deal with his emotional baggage right now. Or mine. There were more important issues.

"Then you can start by finding us a mage with memory skills."

He nodded, obviously relieved I was being reasonable. "What type of memory skills?"

"The ability to find missing memories. The ability to remove memories from a person's mind." I scowled at the possibility. "The ability to tell us if such a thing is possible and, if so, what the process is."

"And what type of person would have that particular type of ability?"

I thought of Storm.

"Exactly." I nodded, then said, "Oh, and I may want to take them with me to the Graylands."

"What for?" He didn't ask how I'd carry off such a crazy plan.

"It's probably the best way the mage will have of accessing the minds of the agent—Daniel Chou—and the two kids. The kids were both pretty sure something had happened to their memories." My fingers curled into fists at my side. "Whatever it takes, I'm damn well going to do it."

Logan made a soft grunting sound which I took as his agreement. "Just know that it will take a little while to get the right person on board."

My brow furrowed. "Why?"

Logan cleared his throat. "My security clearance has been downgraded. I don't have the access I did. I think it's best we move covertly so we don't alert the wrong people at Omega."

"Shit." How could I have forgotten Daniel's warning?

"What's wrong?" Logan was frowning.

"I'm not used to this level of intelligence gathering," I said, my tone angry, both at myself and Omega. "They have their eyes on all of us. Be careful at your apartment too."

"Why?"

"Chou said we're all being watched, and he mentioned your name. You have agents watching you. Probably listening too."

"Great." Logan scratched his head. "I'll sweep for bugs when I get home." He looked around the apartment, raising a questioning eyebrow. When I nodded he began to do a sweep.

I followed slowly.

Whatever we'd said up to this point was incriminating enough that I didn't care what else they heard. Our personal dramas had no impact on the greater scheme of things.

"We still have unfinished business between us." I spoke softly, but with a rock-hard firmness "I'm putting it on the back burner for now but we *will* revisit it."

He merely raised an eyebrow and continued his scan of an air vent.

"And," I continued, "When this is over, even if you don't want me in your life anymore, I plan to help you find the truth behind your dreams."

He didn't respond, just headed into Grams' bedroom, his expression bland.

Another few minutes and he returned with a handful of listening devices.

Crap.

Well, it wasn't as if they hadn't already heard everything else that had gone on in our apartment.

And how the hell had they managed to install them without leaving a trace of their own scent behind? I sighed silently. This was Omega we were playing with. I wouldn't put it past them to come in wearing hazmat suits.

Logan put a finger to his lips and went to the kitchen. In a cupboard beneath the counter he found an empty canning jar and placed the devices inside it. Then he put the whole thing inside Grams' glass cookie jar, and dusted off his hands.

"That should dull the sounds," he said, "but still make them think the devices are functioning."

And that, apparently, was the end of our conversation because he dug into his pocket for his phone and began to make a flurry of calls.

While I listened in I made coffee and then sliced some apple and cinnamon cake I found in the fridge. Caffeine and carbs. They weren't a cure for frustration but they made it possible to handle in the short term.

Logan's calls consisted mostly of requests for an 'Eraser'. When he mentioned a Darcy Graham who contracted to both Omega and Sentinel I felt a jolt of relief.

He ended his call and I pushed the plate of cake and a mug of steaming coffee toward him.

He keyed in another number as he took a seat, and as soon as someone answered he asked for Darcy's assistance at an external location. I mouthed *Dad's* and he nodded before he made arrangements for Saleem to bring the mind mage to the *location*. Perhaps he thought Dad's place should remain secure, but I didn't ask.

No doubt Omega had cameras on all their agents.

My cheeks went hot at the thought. I'd visited Logan at his hotel room a couple times already so our personal relationship was probably general knowledge at Omega. But I hoped our physical activities weren't.

When he ended the call Logan inhaled his cake, slugged back his coffee in a gulp, and shoved to his feet.

"Come on. Saleem will get Darcy and be there before we do." He fished inside a pocket for his keys. "Sometimes I hate being plain old human."

I snickered as I headed out the door.

Outside, Logan swung a leg over the seat of his motorbike and gunned the engine.

"Don't have a spare helmet so you'll have to use mine."

He handed it to me and I took it without argument. I'd survive a crash on this machine easier than he would, but there wasn't any sense wasting time in an argument.

I jammed the helmet on my head and swung up behind him, feeling the vibration of the bike beneath me as we started into the quiet street.

With the landscape of concrete and steel fast turning into trees and grass, we headed into the hills.

The ride was a too-brief respite from the turmoil of our world. But however brief it was, I savored every second.

CHAPTER 45

WHEN WE REACHED TUKATS AND entered Dad's house, the place was quiet so early in the morning. Not unusual in a building in which both Dad and Iain worked. Add the goblin kids to the mix, and it should be filled with noise.

I blinked, scrunching up my eyes. I hadn't had any sleep since I'd returned from the Graylands and it was bound to catch up with me soon.

I walked into the front room. My father crouched in front of the fireplace striking a match and watching the flame burn. He touched the match to the paper protruding between the lower logs, then looked up with a smile.

I rubbed my arms as I went to him, and was glad for his hug, however brief it was. My father had been slowly learning how to deal with the physical affection side of our relationship when Greer died, and for a while he'd retreated into his shell as he dealt with her loss.

With Mom back he seemed to be shedding more layers. It was all I could ask for.

I stepped out of his embrace and shivered. "It's cold here."

"Hence the fire," he said.

I rolled my eyes and spun on my heel leaving Dad and Logan to their awkward greetings while I rummaged in the hall closet for one of Dad's old cardigans.

I was shrugging into it when rapid footsteps clattered on the kitchen floor tiles and a moment later a small body slammed into me.

"Hi," sang Alina, her arms around my waist, a wide grin on her face as she stared up at me.

"Hello, you," I said, tapping her nose. "What are you up to?" I picked a leaf from the mess that was her red hair.

"We've been rolling in the leaves," said Alix, looking on from the kitchen doorway. He was watching his sister with an almost jealous expression, as if he too wanted a hug but didn't want to admit it.

I walked over to him and knelt. "Looks like too much fun," I said, grinning. When I saw the tiny lift to the corner of his mouth, I took that as my cue. "How about a hug? I came all this way so I might as well collect."

He hesitated but I pulled him close. He resisted for the briefest moment, then squeezed back.

Satisfied I'd breached at least one of his defenses I let him go, not wanting to overwhelm him with emotion.

He wasn't the only one on the edge of emotional overwhelm. I found myself far too happy to see them too. It felt strange to find that my affection for them had grown since I'd met them. Seems I was a kid person after all.

The air beside me shimmered and Jess coalesced beside me, holding onto a young woman whose blonde hair was tied up in a ponytail at the top of her head. Was this really our Eraser Darcy?

Alina gasped as the two women solidified a foot from her, and Alix jumped back into the kitchen.

I squeezed Alina's shoulder. "It's okay. Why don't you and Alix go and clean up? I'll see you both later."

Alix watched Jess and Darcy suspiciously and didn't move until Alina went to him and held out her hand. Then together they walked past us and up the stairs without a backward glance.

They still needed to adjust to other paranormals but they seemed to be pretty resilient. I only hoped that we were able to help them in the long term.

"Hey," I said to Jess, giving Darcy a smile. "This must be Darcy?"

The girl nodded while Jess said, "Kailin Odel, meet Darcy Graham. I have already apologized to Darcy for the early morning request."

"And I've already assured Jacinta that I am happy to help Logan out." She glanced at Jess, and I sensed they were having a conversation that went beyond the words they spoke, as if they both knew something that I didn't, and were reaching some sort of understanding.

"I'm so glad you're here because we seriously need your help," I said holding out my hand to shake hers. Her handshake was firm and confident and I found that I liked her already.

"Was Saleem busy, Jess?" I asked, wondering what had happened to our expected transport.

"He was unreachable." She gave me a teasing smile. "I was the second choice."

I grinned, hiding my worry for the djinn. It was rare for Saleem to be unreachable.

I waved them inside the living room where the fire was crackling nicely, and where Dad and Logan were deep in conversation beside the floor-to-ceiling window.

Truthfully, I was surprised that neither appeared to be uncomfortable or want to rip the other's throat out.

Good.

We'd just completed introductions when my brother, Iain, arrived. I was tall, but Iain towered over me by a full head. His bright smile and fast, hard bear hug warmed me more than the fire did.

When I introduced him to Darcy, I didn't miss the rosy tinge to her cheeks, or the way Iain's gaze stayed on her face for a bit longer than was normal.

Since his wife Sonia had been killed, Iain had kept his relationships light and fun, and never too serious. But he seemed to have taken a shine to our Eraser.

Interesting. It could be a relationship worth prodding in the right direction.

But first, our current business.

"Darcy," I said. "Thanks for coming. We need help urgently."

At my words Logan and Dad ended their private conversation and joined us. "I have reason to believe," I continued, "that someone's memory has been erased against their will."

Darcy's gaze flicked immediately to Jess and again they appeared to share a look. "Such a thing is easy enough to accomplish if the subject is sedated."

"Is sedation necessary?" I asked.

She pursed her lips. "Not necessary, but recommended. Mind-melding in any form takes time, and with a conscious—or even semi-conscious—subject it's far too easy to lose concentration."

"How long would such a process take?" Logan asked. His expression was off—tense and strained as he studied Darcy's face.

I wondered if he too was taken with the lovely mage but decided his expression appeared to be more like he was struggling to figure out where he'd seen her before.

She hesitated then, her discomfort clear. "It depends on what I'm doing. For a full erase it's quick, although extremely painful for both the subject and myself."

"And if you're just removing specific memories?" I asked.

"It takes much longer. Anything between eighteen hours and two days, depending on how intensive the wipe needs to be."

Logan frowned. "So you can remove specific pieces of information from a person's memory?"

Immediately I understood what he was getting at.

Could it be possible that the memories he was trying to recall had been wiped from *his* mind? I felt a little ill at the thought and had to focus to hear Darcy's answer.

"Yes," she said. "Imagine you're eating an apple and I go in and remove the memories of what you ate. And replace the apple with a peppermint." She smiled, yet the corners of her mouth didn't rise high enough, as if some form of tension still controlled her responses.

Logan thought about it. "I'll recall that I ate a peppermint?"

She nodded. "If I gave you a new memory of an actual peppermint, yes. But if I didn't replace the actual apple with an actual peppermint you'd recall eating an apple but not see it, and you'd recall the taste as peppermint, not the crunchy sweet apple itself."

"Sounds like a bit of a mind-fudge." I kept it clean since Jess and Dad were present. "Does it ever go wrong?"

She didn't hesitate. "It can. I could make a person recall eating a live snake instead of an apple. Or erase every apple they've eaten in their life. There are limitless possibilities, but few are ethical."

So all that protected us were the ethics of the practitioner. That was scary. "How long do the effects of such an erase last?"

Darcy considered. "It depends on the job and the particular need. It could be forever. Or I could make it only temporary."

"What are the signs that an erased memory is returning?" I asked, my heart beginning to thump harder.

"They usually begin with dreams that allude to what's been erased and odd flashes of memory that are usually sensation-related."

"Sensation?" asked Logan softly.

Jess glanced at Logan as Darcy answered. "Yes. Sensations are often the most difficult to erase. We can remove the apple but the experience of the eating is incredibly hard to remove and replace. Erasing is usually the only viable choice. In the 'eating an apple' case there you won't recall the apple but you'll remember the feel of eating it, the taste of the fruit and the juices. The context in which you ate it will also remain."

I nodded then glanced over at the fire. "So if you removed my mom from my memory, but she always burned toast,"—Dad and Iain both laughed—"then every time I smelled burned toast, my mind would search for the association with that smell and find nothing."

She nodded.

"And I'd feel like something is missing?" I asked, giving Logan a glance. He was staring at the fire, the expression on his face pained. He was making connections.

I turned back to Darcy and found that she too was watching Logan, her expression sad.

Then she caught me watching her and her expression returned to calm professional. "A lot of people never feel they're missing something," she said, "but there are a small number of subjects whose emotional strength can override the erase." She tilted her head. "Is this the problem you have for me?"

Somehow I knew she was aware it wasn't.

"I have two kids," I said, "whose memories of an attack on them have been taken. Their recollections are more in terms of association and feeling—which means their descriptions can't be fully trusted. Are we able to do anything to help them remember? Or to overturn the erase?"

Darcy tapped a finger on her lips. "I can try. If you arrange a meeting with them, I'll try a few exercises. Perhaps I could even do a search within their minds to find out if their memories have been erased to begin with."

I nodded but glanced over at Logan.

Darcy leaned forward. "I really am happy to help, Kailin. When can you arrange for me to meet them?"

No help from Logan, then. "And that," I said, "is where we have a little problem."

Her eyebrows lifted slightly. "Why is that?"

"They're dead."

Her eyebrows hit her hairline. "Yes," she said. "That does complicate things."

CHAPTER 46

IT WASN'T UNTIL EVERYONE LAUGHED that I realized how tense the conversation had become.

"*Can* you examine the mind of a dead person?" I asked.

Expecting Darcy to give a flat-out *no*, I was surprised when she smiled and nodded.

"It will be a complicated exercise," she said. "But yes."

I let out a relieved sigh. "We can do 'complicated'. It's the 'not possible' we have a problem with."

She laughed softly. "I understand. I'll need a DeathTalker to set up the mind-link. A person's mind doesn't disappear once they die. It exists within the soul-aspect—or the spirit, as some people call it. It's much, much harder to access, but if the subject is willing then their willingness removes a number of the mental barriers. So yes, I can help. Although it does depend on what you expect of me."

"How do you mean?"

She lifted a shoulder. "Do you just want information? Or do you want me to erase something from their minds?"

I thought of the ghosts and their desire to help me. I wanted to give them something in return. "To be honest, I'd like you to put their memories back the way they were. But if you can't, I'll be happy with just information."

She nodded. "Unfortunately, information is the best that I can offer. Only an Immortal can manipulate the memories of the dead."

The temperature in the room seemed to plummet and the chill lifted the small hairs on my arms.

Only an Immortal can manipulate the memories of the dead.

Logan's dark look told me what he too was thinking.

Storm.

Beside him, Jess's face tightened with shock. Now, she too had to admit that Storm was a strong contender for the guilty title.

And then time froze as Jess decided we needed a private conversation.

"Sorry to do this to you again, Kailin," she said, her expression strained. I nodded my understanding, and she continued, "Are you *absolutely* positive about what the children said?"

I was no longer struggling with the idea that Storm could be our killer/mastermind, but the Titan certainly was. It was clear that whatever previous relationship she'd had with Storm was influencing her current state of mind. A good thing I'd always been a little intimidated by Storm and kept our relationship merely cordial.

"I'm sorry, Jess." And I truly was. "I know this is hard for you to wrap your head around. He was your friend. Sorry, he *is* your friend. I understand if you need more proof."

But the Titan was shaking her head, a blonde strand escaping from the low bun at the back of her head. Her eyes, usually blue and sparkling, were now just a dull gray.

"I am trained to be impartial in all matters, but I now understand how humans think and feel, always swayed by emotional attachment. As much as I want to believe Storm incapable of such dreadful crimes, I cannot ignore the truth. I understand him to be *able* to do the things you accuse him of. I had thought him too ethical to do so. And yet—"

She broke off suddenly, her pain and disillusionment obvious. "It is the last thing that I would ever want to do, but I fear I have no choice. I confess that I am now afraid Storm is complicit in some way, if not the mastermind himself."

I was already shaking my head. "We might still be wrong about Storm," I said with a shaky sigh. She didn't seem appeased by my words though so I continued. "The only reason that we're focused on Storm is he seems to be the common factor according to our witnesses. And the agent I met in the Graylands, Daniel, described Storm almost perfectly. I also hate to think it, but he could be the one."

The Titan nodded, her face paler than was possible. "And if he is the killer, he needs to be stopped. The Immortal High Council would never allow him to continue. Power in one such as Storm is something that could easily explode out of control. Your world is not ready for that."

I nodded, my heart tightening within my chest. "We also have another important reason to find him. Lily. If he doesn't have her, then Omega probably does."

The Titan must have seen something on my face—perhaps my determination to take the next step no matter how hard it was— and she gave me an approving nod.

Then time flowed back into the room and the discussion moved on.

I let it move. I'd made my decision, determined what I'd do next. So I took a moment just to watch the people I loved. The expression on Iain's face as he looked at Darcy. Dad talking to Logan without judgment. Logan himself, the strain at the sides of his eyes, the hollowness to his cheeks, the dark bruises under his eyes that screamed lack of sleep—

"Can I take you home?" Jess's question broke into my

thoughts, and I'd almost started to answer when I realized she was talking to Darcy.

"Thank you," Darcy said with a smile. "I think I should go." Although it was hard to miss the reluctance in her eyes as she gave Iain one last glance.

"Where do you live?" asked Iain, unconsciously taking a step closer to her, as if already he didn't want her to leave.

This is going to get interesting.

Darcy looked up at him and smiled, "New Orleans." Then she turned to me. "As soon as you need me, Kailin, I'll come. Just get the DeathTalker. I don't need to go to the Graylands and I would suggest that you not go back there either."

I frowned. "Why is that?"

Darcy shook her head. "It's far too dangerous to move back and forth between the planes. It's bad enough to jump from one world to the next, but the Graylands have a way of sucking energy and life from a person. That plane was not made for the living. If you want a long and healthy life then always make a visit to the Graylands your least acceptable option."

All I could do in response was to nod.

Now that Darcy mentioned it I realized that every time I'd been to the Graylands I'd come back exhausted and hadn't regained full-strength until days later. I wouldn't challenge her on her opinion.

We all got to our feet and Jess and Darcy started for the hallway. They could have just vanished right there but Jess preferred to look as though she came and went like a normal person. Unless she had no choice.

As they walked off, Ian said, "Let me accompany you out," as if they were going to grab their jackets or something. I was amused, yes, but it was also cute to see him so obviously enamored of someone.

As they left I turned and caught Dad's grin and narrowed my eyes at him. "Whatever you're thinking, stop. Leave him alone."

"I have no idea what you mean," he said, trying to look innocent.

"You know exactly what I mean. Don't go sticking your nose in his business. We all want him to find someone to settle down with, but if you nose around trying to find out how serious the relationship is, it'll die a very quick death."

Logan grinned.

Dad made a weird sound and even opened his mouth to respond.

I didn't wait. I raised my hand and began counting off on my fingers, "Lizbeth, Annamarie, Patrice, Mary, Tina." I raised my eyebrows. "And those were all in the space of a year. Shall I continue?"

Dad folded his arms. "I had no idea you were paying such close attention to your brother's love-life."

I smiled serenely. "When you don't have one of your own, the love-lives of others become very interesting. Besides, brothers were invented so that sisters could mind their business."

I grinned and walked over to slip a hand into the crook of Logan's arm, not yet ready to reveal to my parent that my own love-life was dying as we spoke. Thankfully, Logan played his part, leaning forward to shake hands and say goodbye.

"Speaking of love-lives, where is your special squeeze?"

Dad frowned. "I'm not sure. She headed out with Grams to do some of their own investigations." He scowled. "And they wouldn't tell what they were up to. Those women are courting trouble."

I laughed. "You're talking about two high-profile intelligence agents, one a no-nonsense walker and the other a demon-hunting tracker. I think they can take care of themselves."

Dad merely grunted before shaking Logan's outstretched hand.

When we headed out into the hall, Iain was nowhere to be

found. As we stepped out into the cold night Logan threw an arm around my shoulder and drew me closer.

"Should I order a cardigan for you?" He quirked an eyebrow.

I glared at him, pulled Dad's cable-knit around me, and lifted my chin. "No thank you."

He handed me the helmet, mouth twitching. "Are you sure?"

"Just drive, smartass." I put the helmet on, climbed onto the Harley behind him, and we sped off.

On the return home the landscape was the last thing on my mind. When Logan eased the bike to a stop outside my apartment I slid off, drawing the helmet off my head.

"I've made a decision," I said, and handed him the helmet. "I'm joining Omega."

$\mathcal{L}$OGAN'S FACE WENT TERRIBLY STILL and he watched me, dark eyes going darker than I ever thought possible. Very slowly, he swung his leg over the seat and came to a standstill in front of me.

"Are you *insane?*"

"What do you mean?" I asked. "You've been wanting me to join Omega and now suddenly you think it's a bad idea?

"I don't think it's a *bad* idea." He sounded like he was talking to a mentally incompetent three-year-old. "I think it's an *insane* idea. With everything that's been happening, with the likelihood that an Immortal could be behind these killings, with the possibility that Storm could be working with Omega, you really think that I would condone you doing something that could endanger your life? You should be joining The High Council's Elite."

I folded my arms, even though the action proved quite awkward with the helmet within my grasp. "Don't you see? This could be the best opportunity possible. And besides, I have this whole blood promise thing hanging over my head, remember? I promised them that I wouldn't jeopardize their involvement until I fulfill my end."

Logan frowned. He still hadn't confirmed whether he would join the Elite with me, either. No judgment.

"If I agree to join Omega, it'll look like I'm going over to their side. They'll think I'm softening toward them. Maybe drop their guard."

"It's too risky, Kai"

I shrugged. "Your clearance has been downgraded for a reason. They're suspicious. Maybe if they believe you've recruited me like they asked you'll be reinstated. Have you considered that possibility?" I could see he hadn't. But he still wasn't happy.

Logan narrowed his eyes. "Fine, I'll take you in tomorrow."

He started past me, but I grabbed his arm. "I want to go now."

He shoved both hands through his hair. "You must be crazy. At least take some time to think about it."

I shook my head. "I don't need time. I don't *have* time. I've already thought about, and I think we're out of choices. Sentinel came up with nothing new—nothing. It won't hurt for me to try."

He made a rude sound under his breath. My heart twisted and I pushed the feelings of rejection deep inside me. I had a job to do. I had no time to sit here bemoaning my broken heart.

I shoved the helmet back on and hopped onto the bike. He stood on the pavement for a couple of breaths and then took his place in front of me.

His back was stiff, bleeding suppressed frustration and fear as he drove to the Omega headquarters.

It was obvious that Logan was wondering what the hell I was up to. Was it desperation that was making me do something that I'd said I never would? I really wasn't sure.

We entered the building and as we traversed the lobby and threaded through little groups of people I drew on my calm.

We stopped in front of the elevators and Logan thumbed the button. He didn't say a word to me as we waited, staring at the numbers lighting up in a row above the doors.

At last, the elevator opened and a group of people exited, all hurrying off to whatever lives they had. As they were Omega people they probably had no lives at all.

I entered the elevator with Logan and was about to turn and face the door when Logan touched the base of my spine—a gentle warning.

I didn't have to look far for the reason.

A man had entered the small space and stood inside the doors, his back against the side wall so I could see only his profile. And then he turned his head.

A flare of fury raced through Brett Nevins's fiery golden eyes and as the elevator doors closed the temperature within the small space dropped low enough to bring goosebumps to my skin.

Seconds later the temperature rose again, his expression smoothed, and he focused on the passing floor numbers as if the other occupants of the elevator were not worth his attention. At the next floor he brushed through the barely open doors and made a left into the corridor.

I didn't move.

I stood there until the doors sealed shut, with Logan's hand warm on my lower back, and wondered what the hell had just happened. If I hadn't seen that initial flare of rage in Nevins's eyes I'd have thought he hadn't recognized me.

But the fact he'd recognized me wasn't my only concern. The cheek my panther had ripped up only yesterday was perfectly smooth, unmarred by anything except a faint five o'clock shadow.

A glance at Logan's face confirmed that he too had watched Nevins's little acting job. "He pretended he didn't recognize you."

I waved that irrelevancy away. "Did you see?"

Logan's lips curled into a cold smile. "You mean the lack of damage to his face?"

"How observant you are."

Logan snorted. "Now, how do you suppose he's managed to heal his face this fast?"

I had no idea. "I feel like I'm in *The Twilight Zone*."

"Didn't peg you for an old movie buff."

"I'm not." I let out a slow breath. "What now? He's seen me. And I didn't exactly play it cool and pretend ignorance the way he did. He knew I knew him."

"Best thing is to go with the flow. Be natural. Keep it cool. Fill the forms and go through the motions. Do nothing untoward. You're just a walker joining Omega."

I nodded. "We have to find another way to get into the computer system undetected." I let out a short laugh. "As long as we don't do a Grams we'll be fine."

Logan frowned, but I waved the question away. "I have an idea. I know someone who has the particular skills we need."

And now I was grinning. We had just the ticket to get this job done. And he'd been there all along.

Baz.

CHAPTER 48

REGISTERING AT OMEGA WAS ANTICLIMACTIC. I filled in forms, smiled blandly at the enthusiastic registration officer who seemed thrilled that I was 'joining the team'—albeit on a contractual basis, and then we headed home.

This time, when I got home I intended to rest. The whole awful day was taking its toll.

But first, I needed to check on Anjelo. So as soon as I got off the bike and gave Logan his helmet back I called him. A quiet Anjelo tended to be a dangerous one, and I hadn't heard a peep from him for hours now and I was beginning to worry.

After a few rings the call went to voicemail.

Not a good sign.

Entering my apartment, I came to a sudden stop, so sharply that Logan almost ran into me from behind. He stopped with his hands on my shoulders to support him.

In the end it was me who need the support.

The apartment was in shambles, completely trashed. From where I stood I could see into my bedroom where my mattress had been tossed onto the floor, its insides ripped open and its foam and springs spilled out like the guts of a dead animal.

I raced into my room and shoved my closet door wide open. Although my clothing had been torn off the hangers, and the shelves rifled through, the back wall appeared to be intact. The hidden space containing our weapons was still secure.

I returned to the living room grateful we were at least still armed.

"Why the hell don't I smell them?" I mumbled. Then I let out a sharp laugh. "Hazmat suits."

"What?" asked Logan as he checked the windows.

"Never mind," I mumbled, heading to look through the rest of the apartment. It was a mess. When I got back to the living room Logan was busy straightening furniture and putting the totally ruined stuff in a pile beside the kitchen counter.

"Whoever they were, they were looking for something," Grams said. I turned around to find her leaning against the front door jamb looking slightly sick.

"At least they didn't get into the safe," I said.

Grams nodded, and some of the sick look faded.

"What do you think they wanted?" I asked softly. Was it my fault?

"Could be my fault," she said, watching Logan answer his buzzing phone. "Maybe digging around in top secret files wasn't a good idea." Her gaze returned to me and grinned. "More likely your fault. What have you been up to?"

Little did she know.

So I brought her up to speed; Lily's disappearance, visiting the Graylands, ripping up cheeks that now showed no sign of damage. I skimmed lightly over the fact that I'd joined Omega and took her raised eyebrow and lack of comment to mean she'd deal with me later.

So I went on the offensive first.

"What happened to you today?" I asked. "Why didn't you come to Dad's? And where's Mom?"

Grams shrugged. "I don't know about Celeste. She said she

had something to look after. And nothing happened to me. I went in to clear the air. I said I used to have full security clearance, and if that had been changed it was certainly done without notifying me. I told them that now I know the new protocols, I'd keep my nose out of things that my security status didn't allow. And I didn't pretend I wasn't pissed off either. They seemed to believe me."

She sighed, then gestured to the ruined room. "This, however, might indicate both of us were lying."

"It could." Logan pocketed his phone and wove his way through the mess toward us. "And then it could just as easily be something else. Maybe Omega got suspicious of Kai. Maybe Nevins alerted the mastermind and he wants to know what you know."

I nodded. They were good points.

Grams raised her eyebrow again and walked over to the television as Logan joined me.

"Jess is collecting Baz for you," he said, and the air in the middle of the living room began to shimmer. Jess materialized with a stricken Baz in tow.

"What the hell happened here?" he asked, his eyes widening as Grams straightened from her failed attempt at setting the television right. "Oh, I do apologize for my language, ma'am." His skin flushed a darker shade of chocolate, and I hid a grin.

Grams, on the other hand, smiled brightly. "Young man, you should teach that particular brand of manners to a few people I know."

I laughed. "Sorry, Grams. Only the Brits can do manners that well."

She made a face then moved away to talk to Jess.

"Right, Baz," I said. "Let's get to it. What do you need?"

"A terminal to access the Omega servers," he said.

Okay.

"Just a moment." Grams abandoned Jess and hurried to my

bedroom. "You can use my laptop. I think someone took it when they trashed my apartment."

"Very sad," I said.

Jess came to stand beside me, giving a soft huff in agreement to Grams' idea.

Grams returned with the laptop and handed it to Baz. "You have one hour, and then I'll report it stolen. Off you go."

"Let me deal with the GPS first." He sank to the floor. Opened the laptop and tapped away. Then he looked up with a grin. "I wonder when your burglary happened. The tracking system was activated two hours ago. I've disconnected it. We can go."

"Give us half an hour," I told Grams. "Then report it. That way it'll look like the place was trashed, the GPS disabled and the laptop taken, then you arrived after they left."

"If it wasn't Sentinel." Grams' mouth tightened and she glanced at Jess then me. "You kids better go somewhere far away. And fast." Then she met Baz's eyes. "And you, young man, had better work faster than you've ever done in your life. All our lives are depending on it."

Baz nodded, looking like he was about to choke. Grams did have that kind of effect on people.

I waved at Logan and grabbed hold of Jess's arm as Baz did the same. Seconds later we materialized on the rooftop of a high-rise. I blinked and—doing a complete circle—scanned the horizon.

West of us a gleaming pyramid rose out of the desert, and with the conflagration of city lights I knew where we were. Las Vegas.

Baz had already made himself comfortable on the tile of the roof patio, crossing his legs to lay the laptop on his lap. He pulled on a pair of gloves, then shook out his hands in preparation. Soon, he was tapping away at the keys so fast I could hardly see his fingers move.

"Making good use of the vamp virus, I see," I said.

"I do believe it does have its advantages."

"Just don't fry the keyboard, okay."

He didn't even look up.

Jess and I waited a few feet from the vamp, watching the twinkling lights that surrounded us like a sea of glowing bugs.

Baz had been working for only a few minutes, yet I felt like hours had passed. I began to tap my foot. "Baz. How's it going?"

"I've written a program that'll search the Omega system for files containing certain keywords. Termination, ammunition, certain locations, Section Seven—anything that could be considered a connection."

I nodded. "Sounds good. So now we wait?"

He grunted, and began to type again.

"Something happening?"

"I'm refining the search fields."

As he worked I moved over to Jess. The look she gave me made my stomach drop.

"What did your High Council say?"

"They want him brought back to our headquarters in Italy," she murmured. "He will stand trial there. And they want it kept secret."

"I understand why, but keeping it a secret won't be easy." I gestured to Baz. "We're all involved. What will you do? Wipe out all our memories?"

Jess shook her head. "The High Council understands certain key people will remember. We will just have to trust you will honor your word."

I hadn't yet given any such word—but I didn't think that fact worth mentioning.

CHAPTER 49

THE LAPTOP PINGED AND I flew to Baz's side. "What is it?"

He pointed at the screen. "Here. A file belonging to a Colonel Gunther. It's a confirmation that Agent Nevins's services will be on loan to Division Seven for an unspecified time, on a top-secret mission. The name of the requester has been redacted, even from the Omega top secret files. Which is weird. I'm four levels deep so this far down nothing should be hidden."

I frowned. Could those redacted portions be reference to Storm? I glanced up at Jess and saw the hardening of her jaw. She was thinking the very same thing.

Then he tapped again, and leaned closer to the screen. "And here, a list of orders for items from another facility called Area X." He laughed. "Yeah, it's really called Area X. The files are marked Top Secret too, and it looks like someone has tried to wipe them."

I nodded, my gut tightening. Those would be products made as a result of experimentation done on paranormals like Mom.

"This is proof that Omega is guilty of experimentation."

I sounded dead. I felt the same. All along I'd wanted to find the proof that Omega was dirty and now that I had, my emotions were all twisted. Was it Logan's connection with Omega that made me feel this way?

"I can see a solid paper trail from Omega HQ to this facility," Baz continued, unaware of the hurricane that was my emotions. "They were commissioned to create something—what it is and what it does has also been redacted."

"As they were experimenting on paranormals," I said, "I'd bet they're working on a weapon designed to kill or weaken us."

Jess merely nodded. Baz continued, muttering things like 'confirm design and makeup', 'design and construction of paranormal energy detector', production quantities, and shipment destinations.

He let out a dissatisfied grunt. "Destination: classified."

"Check if the code has military prefixes," suggested Jess.

Baz gave her an odd look, then continued tapping. Good thing he'd been turned or this business would have taken much longer. As it was, we were running out of time.

"Can you copy the files?" I asked.

He shook his head. "Not to this laptop. But I can reroute the files to a secure online server I use. I can reroute and cloak the destination enough times to stay ahead of them long enough to download the files before they discover they've been taken."

He focused for a few moments, and suddenly a low buzzing started.

"Bloody *hell*," he snarled, resuming his frantic typing. Seconds later, he dropped the laptop on the ground in front of him and spun away. The device began to smoke, then spark, and emit a metallic burning smell.

"Self-destruct?" I asked.

Baz shook his head. "No. It's a program written into the Omega server. It found us and followed us back to the laptop."

"Did you get the files copied in time," I asked. He nodded. "Right, then let's get the hell outta here."

I turned to Jess. "Could you take us to my Dad's. We need to keep Baz safe."

We both knew I meant safe from Storm.

We left the laptop on the roof of the building in Las Vegas and were inside my Dad's front hall within seconds.

"What do we have here?" asked Mom as she walked out of the kitchen, a steaming mug in her hand.

"Mom, where have you been?" I asked, giving her a hug.

She laughed. "In hiding. There's been a bunch of strange things going on with the High Council, so Dad figured it was best for me to lie low."

"So the best place is *with* Dad?" I asked, arching an eyebrow.

"Seems ironic eh?" she laughed. "What's happening?'

I introduced her to Baz, and gave a brief rundown telling her we had to keep him safe.

She nodded and crooked her finger at him. "Come get something to eat and then I'll show you a room. You'll have to put up with a rowdy pair of goblin twins, though."

Baz's eyes widened. "I appreciate any help, ma'am."

I touched Baz on the shoulder. "I have something for you to do as well." I pulled Grams' chip from my pocket and handed it to him. "Can you find out what's on that drive that could be dangerous or liable to get someone killed for knowing it?"

He grinned. "It will be my pleasure. And how convenient that I wouldn't need to be killed for it?"

I shook my head as Mom laughed softly, giving the flash drive a glance. "Something of yours?"

"It's Grams'," I told her. "Maybe you could lend Baz a few gray cells?"

Mom nodded and headed into the kitchen. "Do you girls need food?" she called over her shoulder as she went.

"No, thanks Mom." The thought of food made me want to hurl. I looked at Jess. "You?"

Jess shook her head. "Thank you, Celeste but I have to leave soon. I will return Kailin to her apartment. I will be back to see you as soon as I can. It is past time we caught up."

More secret relationships between Jess and my family. I was no longer surprised.

I called out a quick goodbye to Mom as Jess took my arm. Mom's farewell echoed around me as we disappeared and materialized in my apartment.

Sounds from Grams' shower confirmed she was home.

We had scarcely solidified before Jess spoke. "There is much that I have to tell you, but perhaps I will begin with Logan's past."

That took the wind from my sails.

"Logan's memories," she said, "the ones that are returning, pertain to something crucially important from his past."

"He thinks he's remembering a girl, around his own age." I told her, hoping to open her up more.

Jess nodded. "She is very important to him, to his past, and—quite honestly—to who he is. As I have told you before, there is much about Logan that nobody is yet aware of. I must stress again that Logan is far more important than he realizes."

All good to know, but she still wasn't giving me anything concrete.

"I know this may seem like I am telling you very little but I am not yet allowed to provide you with direct information."

I thought I knew what she was saying. She couldn't feed me direct information but she could point me to what lay between the lines.

There was still one more thing. She had promised me more information about the Ni'amh. Before I could form the question, she held out a hand. A white envelope shimmered into solidity on her open palm.

She held it there, saying not a word. I took it and pocketed it in silence. I didn't even say 'thank you' but she seemed happy that I hadn't.

"If you want to help him," she said, "you must ensure he

pushes himself harder to break the wall between him and the truth of his memories. The secret is there, locked deep within his mind, and only he is able to break through. No matter how painful it is, he must keep trying."

"Why?" I whispered. "Can you at least tell me why?"

"Because if he stops trying, he will be lost."

CHAPTER 50

WE'D COMMANDEERED MY FATHER'S DINING room and split the files among Logan, Mom, Baz and me, working late into the night.

Mom had confirmed that the Walker High Council had requested she be brought in for questioning and so she'd spent a lot of time inside Dad's safe-room.

The High Council wasn't aware of the safe-room so they hadn't checked there, and the people they'd posted to watch the house had had to remain outside to do their watching. According to Dad, they'd need an official warrant to search the property. So Mom was safe for now.

She was certainly safer there than our apartment building with all the attacks and home invasions.

I'd tried to contact Anjelo repeatedly over the last few hours and I didn't intend to stop trying. I wished he wasn't the type of person who would close himself off when he was hurting.

We'd scoured the files which we'd downloaded from the server, and they managed to fill in a number of gaps in our knowledge.

A secondary layer of protected files confirmed communication between the US military and Omega's munitions design division. The reports had been lightly coded—easy enough for Baz to break—and revealed that Omega had been experimenting on a wide range of paranormals, extracting DNA, and redeveloping it in order to enhance the government's human soldiers.

More importantly, the humans had had their memories of the enhancement removed, leaving them with psychologically planted triggers that would engage those enhanced powers on demand.

One entire file contained details of Brett Nevins' recruitment dating from two years previously. He'd been convinced by his handler that something called *inferior paranormals* existed, and then empowered with the task of eradicating those paranormals, and named Omega Liaison.

Logan closed the file and then sat back, rubbing his eyes. The endless pots of darkly brewed coffee had helped, but fatigue was starting to take its toll on all of us. I felt it particularly hard since this would be the second night of no sleep.

"I'm still trying to figure out why Omega would get in bed with the US government," he said. "If the aim was for humans to benefit from paranormal enhancement then it would make a sort of sense. But the order to eliminate paranormals doesn't make any sense at all."

Still thinking of Storm, I said, "Maybe there is someone else orchestrating all of it. Someone outside both Omega and Sentinel, someone outside the government hierarchy, too. Getting the US government on board would help to maintain secrecy. Nobody wants to piss them off, or endanger their organization's relationship with the military. Sentinel and Omega both respect the governments of countries around the world. Nobody wants to get on the wrong side of either agency. Creating official, if top secret, associations with them would ensure any nefarious activity would remain secret, by order of both organizations."

"And maybe this same mastermind has more to his plans than he's shared with either the military or Omega. He's using both of them." Logan gave a nod of begrudging admiration.

"And he pulls the puppet strings as and when he wishes," Baz said.

"Which explains why there's nothing in the files about killing or massacres." I twisted to ease the tightness in my back.

"Do you think the government is unaware of the murders?" asked Mom.

"Who knows?"

"I have to speak to Nevins," said Logan. "For all we know, he's been lied to or even brainwashed into this."

He had to be joking. "Are you insane?"

Baz glanced up. "He's probably right. If he speaks to Nevins directly, Logan can figure out if the guy's mind's been effed with."

"It makes sense," Mom said, although she didn't look happy. "I don't like it. You'll be putting yourself in too much danger. But it makes the best sense."

She gave me a 'sorry for agreeing with the guys' look, but I'd already realized they were right. That didn't mean I had to like it.

Logan got to his feet and looked at me. "And as much as I don't like the idea, you should come too."

"I'm flattered," I said as I got to my feet. "And I'll agree on one condition."

His eyes narrowed. "Which is?"

"Get Jess to come too. She can hide and watch him, poke around in his head to see if he's got any blank spaces."

Logan smiled. "I like the way you think," he said with a yawn.

"You'll do nothing of the sort until you both have some rest." Mom's stern tone implied we had no choice and I was fine with that.

I went to the front lounge and crashed on the sofa, barely listening as Mom sent Logan to the library.

A few hours later, rested and fed, Logan was allowed to make his calls. Mom had been right though, tired could easily have translated into careless.

Soon, Jess arrived and transported us to a spot at the edge of the forest, a few miles from Tukats on the side closer to the city.

She didn't seem to be in the mood to talk and disappeared into the bush muttering something about recon. Logan let her go without a question.

I studied the trees and foliage, and the great old oak behind me. "Does it bother you that he agreed to meet you so easily?"

"Yeah. Could easily turn into an ambush."

Good to know I wasn't the only paranoid person there.

"Tell me more about how you know him?" I asked softly.

I expected him to evade and avoid so it was a complete surprise when he actually answered.

"When Omega recruited me, I joined an agency-run school. It was normal learning peppered with a good deal of paranormal military training." He took a deep breath and looked away. "Nevins was one of the older kids. A couple of years ahead of me."

"And a bully."

He flashed me a wry grin. "How did you know?"

"I've met the guy."

Logan nodded. "He tried to hurt me once. Another kid saved Nevins in time."

"Saved *him*?"

A muscle in Logan's jaw tightened. Released. "Yeah. Mikael. He's a weather mage. Storms and lightning and stuff. I'd grabbed hold of Nevins' wrist before he punched my lights out. His performance saved Nevins from being burned alive." Guilt flitted across his face.

An image of a badly burned wrist shimmered in my mind. "Don't you dare blame yourself. Blame the bully."

"And who's to blame for making the bully?" he asked softly.

"That's not your problem."

He shook his head as if the movement would dismiss my comment. "I think I owe it to him to at least give him an out."

"It's more than he deserves."

I sounded bitter, I knew it. I didn't care. But I couldn't change his mind and I wouldn't presume to try. "I still think it's too dangerous, but you have to do what you need."

I hesitated, caught between wanting to hug him and wanting to punch him. Physical confrontation I could handle, especially when it meant using my fists or my panther. But personal confrontation had never been my strong suit. I'd rather swim in bloody water with sharks.

So I didn't hug him and I didn't punch him. Instead I climbed a tree and settled along a nice thick branch several feet above where Logan stood. It was sheltered and comfortable. It also gave me an unimpeded exit route if I needed to turn panther, jump down, and rip Nevins's head off.

It didn't take long before there was rustling in the trees ahead. Bushes swayed as they were thrust aside and dirt and leaf litter whirled like small tornados. Nevins certainly wasn't keeping his presence a secret.

He finally strode into the clearing, shoulders stiff, spine erect, every inch a soldier. The look he gave Logan could have frozen a lava flow.

"What do you want, Westin?" Nevins grunted the question, arms tense at his sides.

"To talk," Logan said.

"Then talk," Nevins said, and folded his arms across his chest. I figured it was a good sign considering he used those very hands to ice things to death.

Logan did the same and I watched as Nevins nodded.

Peace, for now.

"You're being used." Logan launched into the conversation.

Talk about being subtle.

"What the hell do you mean?" asked Nevins, scowling.

"You're being lied to and used and in the end, you'll be killed by the very people you're working with."

"You are insane."

"I've been getting a lot of that lately." Logan laughed. Then his features smoothed and the look he gave Nevins was serious. "The man you're working for— You're just a pawn in his bigger plan."

Nevins took a step closer. "The man that *I* am working for would never do such a thing. I trust him. His intentions are pure."

His hands curled into fists, although his arms stayed folded. "His *plan*, as you call it, is to create a better world. He's done research into paranormals—research that shows some of us are a danger to our world. Some of *us* need to be removed from the equation."

"So, based on the conclusions of one man's supposed research you've become an active participant in genocide."

Nevins blinked. "Of course not. This isn't genocide. Targets are specific. We test for certain markers. Only those who show signs of becoming a danger to society are eradicated."

Like cockroaches.

Logan didn't back down "You didn't eradicate pests, Brett. You killed people."

"You don't understand," Nevins said "They were no longer people. It was in their DNA, right there for us to see that they would eventually be a danger."

He paused and met Logan's eyes. "Don't you see? They *deserved* to die."

CHAPTER 51

"AND WHO DID THOSE INVESTIGATIONS and the experimentation that confirmed these dangers existed?" Logan asked, his tone hard.

Nevins hesitated. "I wasn't told who did the research. I was just shown it." For a moment he looked lost, as if he realized there were missing pieces in his reasoning.

Then his features tightened. "I know what you're doing, Westin. Still the same little upstart, wanting to push his way into things he doesn't understand."

His dislike for Logan was palpable, and I let my panther surface slowly, fingers forming paw and claw, mouth filling with sharp, deadly teeth.

Logan shook his head. "I don't want *in*, Brett. I want to help you *out*. If what I've seen so far is true, then you're in danger from the very people you trust."

"No." Nevins jerked his head back as though a poisonous insect had buzzed in his face. "That's a lie. You're envious. You weren't chosen. You, with your power and your security clearance. You with your so-called friends in *high places*."

He sneered the last two words and his expression spoke volumes. "You weren't the one they wanted in the end, were you? It was *me.*"

And on the last word he unfolded his arms and whipped them behind his body. Even as he swung them around to aim the pistol at Logan, I was flying through the air.

I slammed into his chest, ignoring the ear-splitting shot past my ear, the fabric of clothes ripping under my claws, the scent of blood and skin as I peeled it from his body.

Then he hit the ground with me on top of him.

I tilted my head and growled, my roar reverberating through the trees. My canines were a mere inch from his throat when Logan yelled, "Kai, don't."

Even though Logan begged me to stop, my panther roared for the kill. She was so close, thrusting against me, her need for blood and death a living thing.

I stared into Nevins' terrified eyes and smelled a hint of urine. The big bully had been beaten by a bigger one. That ended it for me. I wasn't a bully. I didn't want to debase another person.

And I stepped away, more because it sank in how badly he'd been manipulated. Total mind-fuck.

As I pulled my panther back Nevins scrambled onto shaking legs.

"What the fuck is wrong with you?" He glared at me. Then at Logan. "Keep your bitch away from me, Westin."

"She's not *my* bitch." Logan smiled. "You're hers."

I took a step closer, surprised that he didn't run for his life. "What happened to the scar?" I asked studying his cheek. "I thought I left you with a pretty memento of our last meeting."

He shrugged, trying for nonchalant. The shiver in his knees, however, revealed his true state of mind. "Part of the post-mission restoration. Something to do with reconstruction of the wound that brings it back to its original state." Then his mouth snapped shut as if he realized he was revealing far too much.

Too late, Nevins.

"Look, Nevins," Logan said. "I'm trying to help you before it's too late. Before you're either too far gone, or too dead to get out of his clutches."

Nevins shook his head. "I don't believe you. He's not capable of what you're implying. Any deaths were specific, and the massacres you're talking about were just training exercises."

Training exercises?

"Which ones were just training?"

"The goblins, and the kids in Cicero."

So he did kill Mika. My gut twisted as I accepted that he was my mark now.

Just one more question. "And the Masai tribe?" I asked softly.

He shrugged. "I wasn't part of that one."

"How did you know these were just training exercises?" Logan asked.

Nevins rolled his eyes. "Because they were. He said they were."

"Then," I said, "how do you explain all the people you killed and all the bodies left behind after you were done?"

"Bodies?" He roared out a laugh. "There were no bodies afterward. The people were just projections made for us by the telepaths he hired. They created images for us to use as training."

It looked as though Logan was right after all. Nevins was as much a victim—in his own way—as the people he'd gunned down. The difficulty was how to make him see it.

And then I asked, "Did you pick up your shells and bullets afterward?"

Nevins hesitated. "Why would we do that?'

"Because if you were shooting at projections the bullets wouldn't hit anything. Ammo would be lying everywhere on the ground. Did you do a cleanup?"

"I . . . yes . . . maybe." He shook his head. "I don't . . . recall. We must have. Or even if we didn't, they would have called in a cleanup crew anyway. What difference does that make?"

"It makes a huge difference if the projections were real people who actually died at your hands and who actually told us what happened afterward."

His face lost color. "DeathTalkers?"

"Uh-huh." I nodded.

He shook his head like it hurt. "No. This makes absolutely no sense. He wouldn't do something like this."

"Who is *he*?" Logan said softly.

He snorted. "There's no way I'd tell you that."

"Why not?" I asked stepping around him. "Is it because you can't *remember* who he is?"

"Of course I remem—" His expression was pained as he frowned at me. Then shocked as he concentrated, clearly trying to recall the name of the man who controlled him. "I . . . No. You're just trying to manipulate me."

"Nope," I told him. "You've already been manipulated. It would be evil of me to do such a thing now."

He made a strangled sound then turned and fled into the forest.

I shifted to follow and catch him but Logan touched my arm.

"Leave him. It's sinking in."

The sounds of Nevins crashing and thrashing through the undergrowth, sending the wildlife squawking, echoed behind him.

"Even if he doesn't want to believe it, a part of him knows the truth."

Jess emerged from among the trees. "That depends if that part of him has been erased."

"So he has been erased?" I turned to her, sure now I'd been right all along.

"That was a good move to try and get him to remember the mastermind's name," said Logan.

"It made sense that he would have been tinkered with," I said. "What paranormal would agree to kill his own kind when the method used would make him vulnerable too?" I looked at Jess. "Did you find anything in his mind that would lead us to the main guy. Is it—?"

I stopped myself just before I spilled out the name but Logan was on his phone and talking quietly. I let out a breath.

"I am afraid the erasure of his memories was very thorough. And permanent." Jess's voice held a dull note of hopelessness. As if she felt that finding something solid to connect Storm to the killings was impossible.

I knew how she felt.

"I have to go now," she said. "I must make my report."

"Omega?" I asked, giving Logan a glance. Done with his call he was heading back to us.

"The Immortal High Council," she whispered in my head.

Startled I glanced up at her, but she was looking at Logan. "Let me take you two back to the city," she told him. "I have some errands to run."

I grinned. "We appreciate the ride."

"I do believe Logan appreciates it more. *You* could just run home. He has only human strength."

This time I had to laugh. I'd never heard Jess utter such a smartass remark. It was quite refreshing.

Logan met her smile with a broad one of his own.

"Where to?" she asked.

"O'Hagan's please," we said in unison. I was eager for food, less eager to face the shambles that was our apartment.

Jess dropped us off in the shadows of an alley around the corner from the pub, and we scanned the sidewalk before exiting the darkness and hurrying toward the sound of relaxation.

I made another round of calls and texts to Anjelo and came up empty. Despite the heavy weight in the pit of my stomach, I dug into my meal with gusto.

After a satisfying double cheeseburger for me, and a steak for Logan, we sat back replete but exhausted.

I yawned. "I feel like I've been going for days."

"You have," he said dryly.

"Not as if I've had a chance to nap, you know."

He sighed. "I know all too well." He wiped his mouth with his napkin and tossed it onto the plate. "I hope tonight I can get some sleep."

"They're getting stronger?" I asked, stirring my milkshake with my straw.

He nodded and gave a tired sigh. "The littlest things set me off. Like the thought or the taste of chocolate cake, or ice-cream, or a strawberry milkshake."

He looked down into the glass in his hand. It was an apple cider. He told me he'd gone for the cider because it wasn't strong enough to knock him out. The last thing he wanted was to pass out before he got home.

"I can see a figure in the dreams now." Logan was still staring into his glass. "It's not just a feeling anymore. There is someone there that I can't remember quite so clearly."

I didn't respond, what with Jess's words ringing in my ears.

"What Darcy said made me think about these dreams and memories." He tilted the glass, let the cider edge up to the rim. "This girl is just a ghostly shape, I have no idea who she is, but somehow I know she's real."

"Do you think you should see someone?"

"See someone?"

"Don't be obtuse. Speak to someone about it. A therapist or even a telepath. Someone who can look under the hood and see if anything is missing in there." I gave him a teasing smile.

"Not about to take such a chance."

"Why not?" I asked. "Maybe speak to Darcy about your missing memories. Some of the stuff she said had to make you wonder if she could help you."

Logan studied my face for a long moment. Then he sat back. "As soon as this craziness dies down, I'll think about it." He smiled and leaned toward me. "I promise."

That was all I could ask for.

CHAPTER 52

WE'D BARELY GOTTEN BACK TO the apartment when Logan's cell phone began to ring. When he recognized his caller, his expression turned from resignation to suspicion.

"Westin." His tone was hard but not unpleasant. "Is that right? Yes. Where? I'll meet you there in half an hour."

He cut the call and met my eyes.

"And why," I asked, "do I get the feeling that this isn't good?"

"Nevins wants to meet us. Someone blew up his house."

"Oh." I blinked. "Is he considering his options?"

Logan nodded. "Seems so. After what we told him, then finding his place blown to bits, I figure he's thinking someone wants him dead."

"With good reason." I folded my arms.

Logan laughed softly. "He sounded frantic. And shocked."

I wasn't surprised. "Why does he want to meet?"

"He says he knows the location of a meeting with his boss." Logan paused. "He did sound odd though."

"Maybe he's not himself. It's not every day you get your

personal beliefs and your personal possessions destroyed within a couple of hours."

"I guess not."

"Maybe it's a trap?"

"Likely."

I rubbed my palms together. "Great. When do we leave?"

CHAPTER 53

*J*ESS TRANSPORTED US TO THE location; a narrow sandy canyon where the sides of the mountains rose so high above us that we had to crane our necks to glimpse the peaks. From the red rocks around us I guess we were somewhere in Nevada.

It was cooler down there, away from the sun, and I shivered. But it wasn't the temperature that gave me the goosebumps.

Gigantic rocks lay strewn across the red sand of the ravine. Great hiding places. Perfect for an ambush.

I slipped my fingers into my pocket for Nerina's key and sent her an urgent call. I'd promised she'd be part of the effort to apprehend Mika's killer, and I was a woman of my word.

As I studied my surroundings she responded, sounding worried. I kept it brief, and within seconds Nerina solidified next to me.

Paranormal instant messaging rocks.

Logan stood beside us, the four of us back to back, watching and waiting.

"This isn't good." I kept my voice soft.

"It's probably a trap so watch the rocks."

"Heads up. I got movement." Logan's whisper barely reached me when I saw someone peer out from behind a large stone about ten feet away. Military gear, smelled human, but a little odd—with that strange, metallic odor again.

My sense of smell had picked up on the changes to the human DNA. My panther could sense their 'paranormalness'.

Creepy but advantageous.

I relayed this information to the team in a soft whisper, and said, "I'm downwind from this lot, but I'm blind behind me."

"You just concentrate on your end," said Jess.

The silence that followed was strange and tense, a portent of the fury to follow.

Suddenly, one of the enhanced humans came flying through the air at us. As he flew, he performed a double somersault and slammed to the ground behind me, right in the middle of our safe zone.

"I got this," yelled Jess and threw herself at the soldier. Even before they hit the ground they disappeared into nothing. A shout from the top of a nearby rock revealed the Titan's strategy.

The soldier was now buried knee-deep within the solid stone, his arms flailing as he tried to remain upright.

"Hope you didn't hurt him," I said as she rematerialized beside me.

"Only his pride," she said, and waved a two-way radio at him.

He patted his hip, scanned the ground around him, and then glared down at her.

She smiled serenely as she slid the radio onto her own belt. "And he'll have to be teleported out, or chiseled out. Either way he's not a problem."

"But *they* are." I nodded at the two dozen soldiers now emerging from their hiding places behind the rocks.

Even the fact that one sent repeated flashes of fire, while another drew a hurricane of sand and stone from the ground and hurled it at me didn't stop me. As I ran I shifted into that comfortable spot balanced between human and panther.

I didn't like the idea of killing humans, no matter how enhanced they were, but *our* lives counted for more in this battle.

The fire-human sent balls of flame straight at my face. I ducked and he got careless in his enthusiasm.

And too close.

I punched him in the stomach, keeping my claws in check. I'd worried about ripping his gut open and giving him a mortal wound, but when my punches did absolutely nothing to him, I grew a little afraid.

Though the hurricane had disappeared it seemed that the wind had picked up. In the distance a large man stood very still, watching the melee.

Storm?

I squinted, evading a barrage of flame from more fire-humans. But I knew in my gut it was him.

Nevins walked up from behind him, and a flash of fury ripped through me. So he *had* sold us out. He owed us no loyalty. Now we owed him none either.

Keeping him in my sights, I battled with another half dozen enhanced humans, a medley of powers aimed at us; flames, water, heat, ice and wind, each forced to be deflected, and their owners to be defeated.

Nerina faded into the ether to remain untouched and yelled out warnings, repeatedly saving us from a variety of terrible deaths.

Nevins stood at Storm's side, watching us fight for our lives, a cold sneer at his lips. Only when Storm gestured in his direction did he finally move.

Nevins ran straight for us, and Logan moved to protect me while I deflected the blows of a furious lightning mage.

Nevins closed in, his face a picture of passionate fury as he began to throw blades of ice at Logan.

Logan calmly melted them with a mere flick of his palm as they came.

Frustrated, Nevins circled him, gained a little distance, and lifted his hands to the sky. Wind howled, and a freezing hurricane surged around him spitting blades of ice at us.

Logan aimed his fire, building it up so hot that I felt the burn on my cheek. Then he threw out his power. The hurricane spun into Logan's heat. As it spun it lost momentum and power, slowing, slowing, until it faded to nothing, and its icy missiles fell to the ground at Nevins's feet

Furious that he'd been bested, Nevins raised his hand and sent a volley of icy javelins at us.

Logan responded with another wave of heat.

I evaded the blows of another enhanced human, one whose power made him so fast I could barely see his blows coming. My concentration was so focused on maintaining walker speed to defend myself from him that I didn't see the ice-spear until it was embedded in my hip.

I didn't fall, but I uttered a low groan and clutched my side as agony tore through me.

Logan heard my cry and spun around. His horrified gaze fell on the frozen weapon, but all he could do was send heat at it with one hand before he was forced to turn his attention back to Nevins.

But that brief moment of inattention was enough. He didn't see Nevins draw his weapon. Didn't see him aim. But I saw, and in a burst of panther energy launched myself in front of Logan.

I took two bullets to the abdomen. Hit the ground. Rolled straight into a somersault and onto my feet.

Then I raced, for Nevins, ignoring my wounds, ignoring the fiery agony ripping through my gut. I body-slammed him and took him down to the ground. He lay there, stunned, and I wasn't sure if it was his ego or his body that had taken the harder hit.

I bit back my pain, ignored the scent of my blood, the fading light that told me I was badly hurt. I focused only on the murderer who would destroy the man I loved if I didn't kill him first.

He reached for his gun with almost inhuman speed, the nasty gleam in his eye alerting me to his intention even before he aimed again at Logan.

As I swung my hand at him, my panther claws shot out, connecting with neck and flesh and muscle, swiping through it all with satisfying ease.

Blood slapped me in the face, hot and slick.

I stood over him, watching as he struggled to speak, the sound gurgling in his throat. His eyes shifted from my face to somewhere behind me and his expression turned from hopeless to triumphant. A nasty, ragged laugh escaped his ruined throat, but I was no longer paying him any attention.

I swung around, realizing too late that, while I'd fought with Nevins, Logan had been left wide open. Storm now stood two feet from him, his eyes a fiery blue, a gun gleaming between their bodies.

Jess took a step closer to Logan, and her eyes met mine. I gave a slight nod, knowing she intended to run at Logan and jump him to safety.

But his shouted, "No!" froze Jess in mid-step.

He lifted his chin and stared Storm in the face. "I don't care what you want with me. I'll go with you. On one condition."

The Immortal smiled. "You are not in any position to make bargains."

Logan ignored him. "Release Lily, and you won't have any trouble from me."

Storm considered, then inclined his head.

Then, he, Logan, Nevins, and all the men with him disappeared—and standing in the middle of the valley floor, a stunned look in her eyes, was Lily.

CHAPTER 54

"WH-WHAT HAPPENED?" LILY ASKED, her eyes round and shocked as she scanned her surroundings. Then she saw me and launched herself into my arms.

I fell to the ground, pain exploding in my body as adrenaline bled away.

"Kai!" Lily let go and scrambled away from me, frantic. "Omigod you've been shot."

"More than just shot," said Nerina as she solidified at my side, dropping to her knees to lift my shirt for a quick inspection. "Kailin, they have taken all their dead with them. There is nobody left to question."

"Yeah," I gritted my teeth, brushing her hand away. "My fault. We told Nevins that's how we got our first clues, so he must have told . . . him." I didn't want to say Storm's name. I grunted, feeling the pair of bullets move within my flesh. "It's fine though. The bullets will be expelled in no time, and I'll be just as good as new."

Nerina shook her head but said nothing.

Don't antagonize the patient? Or was that the insane?

Jess moved closer, her hand closing over the walkie-talkie at her waist, as if she wanted to do something with herself. "Lily, don't worry about Kailin. She should have developed a good level of resistance against the poison in those bullets, so she'll heal soon enough." The Titan gave me a glance, as if she wanted reassurance for her assumptions.

I smiled. "I'll be fine, kid. The important thing is how *you* are."

"I'm fine . . . I think." She stared around her. "How did I get here?" Lily asked, her expression perplexed and a little disoriented.

"Logan traded himself for you." I watched her response.

"He set me free?" she asked, her voice faltering.

"Who was he?" I asked softly, wanting to hear if she too couldn't recall Storm.

"I . . . I don't . . ." Then she gazed up at the sky. "Funny, but I just don't know. I know him. When I look at him, I *know* I know him. But now, I just can't put my finger on a name."

"Her memory has been erased," said Jess from behind us. Her voice was soft and filled with regret.

Nerina touched my arm. "Kai, the blood promise . . . It's fulfilled. You did kill the man who murdered Mika, didn't you?"

I nodded. "Yes, I've fulfilled my promise. Nevins is dead." I smiled at her. "You can go tell Kira that her daughter has been avenged."

Nerina nodded. "If you don't need me anymore?"

I shook my head. "If I need you, I'll call." I managed a breezy smile and she got to her feet.

"Make sure you get those wounds looked at." The sound of her voice faded with her.

I'd fulfilled my blood promise, yes. And Lily had been returned safely, if a little shocked and confused. But Storm had taken Logan.

I turned to Jess. "He may have been able to mess with everyone else's mind, but we saw him."

Jess let out a ragged sigh. "The Immortal High Council wants him alive. They will mete out the appropriate punishment."

"That's not fair," I said, shifting to sit upright. Even as I spoke I knew we'd all be better off with the Immortal High Council meting out Storm's punishment and yet a big part of me wanted the satisfaction of seeing him charged, and judged and punished.

"I apologize, Kailin. These are not my personal wishes. The Laws of the Immortals are too powerful to disobey."

I clamped my mouth shut and gave a tight nod. Safer that way. I'd gotten a little bit of vengeance today. I guess I'd have to be satisfied with that.

"This is so weird," Lily said, holding the side of her head and wincing. "Okay, I think I'll pass out now."

She fell sideways and Jess grabbed her, settling her gently on the ground.

I crawled over to Lily's side, thinking about Anjelo and how relieved he'd be to know she was safe. Now, if only we could get a hold of the damned kid.

"What happened to you, Lily?"

"He hid me in . . . his apartment," Lily mumbled "There's a secret room behind the kitchen in his apartment."

"Whose apartment?" I asked, not wanting to push her too hard.

Jess moved me out of the way. "Let me," she said, and placed her hands on either side of Lily's head. "Hold still and do not be afraid."

Good luck with that.

Lily stared at me, eyes wide, her expression more like 'what the hell is going on?' than fear. But she allowed Jess to do her mental examination and only let out her breath when the Titan sat back.

Lily glanced at me, puzzled. Then she frowned, her expression darkening. "Oh," was all she said, and her jaw went tight. "*Oh!*"

"Do you remember?" I asked, studying her hard features.

"The bastard." She looked up at me, outraged. "I can't believe he did that to me . . . and those kids . . . Dear *Ailuros*."

Jess shifted to her feet. "Let me know the moment you feel anything unusual."

"The only unusual thing I feel," Lily snapped, "is the urge to kick Storm in the balls."

I snorted and I grinned at her. At least she was getting back to her old self.

Then her fierceness died away and she met my eyes, hurt filling her face. "He told me himself that he hated humans . . . It didn't hit me then that I was talking to him. It was like I knew him all along, but his face wasn't recognizable. Not until Jess did her weird mind mojo."

She made circles with her finger beside her head and Jess smiled. "No offense," Lily said, her cheeks going pink.

"None taken," Jess assured her.

I cleared my throat, finally having gotten enough strength back to get to my feet. "You said he was in his apartment? We have to find him before he hurts Logan." I dusted myself off. "*Ailuros* only knows what he wants Logan for."

"He knows who Logan is," said Jess, her voice dead.

I arched an eyebrow. "Who *is* Logan?" Maybe now she'd tell me.

Jess shook her head.

Not happening, then.

"I cannot tell you, Kailin. All I can say is that his identity is one well worth concealing."

"She's right, Kai. He hates Logan. He's been the target all along." Lily's voice broke.

I turned to Jess. "Can you find him? Sense him or something?"

Jess nodded. "I can sense him. I can tell you he is still alive, he is very angry though, so I hope he does not do something stupid."

"Can you tell where he is?"

Jess shook her head. "Not exactly. It depends on whether Logan has any thoughts that he has consciously decided not to block. From this distance, I would need him to *want* me to hear him."

"Like he projects his thoughts?" I asked, frowning.

"Yes, and at this point I am getting a sense that they are at Storm's apartments. Logan is familiar with the place and so am I."

"You've been there before?" I asked, recalling that someone has told me they'd seen Jess with Storm.

"Unfortunately. I have to confess that we were friends. I had thought I understood him and that we trusted each other. In truth, I was mistaken."

"Not mistaken. Used." My voice was hard.

She inhaled sharply and straightened. "I'll take you back to Chicago, and I must alert the High Council. I'll be back immediately."

"Why do you need to tell them? Can't we just take him down now?" Lily asked angrily.

"I'm afraid only Immortal bindings can hold an Immortal against their will. Only the High Council possesses the necessary means to hold God, Immortal or Titan."

"Oh," said Lily, as Jess held out her hand.

Jess spirited us away, back to the front room in Storm's apartment building where we'd left Baz the last time we'd been here. She disappeared immediately and I turned on my heel and ran to Storm's office, on the off-chance that he would be there.

He was.

He was sitting behind his desk, as calm as always, head bent over paperwork. He looked up as I opened the door and entered. Lily had stayed in the front office, clearly unable to deal with facing him down.

"What's going on, Kailin?" he asked rising to his feet, the picture of concern.

"Why?" I asked, my voice vibrating with fury.

He tilted his head. "If you want me to answer a question, you will have to ask one."

His words made me remember that my mind was blocked from him. He couldn't tell what I was thinking and surely he'd be wondering why.

"Why did you do it?"

He sighed and leaned back, his blue eyes bright. "I'm really sorry, but I have no idea what you're trying to ask me." His expression remained clear, not a hint of concern or fear, nothing to indicate he was guilty.

I frowned, wondering if I'd had the wrong person all along. Had I made a huge mistake?

"I—" I paused and swallowed, blinking against a wave of fatigue. My jacket hid the worst of my injuries, but my hands and face bore the bloody marking of the battle.

He rounded the desk, his gaze traveling over my body.

"What happened?" He came to stand in front of me and I blinked as I tilted my head up to look at his face. "Are you hurt?"

All I saw was Storm's concern, the care he'd always given to us. Our Storm, not a killer.

I inhaled and looked down, my cheeks heating up with shame.

And then I saw his shoes.

Black sneakers. A Stygian darkness—that contrasted sharply with a fine layer of red sand.

I backed away, my gaze lifting from his shoes to his face.

He frowned as if confused. Then he looked down at his feet and let out a laugh, his expression now apologetic.

"Let Logan go," I said, proud that I hadn't screamed the demand at him.

He smiled.

An invisible hand closed around my throat, its fingers gripping hard, cutting off my air as it lifted me off the floor and held me suspended. Terrified to swallow, I stared at Storm as he watched me, a cold smile on his lips.

The air in the room shivered, moving faster and faster, rising like a thunderstorm. So apt for the Immortal named after that furious aspect of the weather.

The wind ceased and I fell to the ground. My hand went to my throat as I coughed and hacked, sucking in air, the sound wheezing out of my mouth.

"Who are you?" I asked, my voice ragged.

"I am Ares." He took a step back. "You may have heard of me."

"The god of War." I laughed harshly. "That explains a lot."

I was beginning to feel lightheaded so I perched on the edge of his desk while I waited for it to pass. We'd heard Ares had been banished from the heavenly realm centuries ago for a bunch of unnamed crimes. "Wasn't he sent to this plane to serve mankind as part of his rehab?"

He shook his head, his blue eyes now so dark they looked almost black. "Nobody tells me what to do. I am the god of war and I will avenge myself against the creatures who took everything from me. They took my power, the devotion of my followers, my godhood. They will pay."

"Nice speech. Doesn't explain why you took Logan."

He laughed, the sound echoing in my head. "If you only knew."

I opened my mouth to ask him what he meant but Jess solidified next to me.

"I am here to take you to the High Council," she told him without expression. "Your presence has been requested." He stared at her, not moving a muscle. "Please come peacefully. I do not wish to shame you by taking you back in chains."

"There is no such thing as peace," Storm said. "Surely you know that you are all chasing a dream."

"Is that the reason you have been killing paranormals. I am afraid I do not see the sense in it."

"When every last one of them is removed from the earth, then and only then will there be peace. They are the reason the gods fell from favor."

He paused to look at me.

"You people are the reason I have lost everything."

CHAPTER 55

"ONLY WHEN WE REMOVE EVERY paranormal from this plane, then there will be peace. The paranormals are the reason the Gods fell from favor."

Jess shook her head. "You are confused. The paranormals were created at the same time normal humans were made. Why do you now want to kill them? They have existed all this time."

His lips twisted in maniacal fury. "It would have been fine if they had just existed, but they are growing stronger. Soon they will rule."

Jess stared at him without expression. "You are talking nonsense. Has your brain become addled?"

Storm shook his head. "What about Logan? You know his true identity. Do you not see that the power will be too much for him? Just like the Ni'amh had to be given to five different hosts, so the power he has should be disbursed."

Jess frowned. "That's why the power is dispersed between *two* hosts right now."

Storm smiled. "I'll have it all when I find her."

"You won't find her."

"The High Council knows where she is. Sooner or later I will find out where they have been keeping her."

Jess shook her head. "Not if I have anything to say about."

"You cannot stop me. I am a God."

"Watch me." She raised her hand and lightning sparked from a fingertip. When she aimed her hand at Storm the lightning wove a cage of gold around him. Its energy throbbed as if in time with his heartbeat.

I grabbed her other arm before she could disappear with him. "Make him tell us where Logan is."

The Titan looked at me over her shoulder. "Lily knows," she said, and disappeared, taking Storm and the cage of lightning with her.

Or was that Ares and the cage of lightning?

Yeah, a total WTF moment.

Adrenaline buzzing again I shoved the door open and ran straight into a pacing Lily. "Can you remember where he kept you?"

Lily looked confused. She glanced at the open door, her eyes going round when she saw the office was empty. "Where—"

I raised a hand. "We don't have time, Lily. Focus. Where did Storm keep you."

She blinked, frowned. "Upstairs in his private apartment."

"I thought he had an apartment down here?"

"Yes, he does," she said. "But he also has one on the top floor of the building. Nobody is allowed to go up there. Only Storm has the access codes."

With Jess gone and Saleem still unreachable, I rang Mel. She'd helped me find Greer in the Graylands and she was the only other person I knew who could jump us into the room without opening the door.

Mel arrived within minutes, her eyes dark with worry. She looked tired, her black hair almost lifeless, olive skin tinged green.

"Are you okay?" I asked.

She nodded and gave a small smile. "I'm fine. Just a whole lot going on." She tried to make me believe she was fine but the dark burgundy of her blouse just made her complexion all the more drained.

"Is Saleem okay? He hasn't been answering our calls and I'm starting to worry."

Mel shook her head. "He's ok. He had to go home to see his brother."

"Home as in Djinn-world home?" I asked, a little stunned.

Mel nodded and from the strain on her face I knew his absence was hard on her. There was more going on here than she was telling me, and I intended to ask. Later.

Right now, I led her upstairs and we confronted the locked door of Storm's apartment.

"It's made of steel," said Lily.

Mel nodded. "I'll check first." She closed her eyes for a few moments, then opened it with a smile. "All clear. See you soon." Then she was gone and we listened as she fiddled with a lock on the other side of the door.

She swung the door open and we entered, Lily hanging back. I suspected seeing this place again would be hard for her so I let her find her own pace.

A quick search revealed the place was empty. I turned to Lily. "Can you think where they would have taken him? Was there someplace else that you heard him mention?"

She frowned, her eyes going dark. Everyone's stress levels were sky-high and I worried that she'd been through too much to be of any use to us now.

"If you can't manage it, then don't push yourself too hard, okay?" I said, bending close so she would look at me.

"I do remember Storm mentioning something about sending kids away to a special facility. I think they had something special planned for Logan." Lily frowned. "I wish I could remember more. All I know is that Storm would email the people at some facility to keep them updated on Logan's whereabouts."

"Did he actually talk about this in front of you?" I asked, wondering at Storm's carelessness. The only reason he'd do such a thing was if he considered her expendable. Thank *Ailuros* we'd gotten Lily out before Storm had killed her.

Lily was nodding. "Yes. It's like he wanted me to know everything he was doing. Like it was a game. Sometimes he'd keep me tied up in the front room, facing all the monitors on the wall so that I could see what was happening."

"Monitors," I asked.

Lily nodded. "Yes."

She headed to the wall on the left and rifled around on the top of the mantelpiece for something. Found a remote control. She pressed a button and a whirring sound emanated from the wall. Then a panel shifted and slid upward, revealing a bank of monitors—all currently revealing live feeds.

One camera focused on a young woman, her red hair gleaming in the sunlight as she walked through a park, the evening sun giving her a strange glow. The happy, carefree expression on her face led me to believe that she had no idea that she was being watched.

So this was surveillance.

I had no time to waste wondering who the girl was and why Storm was watching her. Now, Logan was my only priority.

But, as I stared at the monitors my heart twisted.

The air in my lungs turned to ice as I stared at the screen. I could barely breathe as I stood there, frozen to the spot, tears surging to my eyes.

Now I knew why Anjelo hadn't been answering me. I glanced away at Lily, and was glad to see that she hadn't noticed that particular feed yet. I moved away, shifting around so that she would look at me and not the monitors.

I had my own feelings to deal with and I had to be selfish

because dealing with Lily's horror as well as my own would take far too much time. Time we didn't have.

Mel came up to my side. "What do you need me to do?" She looked worried and I knew she understood how important the situation was.

"Just hold on for two seconds while I send a text."

I gave a short nod in Lily's direction and Mel seemed to understand. She slipped an arm around the girl, angling her away from the screens toward a sofa beside a picture window.

With Mel taking care of Lily, I concentrated on sending a text to myself, addressing it to Daniel Chou.

I typed his name and a brief message about getting together for drinks. I hoped that it would be enough.

A few seconds passed and I was beginning to wonder whether the ghost had been messing with me.

When my phone beeped, I exhaled softly in relief. A text from Daniel filled the screen. 'What do you need?'

'Can you scan your communication lines for any information on where Logan is being kept.'

'Logan, as in Logan Westin?'

'Yes,' I typed back annoyed with the back-and-forth. Why didn't he just do what he was told?

'One minute.'

With nothing to do but wait, I reluctantly shifted my gaze from the phone to the bank of screens, staring at Anjelo. He was being kept in a small room, strapped down to a metal table. The number of wires and tubes entering his body made my stomach turn. They were planning something for him, and I was afraid to consider what it could be.

As I watched, two orderly types entered the room, faces hidden as they closed in on Anjelo, who remained deathly still.

I watched in horror as they untied him and moved him onto a gurney then pushed him away.

What were they going to do with him?

Panic took over for a moment, and I could barely breathe. Was Anjelo going to die while I looked for Logan? And could I ever live with having made such a choice?

My cell phone beeped again, and when I looked at it my chest tightened.

'Located mention of Logan at the Omega HQ.'

'How did you find it so fast?' I asked, then tapped again. 'Floor?'

Daniel responded. 'I tapped into the GPS on his phone. Although it's not physically on, it still emits a low transmission, probably detected only by someone like me.'

Suddenly I was thanking *Ailuros* that I'd run into Daniel, however roving his eyes were.

I waved at Mel. "I know where he is."

She got to her feet, and Lily followed close on her heels.

"Let's get going then," said Mel. She glanced at the monitors, giving me a questioning look. She'd never met Anjelo so she wasn't aware of what I'd seen. But I didn't have to worry anymore, because Lily wouldn't see anything since he was no longer on the monitors.

Ailuros knew where he was right now.

I sent off another text Daniel. 'Anything on the location of Anjelo Alvarez?'

Daniel came back almost immediately. 'Will check and let you know.'

I said my thanks and then nodded at Mel. "We need to get to Omega. They're keeping Logan in a facility within the building. Daniel couldn't be any more specific than that, so we'll have to do some searching."

Mel nodded. "You two wait here I will do a quick recon."

She closed eyes but didn't go anywhere. Her astral plane thing. Fascinating stuff.

But, all I could think of was Logan and what was happening

to him. From the looks of what was going on with Angelo, I had no hope in hell of getting Logan back unhurt.

Mel, inhaled harshly and opened her eyes. The shock in her expression was enough to make me feel sick. I didn't want to ask her what was wrong.

"Come I found him."

Lily and I both took hold of one of Mel's hands, and we disappeared.

Although my stomach lurched the tiniest bit, I was fine when we arrived in a darkened room. Light glowed from beneath the door to our right.

"Where are we?" asked Lily, her eyes glowing, her lynx surfacing to allow her to see in the dark.

"We're in the room next to the one where they're keeping Logan. See, over there." Mel pointed to our left at a window that gave on to the room next door.

I shifted closer and had to force myself to swallow a gasp of horror. We'd found Logan.

Dear Ailuros, what have they done to him?

Of all the things that I had wondered, I had not expected this.

"He's frozen." I said the words, but could barely believe it.

CHAPTER 56

*L*ILY LET OUT A STRANGLED sound.

I knew how she felt, but I had to stay in control.

We stared through the window into the silent room next door. The walls were lined with glass shelves containing dozens of bottles of liquids, probably chemicals. Countertops ran against the wall, circling the room, covered with paperwork, bottles, and all sorts of strange equipment.

Against the far wall, a strange device emitted a blue glow, the fluorescent aqua light from within revealing Logan's shadowed features.

A layer of ice covered his skin, and frost crept up the glass windows of the cryo-pod.

"How the hell do we get him out of there?" I whispered.

"I had a look," said Mel. She shook her head. "It's very secure. It also has a self-destruct. We need to enter the correct code or the cryo-chamber will kill him."

I stared at Mel, shocked. I was filled with dread for Anjelo and now I stared at Logan, unsure if he'd make it out of this alive.

Could it get any worse?

"Kai?" Mel said. "What do we do?"

Who knew about codes? "There's someone that may be able to help us," I told her. "He's at my parent's place at Tukats. Bring him here as fast as possible. I think he may be the only person who can crack the code without tripping the self-destruct."

Mel nodded. "Be back in a sec."

It only took a few minutes to return, but they were minutes that dragged like an eternity as I watched Logan's frosted face through the glass. Lily's pacing only amplified the feeling that my world was teetering.

Mel reappeared beside me, holding onto Baz whose expression indicated he was struggling not to throw up.

"Geez," he croaked. "How come that was worse than when Jess took us to—" He broke off when his gaze came to rest on Logan in the pod on the other side of the mirror. His eyes widened. "Can you get me in there now?" he asked Mel, not wasting a single second.

The tracker nodded and jumped Baz into the room, landing right beside the cryo-pod. He'd certainly come prepared. He was already opening his laptop and connecting his device to the keypad on the pod with a cable he'd drawn from his rucksack.

He went to work and Mel disappeared, arriving beside me her expression pale and concerned. She held out her hand and took both Lily and me into the room to join Baz.

"Aren't we worried about sensors picking up our presence?" I asked.

Baz looked up from his screen. "Don't worry about that. I've disabled the sensors. They only had one at the door to detect people entering the room."

I nodded and watched him work, my heart thudding in time to the tapping of his fingers on the keys.

Only seconds went by before I began to stress. "How much longer?" I asked, needing to ask something, needing to know that we were going to succeed.

"Give me a minute," said Baz. "The cryo-process has already

begun. Unplugging him now without being super-careful, may hurt him if not kill him."

I swallowed hard, and began to pray.

Then I turned to Mel. "Is it possible to transport him out of the room to safety?"

Mel nodded. "Yes, I could do that fairly easily as long as I don't have to transport the whole pod. I don't have the energy right now for such a huge jump."

Baz looked up. "You don't need to take the pod. As long as you take the wiring and the generator he will survive."

Before Mel could respond, the panel began counting down.

"Crap. You must have set something off."

Baz nodded, neither hurt nor insulted by my criticism. "Take him now."

I looked at Mel. "As soon as you leave him, come straight back for Lily."

She nodded. "You guys ready?"

Everyone nodded and Mel jumped. She disappeared from beside me and I saw her inside the pod with Logan for the briefest second.

And then they both disappeared.

A few minutes later Mel materialized again. "Lily, you can come and look after Logan for me?"

Lily gave me an odd look, but she didn't complain. Within seconds Mel transported her away. When she returned, her face was pale, blue veins dark at her temples.

"Are you okay?"

She nodded, waving the question off. "What's going on?" she asked.

Baz stowed his keyboard and got to his feet, his expression asking the same question.

"Anjelo." I found it hard to say his name. Just voicing it made me want to cry. "He's somewhere here in this facility. When I last saw him on the monitors in Storm's apartment, it didn't look good."

Mel nodded. "Let me go and have a look. I might be a few minutes because I have no idea how big the place is."

As she disappeared, I looked at Baz feeling like I needed to say something. "Thank you so much. You have no idea how much your help has meant to us."

He just grinned. "It's a pleasure. You saved my life. I'll always be willing to help you."

I could feel my mind wanting to shut down. Fatigue, grief, relief and fear, not a very comfortable mix.

Mel reappeared before things got any more emotional. "I found him," she whispered, and held out her hands.

We materialized in a darkened room—a mirror of the one in which they'd been keeping Logan. The only difference was that Anjelo lay on a gurney—probably the same one I'd seen them take him away on—and there were no beeping machines.

My stomach tightened. "Are there any sensors in here?" I asked Baz softly.

He studied his laptop screen. Nodded. "But it doesn't matter now. The facility is empty. There's no sign of anyone around."

"Maybe they found out that Storm has been taken?" I suggested, reluctant to look at Anjelo. My panther sensors had heightened, and I could not detect a heartbeat.

No. Please, no.

I moved to the side of the gurney on legs that felt like wool, and placed two fingers on Anjelo's neck. I didn't know why I was doing it.

His skin was cold against my shaking fingers. I wanted to flinch. I wanted to cry. We'd discovered too late that Storm had taken him. We'd found out too late where he was.

He was gone.

This was my fault. I'd given priority to finding Logan and in the process, I'd lost Anjelo.

"How long has he been dead?" asked Baz, staring at Angelo, eyes wide.

I shrugged, curling my shaking fingers into tight fists. But I couldn't hide the tremor in voice. "He's very cold. Maybe it's just the temperature of the room."

Was I trying to convince myself that he could still be alive?

"Someone came into the room," I said. "And unstrapped him, and took him away on a gurney. But I can't be sure that he was alive at that time."

"He could already have been dead when you were watching him being taken away." Mel was being reasonable.

I didn't want reasonable. It didn't make a difference to me now how long he'd been dead.

It only mattered that Anjelo was gone.

CHAPTER 57

*M*EL TRANSPORTED US BACK TO my father's house, bringing Anjelo's body with us. He deserved a proper Panther funeral and we'd need to notify his mother. Stella Alvarez lived two doors down and often came by to help her alpha with his chores. I wasn't looking forward to telling her that I'd failed her.

That Anjelo had died on my watch.

We arrived in the kitchen, our shoes swishing in the water that covered the terra-cotta tiled floor. I hoped it meant Logan's freezing process was being reversed.

A trail of droplets led into the front hall and up the wooden staircase.

"Help me get him to the smaller lounge." I tipped my head up the hall trying not to look at Anjelo's unmoving face. He looked like he was sleeping, and my entire being wanted to scream out at the unfairness of it all.

Why Anjelo?

I forced myself to focus as Mel nodded and disappeared with Anjelo's body. She returned seconds later. "I've left him on one of the sofas. It didn't seem right to leave him on the floor."

I gave her a bleak nod and she responded with a weak smile. "I hate to desert you, but I really have to go now."

"Thank you, Mel," I said. Despite my lack of enthusiasm, I did mean it. "If you need me, I'm there."

Mel gave me a squeeze, a sad smile on her face. Then she disappeared.

The second she was gone I raced up the stairs leaving Baz to scurry after me.

Using my nose, I found they'd taken Logan to Greer's old room.

Dad and Iain glanced up from the side of the bed as I entered.

Dad gave me a sad smile. "The cryo-process had begun well before you found him. It can be reversed, but it will be more complicated."

He'd told me what I needed to know before I'd even asked the questions, and I was very grateful for that.

Lily sat at the foot of the bed watching Logan, her face pale. When she looked at me, I froze at her expression. The color in her eyes faded as she studied me.

I had no idea how I was going to break the news to Lily. And at this point I wasn't strong enough. Selfish, yes, but I just couldn't do it right now. I shifted my gaze, not ready to launch into that conversation as yet.

I moved to the side of the bed and stood beside my father and brother. Logan still had tubes running into him and the small generator groaned beside him.

"We need to find someone to help us bring him back," I whispered.

"Don't worry. We've got it covered."

I looked up at Dad, frowning.

His eyes were dark. "It can be reversed, Kai. I'll figure it out."

I pressed my cheek against his shoulder. "I had no idea you were scientifically minded, Dad."

He snorted. "Your uncle Niko wasn't the only scientist in our family."

I raised my eyebrows. "You're a scientist?" How in *Ailuros'* name did I not know that?

Dad nodded, unaware of my surprise "I used to work at Sentinel in their labs. It's where I met your mother. I still have enough gray cells left to figure this out."

My father was a geek. "I'm so not impressed with all the secrets."

"You'll get used to it."

I didn't have the strength to fight with my father. And I didn't want to search out my Mom either. I knew I'd break into a thousand pieces the moment I saw her.

I suppressed a sigh and asked, "How are the twins and Baz?"

"Twins are asleep and Baz is trying to crack that flash drive of Grams'. They're all fine."

I managed a grateful smile, then motioned for Lily to follow me.

As I headed down the stairs and out of the house, I sensed her following a few paces behind. Her silence hurt but I didn't stop until I got to the gazebo outside.

Dad had built the little house for Greer, but she'd never used it solely because she hadn't been given what *she'd* wanted. Instead, it'd become a place for me to run away to.

I took a seat on one of the wooden benches inside the gazebo and suppressed a shiver. I'd been so focused on the need to talk to Lily that I'd forgotten how cold it was getting.

Soon it would snow. It would be beautiful. And yet I knew that I would find no beauty in this winter.

Lily sat down beside me. She sat very close, as if she knew that she'd be needing me, or perhaps she sensed that I'd be needing her more.

"Did you find Anjelo?" she asked softly.

I nodded even though she was staring at her hands, folded in her lap. "He must have come looking for you," I said.

Her lips trembled. "I was afraid of that."

My arm shook as I placed it around her. "I'm sorry, Lily."

She looked up at me, her eyes filling with tears. "What happened?"

"I don't know. We brought his body here. There's no indication of what they were trying to do to him." I didn't add that we hadn't had time to remove the papery hospital gown from his body and inspect him for wounds.

"How long has he been dead?"

"It's hard to tell. But it may be a day or two."

Lily laughed softly. "I thought I was dreaming." Shook her head. "He must have already passed into the Graylands yesterday."

What? I frowned. "Why would you think that?"

"Because he came to me." Lily sent me a watery smile "I thought I was dreaming. But now that I know he's dead, I know that he'd come to visit me."

I shook my head, not wanting to believe what she was saying. "I'll get Nerina. Maybe she can help us find out what happened to him."

Lily smiled. "It's too late, Kai. We'd only be able to talk to him if we went to the Graylands."

"Nerina would still be able to find him." My body shuddered as I tried to suppress the sobs rising within me. "Even in the Graylands. She'd be able to tell us if he's okay."

"He's dead." Her tone was tired and it made me want to burst into tears. "How okay do you think he'll be, considering he's dead?"

She had a point. But Nerina would be able to tell us if he'd passed on.

I held Lily close, pushed my grief away. "Tell me what you want to do, Lily. Whatever you want, I'll do it."

She looked up at me and slid an arm around my waist.

"Leave him be, Kai. He came to see me already and now I know that he's gone, I can handle his visits better." She smiled. "If he wants to tell us something, he'll find a way. Just leave him in peace."

I blinked away my tears.

Anjelo a ghost? I didn't want to think about what that meant both for him and for Lily. Would she ever be able to move on when Anjelo lingered in our world? Would I? How would I face him should he ever visit me?

I didn't want to think about it. Instead, I thought about Lily. I put both my arms around her. The warmth of her closeness made the shaking in my limbs go away, and right that moment I needed to not fall apart.

"When did you go and get all smart on me?" I asked her softly.

Lily didn't answer. She wept. She wept and I held her close.

We would both grieve for Anjelo.

And in the meantime, I'd be joining the Supreme High Council's Elite Corp. Maybe with their power behind me, I could make a real difference.

And I would wait for Logan to come back to me.

CHAPTER 58

I SAT ON my bed, staring at the piece of paper. Only a single sheet had been contained within the envelope that Jess had given me. She'd promised me a gift and what I'd received was the last thing I would have imagined.

I glanced at the words again, and managed a small smile. A little ray of hope entered my bleak life.

I bent my head and read the words one more time.

> ***In the Dark World, when the night is black,***
> ***When darkness looms, to swallow you whole,***
> ***A quintet of courage will bring forth hope,***
> ***And reach across the planes to save heart and soul***
> ***She who shreds the Veils and she who hunts the Demons,***
> ***She who mend Minds and she who speaks beyond the Grave***
> ***And she who bears the face of all - these five shall be as one.***
> ***For they are the saviors of the DarkWorld, they are the Ni'amh...***

The poem could mean only one thing, as far as I could understand it. a SoulTracker, a DemonHunter, a MindMage, a Death-

Talker and a ShapeChanger; Mel, myself, Darcy, Nerina and Cassie—we were the Quintet of the Ni'amh.

And we had our work cut out for us.

~ TO BE CONTINUED ~

The SkinWalker Series continues with Scorched Fury.

ACKNOWLEDGMENTS

To my editor Gracie O'Neil - you are amazing. Thank you for going all out for me.
To Rachel & Brina at Mark My Words - thank you for keeping me on the straight and narrow. Your support means the world to me.
As ever, to my amazing family - thank you for all your support, encouragement and nagging - what would I do without you?
And to my readers - Keep on turning them pages...

FREE STARTER LIBRARY - JOIN MY NEWSLETTER

Get the following titles FREE when you subscribe to my newsletter.

Tee's Newsletter

http://smarturl.it/TeesMailingList

ABOUT THE AUTHOR

I have been a writer from the time I was old enough to recognize that reading was a doorway into my imagination. Poetry was my first foray into the art of the written word. Books were my best friends, my escape, my haven. I am essentially a recluse but this part of my personality is impossible to practice given I have two teenage daughters, who are actually my friends, my tea-makers, my confidantes… I am blessed with a husband who has left me for golf. It's a fair trade as I have left him for writing. We are both passionate supporters of each other's loves – it works wonderfully…

My heart is currently broken in two. One half resides in South Africa where my old roots still remain, and my heart still longs for the endless beaches and the smell of moist soil after a summer downpour. My love for Ma Afrika will never fade. The other half of me has been transplanted to the Land of the Long White Cloud. The land of the Taniwha, beautiful Maraes, and volcanoes. The land of green, pure beauty that truly inspires. And because I am so torn between these two lands – I shall forever remain cross-eyed.

Stalk Tee here:
www.tgayer.com
tee@tgayer.com

 facebook.com/TGAyerAuthor

twitter.com/TGAyerAuthor

 bookbub.com/profile/t-g-ayer

www.ingramcontent.com/pod-product-compliance
Lightning Source LLC
Chambersburg PA
CBHW021223060726
47590CB00005B/1617